PAINT IT NOIR

By Steve Bunk

Hidden Shelf Publishing House
P.O. Box 4168, McCall, ID 83638
www.hiddenshelfpublishinghouse.com

Artist: Megan Whitfield

Editor: Robert D. Gaines

Graphic Design: Rachel Wickstrom

Interior Layout: Kerstin Stokes

Library of Congress Cataloguing-in-Publication Data

Names: Bunk, Steve, author.
Title: Paint it noir / Steve Bunk.
Description: McCall, ID: Hidden Shelf Publishing, 2025.
Identifiers: ISBN: 978-1-955893-49-7 (paperback) | 978-1-955893-53-4 (Kindle) | 978-1-955893-54-1 (epub)
Subjects: LCSH Idaho--Fiction. | Crime--Fiction. | Family--Fiction. | Mystery fiction. | BISAC FICTION / Mystery & Detective / General | FICTION / Mystery & Detective / Amateur Sleuth
Classification: LCC PS3602 .U65 P35 2025 | DDC 813.6--dc23

1

Worry clouded the cab of my pickup. I tried to dispel it with the fantasy of a happy dog, gums flapping out the window. Maybe a real pet would have been better if I'd ever been willing to take responsibility for one, but the daydream worked briefly. And then the ominous cloud returned.

McCall's log hotels and red-meat restaurants stuck out their chests as the truck growled by in the morning sparkle. *The Aviator* travel mug in my cup holder was full of organic Sumatran, and from the speakers, Steve Earle issued his confident bobcat snarl. Even so, I couldn't shake the conviction that perilously low cash reserves shouldn't have swayed me to accept a delivery job that would start with a phone call I'd receive any minute now. It was a mistake to get tied up with a character like Cassim Geyer. The gloom of that decision wouldn't go away.

The truck creaked into a sharp left and rambled along the southern shore of Payette Lake. I tugged at the brim of my Phillies baseball cap, which I never would have worn in Philthy, and set a wrist on the wheel to putter between cabins and condos. At the little bridge over the river outlet, patches of blue bled through the lake's ice below the piney mountains, still hooded in snow.

I pulled off the main drag, drove down a paved lane past one of the community's umpteen churches, and crackled to a halt in the gravel space before Myotis Books. Tucked away on this side street, the little building was practically invisible to the crowds from Boise and beyond who would arrive in the warm weeks. Everyone in town assumed the business survived only through the subsidy of its owner, Ellie Crossfield, who had come up winners in the inheritance stakes. It was like an expensive hobby, but my woman Tireia and I appreciated the effort and did our part to keep the enterprise going. She'd hinted, if you could call it that, about a book for her birthday, which I'd ordered.

When I entered, Ellie looked up from a shelf she was stocking and said hello.

"My book's here?" I asked.

"You mean Tireia's book?"

She slung her trademark laugh, a piercing tonal assault that twisted up at the end—the high rising tone gone rogue. She held a copy of Vardis Fisher's *Mountain Man*, which she slotted into place before moving to the register. Shelves ran along three walls and in the center were a half-dozen rows divided into westerns, romance, cooking, war history, fishing. The books were mostly secondhand paperbacks. Passing a section on guns and hunting, I noticed a volume on Glocks and pulled it.

"For a non-hunter, you sure love gun books, Reese."

It was true, the lethal ingenuity of weapons fascinated me. Yet I hadn't owned a gun in years, since the death of a friend at the trigger finger of a punk. In these parts, the hunting-oriented culture was a relief from big cities like Philthy, where guns too often were aimed at other humans. Not that it didn't happen here, especially in the remote communities, like the ones I flew smokejumpers and supplies to during the wildfire season, places where everyone seemed to regard every stranger as a dangerous crackpot. But shootings were rare. People were, too. You could go back and forth on stats like that.

Ellie handed me Tireia's hardback, fearsomely titled, *The Adjacent Possible: General Laws for Biospheres in a Nonergodic Universe.* We exchanged glances, and she ran me through with her whinnying laugh, which seemed to suggest: "This book is beyond you, buster. Kidding! Not really, though."

I said so long to Ellie, took my purchases to the truck, and put them in the toolbox in the tray. The engine gave a split-second refusal to respond when I turned the key, and then rolled over partway like an old man in bed before twisting into action.

"Don't do that," I warned the banger.

My phone rang.

"You need to come over as soon as possible," my friend Fabienne said. "I have a package you're supposed to pick up."

"What do you mean? What is it?"

"He told me you'd bring the money for it."

"Who's he?"

"Just come and get it, will you?"

She hung up. What the hell? Was Fabienne mixed up in this?

She lived a few miles south of town in Long Valley, but I had gone only two blocks to the stoplight at the intersection with Lake Street when the Dodge stalled. I turned the key again. A couple of clicks and then nothing. The battery was fairly new, and the lights worked. Probably the starter. Shit. I got out and put the hood up.

One car went by, two, and then—thanks be to the rural ethic—the third pulled over. The driver gave me a push start and within twenty minutes of the stall, I was back in action. I called Fabienne to say what had happened but was sent to her voicemail.

On the way out of town, I passed my mechanic's place, a two-story clapboard house with an apron of parking in front of a three-car garage. It was tempting, but I had no time for repairs. The rest of the way, I took small breaths and willed the pickup to stay alive.

It was midday, and sunlight showered the tamaracks. In the embrace of these mountain woods, you'd just about expect to encounter talking creatures and gnomes in funny hats. The landscape's allure seemed self-aware. My thoughts floated back to the previous day at Cassim Geyer's place outside Sun Valley, when I did what Tireia had cautioned me not to do.

2

oft footsteps signaled the arrival of Cassim Geyer. Trim and compact, he sported a smoking jacket, slacks, and barefoot shoes with toe pockets, which made me grin. He introduced himself and put out his hand like his mother was making him do it. I took it briefly and said, "Reese Mencari." We sat, and he dangled a gloved foot.

"Let's get right down to business, Mr. Mencari, shall we? No doubt you know about the crowds that flocked to see the centerpiece of the film noir exhibition in Boise recently."

"The little statue from *The Maltese Falcon*? Yeah, I read it's worth more than four million."

"Some say the auction price for the prop was a bargain, considering the fame of the film. When the exhibition ended, the falcon was delivered to me for safekeeping. The owner, Mrs. Pascoe-Leyland, lives in Sun Valley, but we often conduct business of this sort for her when she's overseas."

A lovely young woman appeared in a white blouse over a black skirt. She placed a silver tray on a serving table and poured two cups of tea. As she retreated, Geyer glanced to see whether I appreciated our server. He sipped his tea. I was a little disappointed he didn't hold out his pinkie.

"The problem is—and I'm chagrined to tell you this—someone broke into my safe and made off with it."

"You don't say? I didn't hear it was stolen."

"We kept it out of the news. Nor was the theft reported to the authorities." He twisted his teacup on its saucer but didn't pick it up. "Not long after its disappearance, I was contacted by the culprit, who offered to return it for a price. Mrs. Pascoe-Leyland agreed to the proposal."

"Let me guess. You want me to be the bagman."

"An intermediary, I should say. A skilled interlocutor."

The tea was thin and lemony. The cake was tiny. I grimaced.

"I can understand why you look skeptical," he said. "You'd be exchanging a large sum of money for an extremely valuable object, and you'd be dealing with a criminal. I wouldn't engage anyone for this job who wasn't concerned about that."

My gaze wandered to the wall and alighted on a couple of large paintings. One was a Gainsborough-like portrait of a woman in a pleated gown that covered her feet. It was better than the other one. Right out of the 1940s, a high-breasted brunette in a print blouse sat in a thin chair and stared. She looked familiar, and not being able to place her bothered me.

"You're a film noir fan?" he asked.

"Are you talking about the pictures? The young woman on the left reminds me of someone."

"It's Joan Bennett, playing Katherine March from Fritz Lang's *Scarlet Street*," he said. "The other one is Lady Caroline de Winter from Hitchcock's *Rebecca*."

The names went by and folded into the shadows of other things half-heard somewhere or indolently seen, except for Hitchcock, everybody's dark uncle.

"How did you set your sights on me?" I asked.

"When I was entrusted with this task, I realized it would be essential to contract a person of your special talents."

"Special talents? I fly a plane. Plenty of people do that."

"But your reputation precedes you."

"You're talking about the theft of Fred McInery's airplane."

"Its recovery was an impressive piece of deduction. You made the authorities look hapless."

"My partner, Tireia D'Silva, was the brains. Anyway, we did that because Fred is our friend. We aren't detectives. You need a P.I. to handle this payoff."

"I don't need an investigator. I need a lateral thinker who can function under pressure."

"So you're expecting trouble."

"Not at all. The exchange should be quite straightforward. Yet given the stakes, I'd be foolish not to send a man of the highest caliber."

I was getting buttered up like French toast.

"Why doesn't Mrs. Pascoe-Leyland call in the cops?"

Geyer practically jumped out of his chair.

"No, no, she's adamant the police not be involved. She's had enough experience with the incompetence of law enforcement to be convinced she'd never see the statue again."

This wasn't good. And it was way out of my wheelhouse. Tireia had done some checking on Cassim Geyer and was leery of him. We knew he flapped around the edges of the Sun Valley glitterati, attracted by the light. Yet the exact services he provided were shadowy. Still, I'd spent a long winter on the ground and was cash-strapped. Tireia advised me to steer clear of him but as much as I valued my wise lover's counsel, I decided to hear him out. And what I heard was the fee would be handsome. I wondered how he spelled that in numbers.

"I don't believe in carrying a gun," I told him. "If the thief were to just grab the money and keep the prop, I'd let him."

"That's a risk we're willing to take."

"I'm comforted."

He shot the cuffs of his smoking jacket, which bore his initials in gold embroidery.

"Mr. Mencari, you're a smokejumper pilot, are you not?"

"That's right."

"I'm sure the payment for such work is good, but it is seasonal. I should think a substantial fee for a simple transaction in early spring would amount to a windfall for you. Am I incorrect?"

He wasn't the least bit incorrect. Tireia was loaded, she could tide me over until the summer wildfires began—but the old guard dog of pride coiled somewhere in my limbic system wouldn't allow me to take it.

He reached into a pocket of his smoking jacket and extracted a folded paper and fountain pen.

"I trust this amount will suffice. If you'll sign, please."

He wasn't joking about the dough. Tireia was right, of course: the smartest move would be to walk away. I didn't touch the pen.

"It's a wonder Mrs. Pascoe-Leyland wanted you to handle this, considering the falcon was lifted from your own safe."

He flicked a bit of nothing from his slacks and then regarded me, his eyes as gray as his impeccable coiffure.

"She understood, just as her people did when they examined the scene. They said it was a highly professional operation."

"It'd have to be. I noticed the burglar alarm keypad and the CCTV cameras, and you've got guards. Yet everything was neutralized or avoided."

My host rotated his cup again and considered it askance.

He didn't seem to like the tea either.

"I suppose pilots are trained to be observant," he remarked.

"True." The little cake seemed to want me to eat it. "Strange thing to steal, though."

"Do you think so? An extremely valuable talisman at the center of the Hollywood dream holds no allure for you?"

"I mean it would be hard to sell, because everyone would know it's hot. That suggests the plan from the start was to ransom it back to the owner. But what if she didn't bite?"

He looked away. "Let's not forget the point: the statue was stolen. I'm afraid your analysis of the thief's strategy is too theoretical for me." He gathered a disarming expression around the eyes and said, "If I were a scientist, I'd probably be running the experiments rather than concocting the hypotheses."

"A regular technician, huh?"

Cassim's mouth formed a straight line and he hardened his gaze, which again made me grin. A tough guy in toe shoes.

"Looks to me like there are a lot of prizes people could remove from this place. For example, why wouldn't they grab those two paintings on the wall as well?"

He folded his arms, paused, and then leaned forward.

"I'll let you in on a secret. But it won't go beyond us, if you don't mind."

"OK."

"I did own both original paintings until a while back, but certain financial considerations induced me to divest. And you're right, I received a tidy sum for them. Happily, I have an acquaintance whose skills as a copyist are nonpareil."

"All right, but if they're such good fakes, why wouldn't they fool a burglar?"

"Perhaps, like you, he had no idea what they were."

"He sure knew what and where the bird was. Even though the safe was hidden, I assume."

Geyer dropped his head and exhaled.

"I suppose we could conclude that any thief who knew the Maltese Falcon's whereabouts might well have known the paintings were forgeries. Or at least that they were worth much less than the principal prop in arguably the greatest detective film of all time. Not that any of it matters anymore."

"It might if you plan to put the statue back in the same safe it was taken from. Come on, this had to be an inside job."

"We're very aware of that possibility, Mr. Mencari."

I grabbed the baked treat and chewed. It tasted like cardboard. What was the matter with this guy? All his taste seemed to be outside his mouth.

I picked up the pen, winced at the mental image of Tireia's glare, and signed.

Geyer rose and unlocked a drawer in a table that looked laser-hewn from petrified wood. He took out a fat envelope and put it in front of me.

"This is the payment you'll make in exchange for the falcon. Have a safe flight, Mr. Mencari."

"Oh, I will, Cassim."

My truck took the bend that opened onto Fabienne's cabin. Perched on a ridge with a south-facing view over pine-rimmed pastureland, it was as big-beamed and knotty as a guy in a weight room, but with forest wallpaper. After moving out of town, Fab had reduced her time spent in bars. She'd made progress. A little, anyhow. Parked next to her vehicle was a Jeep owned by Jim Davenport, her latest romantic mistake.

The long dirt driveway's slope would get me rolling fast enough to push-start myself for the drive home, so I backed in. Davenport's presence made me hesitate about the envelope of cash, but then I grabbed it from the glove compartment and got out of the truck. Except for the sparrows and finches, it was quiet on the tree-shielded ridge, neighbors unseen. A lodgepole pine damaged by bark beetle tilted too close to the cabin, and part of my brain filed a note to get it down for her. A chipmunk scrambled off the porch. I took the three steps up and rapped on the screen door. No answer. I called her name and identified myself. Silence. Too quiet. I pushed the door open cautiously, stepped into the mudroom, and peered beyond it into the living room.

Brimful of absence, Jim Davenport stared at the ceiling, the bullet hole in his forehead an empty third eye. I stood transfixed, and then forced my attention to Fab crumpled on the carpet near him, a SIG Sauer P320 in her hand. One eye and the side of her jaw were going a splotchy midnight blue. I remained motionless. A firestorm had ignited in my brain that prevented it from processing any of this. After a moment, I was able to move again.

I checked her pulse. Beating.

I set the envelope of cash on the bar, got out my phone, and called the county sheriff's office in Cascade.

"Sheriff Carmody. Tell her it's Reese Mencari."

"Hello, Reese."

"Darlene, you've got a murder on your hands."

"What are you talking about?"

"I found somebody shot in the head, for Chrissakes. It's Jim Davenport. And Fabienne's lying next to him. She's unconscious. You gotta get over here now."

"All right, calm down. Is Jim Davenport that P.I. from Los Angeles who likes to slap her around?"

"Yes, yes, that's him. And Fab doesn't look good, Darlene. Come now. Bring the ambulance with you."

"We will. When did this happen?"

"Very recently. I talked to her thirty or forty minutes ago."

"We're on our way, and the paramedics should beat us. Stay put."

I started looking around the place. After opening only a few doors and drawers, I located a cylindrical container in the linen closet. Using a towel, I undid the latch. It was the falcon.

I left the container where it was and reentered the living room, stepping carefully. What to do? I eased onto a stool at the bar. If I was still here when Darlene arrived with her officers, she'd take the statue as evidence, and my payment for the delivery would go with it. I slapped the bar. That wasn't the main consideration. It was Fabienne. I couldn't leave her with a gun and a corpse and a four-million-dollar motive in the closet. Still, Darlene surely would realize Fab couldn't have shot him. All that aside, can you leave the scene of the crime when someone's injured and someone else is dead? Why not, if you aren't in law enforcement and you didn't do anything wrong? Nah, running out wouldn't be right. Plus, removing evidence was a dumb idea, even though Darlene had no clue the prop was here. What was Davenport's role in all this? Why had the thief left the statue without first getting the money? Was the killer hanging around outside? Too many questions. I checked the time. Better decide what to do right now.

Davenport lay on his back, no signs of damage except for the hole in his forehead. I went over and looked closely at the wound and his hands. His Walther PPS was still in its holster, inside the waistband at three o'clock. His mouth was open and the vacated eyes ignored a patch of wall near the ceiling. He was brown-orbed, big-toothed and sandy. He looked ageless in his current condition, although I knew he was thirty-eight, same as me.

I straightened up. Fab made a noise louder than the previous groans. Christ. I hurried over to her and then just hovered, helpless. Hang in there, Fab, I thought, the pros will be here any minute.

I stood by the bar, dithering, and then went to the kitchen, grabbed three plastic bags, and took them to the linen closet. I used a towel to pick up the container, which was surprisingly heavy, put it inside the bags, snatched the payoff cash, and strode out the door. I put the bag and the envelope next to the books in the truck's toolbox and reentered the cabin.

Less than an hour later, the pickup's engine bumped alive when I popped the clutch at eight miles per hour in second gear. I took a bend in the long dirt driveway and Fab's place disappeared from the rearview mirror. Swinging along the track, I pictured the container in the toolbox. It felt like I was swapping the statue for her.

I called Tireia, and tried not to reveal in my voice how rattled I was.

"The falcon," I said. "I'm bringing it to your place first."

"OK, but why?"

"There was a problem. We should discuss it."

"A problem?"

I told her about the call inexplicably coming from Fabienne to pick up the prop, and what I'd found when I got there. I said the ambulance had come and gone with Fab. I'd waited for Darlene, who wanted to talk more with me later.

"But you didn't tell her about the statue."

I breathed out my annoyance.

"It wouldn't have been smart."

"Ah. It was smarter to take evidence from the scene. You'd better bring it to her right now."

I drew in a long breath. Silence on the other end.

"Why in the world was Fabienne involved in this?" she said at last.

"No idea."

"I'd be very surprised if she owns a gun."

"Me too. Talk to you soon."

I ended the call.

Back at Highway 55, I turned north, cruised into downtown McCall, and hung a sharp left to follow the lakefront. The truck crossed the river outlet and I headed north again on Warren Wagon Road. Payette Lake sprawled sunstruck on my right, and the steep mountainside on the left was crowded with greenery. Ahead, Tireia's cabin showed itself for a moment on a promontory above a cove that held her dock and then the pines rejoined. Twenty minutes from Fab's cabin, I veered onto the path that wound up and around to Tireia's place.

In the front meadow, Minta looked up from a colony of trumpet flowers. She let out an avian squeak of greeting, stepped carefully away from the patch, and ran to me. I held the hefty sack in my right hand, scooped her up with the left, and propped her on my hip. At nine, she overbalanced the package by far, but her weight was buoyant.

Tireia appeared in the doorway. She wore a long dress of pale green with dark webbing over the bodice.

Despite my agitation, I obeyed an impulse and said at the porch, "You look like a princess from the Middle Ages."

Maybe I half-hoped the compliment would soften her censure. The other half knew it wouldn't work. She ignored me. Minta wiggled out of my grasp and ran indoors.

Tireia took the three-deep bag and glanced into it.

"So Fabienne will be all right?"

"She'll need rehabbing, but I think she's OK."

We followed Minta into the kitchen, where Tireia opened a drawer and extracted a pair of latex gloves. She drew them on, her green-ice gaze internalized. To me, she was the definition of cool beauty: not cold but with enough remoteness that she took effort to reach, which seemed fair for such a reward. Her facial features were maybe a little out of whack, nose a bit sharp, lips thin, but the woman's style arrested me: the straight brown hair, the long dress with its leather lacework, the sudden incandescence when she smiled.

She carried the bag to the dining room table. Minta stood on a chair in the kitchen, butchering a banana with a butter knife to put it on bread that had shared its peanut butter with the countertop. She acknowledged my attention with a flick of her head but concentrated on the banana, as if worried it would be taken away.

The glass pot held coffee, so I poured a cup.

"I'm making a banana," she said.

"Sandwich."

"Of course, what else? Want any? Oh, I'm sorry, there isn't enough for you. I'm too hungry."

She slapped the pieces of bread together, took a huge bite, and stared at me as she chewed ferociously. She had her mother's beauty. If she sensed my agitation, she wasn't letting on. It was as if she were willing me to be normal. I played along.

"That banana sandwich looks good. I'll take it."

She scrunched up her face. "No you won't." She swallowed. "Little man."

This made me smile. "Little man? Who taught you that?"

"I don't know. Mrs. Howard calls the boys in my class little man."

I kissed her on the forehead and went into the dining room,

where Tireia had set the prop on the table. Fully revealed, it looked just like the movie stills. A leaden bird maybe a foot tall, its talons gripping a small block of stone. The wings were folded back like a soldier at attention and the feathers carved into the chest and around the neck resembled a raft of medals. The big shoulders, the scowl, and the dead eyes amplified the martial theme.

"What's that on the side of its foot?" I said. "On both feet."

She bent down. "Bells. It's a hunter's bird." She straightened. "Look, the bent tail feather from when Lee Patrick dropped it in rehearsal."

I remained mute.

"Effie the secretary, remember? Bogart, as Sam Spade, kept calling her angel and good girl."

"I never saw the film, actually."

"Well, you must have read Hammett's *The Maltese Falcon*."

"Didn't get to it."

"That's truly weird."

She kept staring at the statue, as if to stave off her disappointment in me. But it was just a story, I didn't care. Finding out how Fabienne got mixed up in all this was what I cared about. It better not have been my client's doing.

She tipped back the statue and examined the bottom of its pedestal. "There's no serial number, which is good. Warner Brothers wasn't using serial numbers at the time."

"You've been doing homework."

"I did a little research after you told me about the assignment."

Minta wandered into the dining room, expressed mild interest in the statue, and attempted to touch it, which we deflected.

"I don't shitting care," she said, and carried her sandwich

into the living room. We watched her go.

"She knows something's up," Tireia said. "She's cussing because she feels left out."

"She's cussing because of your lecture about what the real dirty words are."

Tireia frowned, and I kicked myself for saying that.

"Too bad we have to return this," I said. "It looks pretty good on the mahogany."

"So we don't know anything about Jim Davenport's involvement," she said. "Or if he was there only as her abusive boyfriend."

"Nope."

"Fabienne can be a handful but …"

"Nah, she didn't plug him."

I retrieved my coffee from the far end of the table.

"If there was another actor or actors, why would they shoot Davenport and then not take the falcon?" she said.

"You got me. I just want to get rid of the damn thing."

"Why didn't you tell Darlene you'd found it at the cabin?"

In a more benevolent universe, this topic would not have come up again.

"She thought I came for a visit."

"Look, if this is about needing the money …"

"It isn't about the money."

That wasn't entirely true, but I was annoyed. Not by the implied offer, which was decent of her, although she knew I wouldn't accept. Just the whole damn thing: hiring on with a dodgy character, and then breaking a rule, which put me in a corner.

"It's Fabienne," I said. "I couldn't leave her there with stolen goods." My voice was already low but, with a glance toward the living room, I softened it to a whisper. "No matter what, she's still Minta's mother, and she can't be in jail."

Tireia rested her fingertips on the table.

"You're going through with this."

"Looks like it."

"I suppose if Darlene never finds out the statue was stolen you'll get off scot-free."

I felt like a chastised child. It was all too obvious that if I hadn't told her about the job in the first place, she wouldn't now have to be a silent accomplice to my misdeed.

"The evidence has to be fingerprinted, and it looks like you're not going to let Darlene do it," she said. "You still have a kit at your place from your college days, don't you?"

"I do. And I will."

I drove back to town and gunned the truck up the winding road to my cabin on a knoll overlooking the marina. Parking backwards was getting to be a habit. In the cabin, I used iodine fuming for the container and silver metallic powder on the bird, old tricks picked up from a forensics course. No prints showed up, which was a relief. Otherwise, I would have had to submit them to be checked against a database, and any hope of staying clear of this mess would be gone. Whether or not Fabienne knew what was in the container, it seemed unlikely she'd say anything to Darlene— although with her, unlikely was no guarantee. I rolled the truck into a downhill start and phoned the hospital. She had been admitted and was in stable condition. I suppressed the urge to visit her right away.

When I pulled up to my mechanic's garage, his feet stuck out from the creeper beneath a vehicle. Not a good place to encounter Marty, for a couple of reasons. First, he'd be pissed off, because whenever he was working on a car he was pissed off. This was a man in the wrong profession. Second, it would be harder to convince him my job was a priority without being face-to-face, and if I made him slide out from under there? Also bad. I stepped out of the truck and left the motor running.

"Hey, Marty."

"Shit. Turn off your damn engine, you trying to kill me?"

"It's just …"

"You're here, safe and sound. Shut it down."

"Sorry, you're right."

Concerning anything vehicular he usually was right, and I suspected he had powerful opinions on other subjects, too, but we never talked because chitchat bored him, and you got the impression all speech not necessary to convey transactional information was babble to him. So I didn't actually know if he had good ideas. It just seemed likely because of the way he zoomed to the point in conversation, even though we always were on his home ground of matters mechanical.

"Pull into the garage and turn it off," he yelled before I had gotten back in the cab.

I maneuvered the truck into a free slot.

Marty stayed under the sedan for another five minutes, during which the only sounds were the faint clank of metal on metal, breathing, muttering, and the occasional whoosh of a passing car. I had turned off my phone's ringtone after leaving Fab's cabin, and now I checked for messages. Darlene had left voicemail and texted. I texted a promise to be at her office tomorrow, but kept the ringtone off.

Marty wheeled the creeper into the open and stood up. He was of average height, on the burly side, and played bigger than his size. Wiping his hands on a rag, he looked at me like I was the insides of a cylinder head.

"In a hurry, are we, Reese?"

"What makes you think so?"

He laughed.

"Relax, have a beer."

"Not the right time for me, thanks."

He went to a bar fridge at the end of a workbench.

"Time," he said, and popped a can. "Imagine what it was like before clocks. People lived by their actions and urges. Now we do it on time, whether we want to or not."

This was the biggest non-car speech I'd heard him make, his first foray into what I had thought was the reviled realm of chitchat. To my relief, he didn't pursue it. He asked what was wrong with the Dodge and quickly seconded my guess it was the starter. He wasn't done with the sedan yet, but almost. He couldn't quit on it now, everybody was in a hurry, but I was in luck, he had a refurbished starter if it did turn out to be the problem. It could be the solenoid.

"Come back later."

"As it happens, I have to fly to Hailey. But I should be back before you close."

"You better be if you want your truck."

I took the bag with the bird and the envelope of cash out of the tool box and started walking. Within five minutes, I passed the grocery store at the end of town and a hangar came into view at the McCall Municipal Airport. The sight helped to calm me down. After this nightmare of a job was done, I'd soon be back in the cockpit of a Twin Otter flying low over wild country on fire. I left the street, cut through a dirt patch behind the airport's buildings, and looked for my Aviat Husky parked on the tarmac, which brought up thoughts of Fred McInery, the pilot whose stolen plane Tireia and I had recovered.

"How do you swipe an airplane?" Tireia had asked before we began our snooping.

I said my question was what do you do with it after you steal it, and she said she'd never seen Fred so agitated. He loved that Cessna like it breathed. Now I got a glimpse of the Husky, part of a wing, beyond the hangar. It still seemed a minor miracle that he'd sold it to me for a price even I could afford after we found his Cessna.

As I climbed up the plane's tire to settle around the center stick, it occurred to me once again how comfortable I was with this aircraft, despite having trained in and flown tricycle-geared planes, while the Husky was a taildragger. True, you couldn't see over the nose when you taxied down the runway, but most self-respecting bush pilots wouldn't tolerate a tricycle. Landing it on dirt was generally no problem, but for the roughest backcountry airstrips it would be like negotiating the narrow and rocky logging roads through the mountains in a front-wheel-drive sedan.

I brought the Husky up to 7,500 feet and cruised at 110 knots toward the razor-backed Sawtooth Range. To the west lay the Boise National Forest, to the east the Salmon-Challis National Forest, and behind me the Payette National Forest, an upwelling of mountain and pine racing away in every direction under the blue ether.

After touchdown at Friedman Memorial Airport in Hailey, I got a rental car and before long pulled up in front of Cassim Geyer's eight-bedroom showpiece of stone and timber. I put the container in the crook of one arm and held the envelope in the other hand. Jonathan, a big guy in black whom I'd encountered on my previous visit, stood in the doorway. He confirmed I was Mr. Mencari, which he already knew, and chewed his tongue as he wrote in a small notebook. I waited behind an invisible velvet rope until he finally led me down the hall peopled by brass effigies and through double doors into the massive study.

Geyer was waiting for me. I placed the container on the coffee table. He removed the statue, put it down, and turned it slowly in a complete circle.

"Excellent," he said. "I'm sure you'll send along your full report as soon as possible."

"There's no full report. You get the bird and your payoff money back for my fee."

I dropped the thick envelope on the table. He stared at it.

"What's this? How did you get the falcon without making the payment?"

"An unexpected turn of events."

I told him about Davenport and Fab, and watched his reaction. He moved his gray eyes around like they were herding his thoughts.

When I was finished, he said quietly, "This is most unfortunate."

"Yeah. I want to know why you pulled Fabienne Sansverrou into it."

He looked up from the envelope, which he hadn't touched.

"I assure you, I had no hand in determining who was involved. I was told the exchange would take place in the McCall area. The thief insisted the transaction be done with someone local, someone well known within the community, and of course not in law enforcement. Hence my interest in you, the best man up there. When he called again, I provided your name and phone number. My understanding was he would tell you the time and place. That's all I know."

"It's a strange coincidence."

"What is?"

"Fabienne is an old friend of mine. Why would the thief pick her as a go-between?"

"You're saying it wasn't a coincidence. Interesting."

He didn't look interested. He looked bored, which made me want to shake him by his silky lapels.

He must have noticed my anger, because he said quickly, "Perhaps the thief preferred to leave the statue with her and collect his money later rather than risking a direct exchange that could be a trap and possibly lead to gunplay."

"Gunplay? I don't think gunplay was avoided, Cassim."

There was something in Geyer's logic, though. The thief might have used Fabienne as an intermediary to remain anonymous during the exchange. Maybe this seemed safer than trying to arrange an anonymous swap with me, especially if the thief figured Fab's involvement would make me anxious to protect her and therefore more likely to cooperate. If so, it was a counterintuitive and risky move, which said something about the criminal.

What I want to know is what are you going to do now?"

"I'll return the item personally to my client."

"I meant what are you going to do about Fabienne's beating, and the death of Jim Davenport?"

He sighed. "I'll contact the hospital to arrange for payment of her outstanding medical fees. As for this Mr. Davenport, there's really nothing I can do, is there?"

"That's what I thought you'd say. But Davenport was a P.I. He might have been mixed up in all this. You wouldn't happen to know anything about that, would you?"

He pursed his lips in a frown.

"I would say he obviously was involved. But who would have hired a private investigator?"

"Did someone hire him?"

"Why else would he be there?"

"You know less than you think you do, Cassim."

He registered this but said nothing. He put a thin envelope on the coffee table.

"Your remuneration."

"Thanks." I pocketed the envelope. "It's a strange thing about Jim Davenport, don't you think?"

"Strange? You mean in terms of someone having hired him to find the statue?"

"You keep saying someone hired him. What I meant is when I went over there, she'd been beaten into unconsciousness, he was on the floor, and the bird was in the linen closet. If he was roughing her up to get his hands on it, why didn't he look around?"

"Yes, I see. That is curious. Another of life's myriad mysteries. Perhaps he couldn't believe she would hide it in her own home. Perhaps he was intending to do a search but time ran out, as it were. In any case, the falcon is safe, and you have my thanks."

"I have more than that," I said, and patted the check in my pocket. "It's interesting, though."

"What is, Mr. Mencari?"

"Well, I don't believe for a second Fabienne did in Davenport, gun or no gun in her hand. Someone else was there. But you don't have to tell me."

"And what is it I don't have to tell you?"

"That it's just another stitch in the mysterious tapestry of life."

"Good afternoon, Mr. Mencari."

"So long, Cassim."

In the air on the return to McCall, I crowed a few bars of Pink Floyd's *Money* and then left off. There was nothing to sing about.

On the approach to the airport, I cut the airspeed and flared into a three-point landing at a powered glide of about forty-four knots. It was faster than old man McInery would do on a meadow of, say, six hundred feet in length, but for asphalt, not bad. I used the brakes only to turn around for the taxi back toward the hangar.

From the airport, I walked to the auto repair shop. It was almost 5 p.m. The boom box in the garage played Jack White's Lazaretto, and Marty stood next to it with a cigarette and a beer, his attention fixed on the guitar break. Marty was a guitarist, that's what he really was, he informed me. This was the first I'd heard of it. Apparently, he had decided to continue in his new conversational mode of earlier. Working on cars was an interlude or at least it better be, he said. He provided a summary of his favorite guitarists, where Jack White fit in, where he himself would fit in, and I listened and nodded and twitched, and Marty paused to blow smoke rings. He was in his early thirties. Two uneasy truths hung unspoken between us: his fitting in had better get a move on, and I wanted my truck. He read my expression and said it was ready, sounding a little surly.

The engine turned over in complete denial of the trouble it had caused, and I drove to my cabin on the knoll. Its front porch not only overlooked the boats in the bay to the north but allowed me to gauge weekend summer traffic arriving from the flatlands in the south. The place was rented but the locale made it hard to think about buying elsewhere, especially given my budget. Anyway, home ownership wasn't the point. It wouldn't magically resolve everything concerning Tireia and Minta and Fabienne and me.

I took off my shoes in the bedroom and put the cell phone in the night table's drawer without checking for messages. In the kitchen, I got a beer from the fridge and put leftovers in the microwave. While the food warmed, I sat on the porch to watch the town electrify in the twilight, and then closed my eyes to let the afterglow fade into a light-rimmed circle of darkness. I ate dinner at the dining room table, looked up a section of the Idaho Code on the iPad, and then read the news. A couple of media outlets and a hyperlocal news blogger had found out about Davenport's death. The reporters had gone no further than the police blotter and questions that were stonewalled by Darlene's people, which sent up a grateful bloom in me. But the blogger was aware of the ambulance and squad cars at Fabienne's place, and she knew about the relationship between Davenport and Fab. She put this together in a questioning fashion, without details.

I grunted, and moved with a second beer to a favorite armchair, where I looked through my new book on Glocks. But I soon set it aside to think about why Jim Davenport was dead.

The quiet of late night descended upon the cabin. I switched off the lamp and put the Glock book on the night table in the bedroom. Sleep came within moments of lying down.

I rose early the next morning, made coffee, and checked my messages to confirm Darlene was expecting me. I rattled down the road to Cascade in the rejuvenated Dodge. It moved through cattle pastureland below the scars of ski runs on the western horizon and past Cascade Reservoir, a flat phenomenon compared to McCall's glacial Payette Lake. You cinch a belt at the waist of the country right around the fortieth parallel, look at the states in the bottom half, and the reason they're overstuffed with humans becomes as bright as the sun in your face. We were just above that belt, a critical five degrees farther north, and only now in late April was winter melting into the sop and shine of spring.

En route, I called the hospital. Fabienne had spent the night there. Her injuries made it difficult to speak and she wasn't taking phone calls. Once again, postponing a visit nagged at me but Darlene had to come first.

In Cascade, I turned at Spring Street and parked in front of the Valley County Sheriff's Office, a couple of connected shoeboxes patterned in brown brick below yellow cement, which always made me think everyone inside must be wearing two-toned brogues. But Tireia was the only one who ever had smiled when I said so.

Darlene made it plain in her expression that she was displeased with me. A sturdy person with a bob cut, clad in the specialized plainclothes of late-term pregnancy, the sheriff didn't rise from her desk. Brusquely, she motioned me to a chair.

"So you gave back the Maltese Falcon, did you?"

She got me good with this opener. Tireia wouldn't have said anything to her. It was Fabienne. She must have looked in the container without leaving her prints, or maybe Davenport was after it and had told her what it was.

"You were hired to make an exchange with a criminal and didn't contact me. Then you came upon a crime scene and didn't stick around because you were too eager to get rid of an object that could be the motive for a murder."

"I wouldn't say 'get rid of.'"

"You wouldn't, huh?" She gripped the edges of her desk. "Regardless of how you'd phrase it, I call it tampering."

"Not really. I looked up the code."

"So you're a lawyer now."

"No, but the intent has to be to prevent authorities from taking the thing into evidence."

"Well?"

"My intent was to give it back to the owner. That doesn't keep you from getting it."

She waved a hand at me, breaking the wrist like a jump shooter.

"You disturbed the scene, you took away evidence. The prints have been obliterated."

"I dusted the container and the statue. Clean as a whistle. It was in a hall closet, under the towels."

"Damn it, Reese, if it wasn't Fabienne's cabin, I'd arrest you right now."

The implication that she wouldn't arrest me was a relief, although I tried not to show it. I offered to describe my involvement. She said don't leave out anything. I gave her the details of the assignment from Cassim Geyer, the phone call, how I had come upon Davenport and Fab, and how I'd returned the money and the statue to Geyer.

"As soon as I got to the cabin, I contacted you."

"And didn't tell me what you were going to do."

To say I hadn't yet decided what to do seemed more like bickering than a defense, so I kept quiet.

"Why did Fabienne have the statue?" she asked wearily.

"She didn't say?"

"She was groggy, and the doc didn't want me to talk to her long. She mumbled something about the falcon, and then I got out of her that you were supposed to return it and leave a payoff for the crook."

"Someone left it with her, I don't know who or why."

"Yeah, that's the question: why would they do such a thing?"

"Maybe they thought bringing her into it would ensure I wouldn't try anything cute. How is she, anyway?"

"She'll survive. Could be you're right about the thief's motivation but I don't know; it's odd, Fabienne being in the middle of this, don't you think?"

"Yes, I do."

We gave each other the poker face.

"And you found her with the gun in her hand and you didn't touch anything, right? Oh, except the bird."

"That's right."

"What really bothers me," she said, "is you stood there and talked to me at the scene and all the while you were concealing key evidence. Just for a buck. Just out of greed."

The blood rushed but I didn't react beyond a glare, aware she was baiting me.

"I had a job to do."

"You had a job."

I gave her a serious expression and said nothing.

"Fabienne takes a beating, she produces a gun from somewhere, shoots the assailant, and passes out," she said.

"What do you make of that?"

"Someone else was there. Aside from me, obviously."

"Oh, obviously, Reese: What reason would you have to gun down a violent P.I. who was paying bad attention to your Fabienne?"

"Come on, Darlene, you know I don't carry. Even if I had a pistol, you think I'd shoot him and then put the weapon in her hand?"

Neither of us spoke for a moment, resting in the ring of our argument.

"I returned the statue to its lawful owner," I told her again. "That's not a crime, is it?"

"If you try to twist the law one more time, I'm gonna break a ruler over your head." After a moment, she said, "There's a guy in town who could be harder to deal with than me. Graham Wheeler, a fed with the Art Crime Team."

"Great." I shifted in the chair. "How did he get here so fast?"

"He said the agency got a tip the statue had been stolen."

We absorbed this.

"Davenport's knuckles were abraded," I said.

"Yeah. He was the one who punched her out."

"And the weapon; was it registered? Prints, aside from hers?"

"No on both counts. But the bullet came from the pistol."

She beat a drum roll with her fingers on the desk.

"I want you to promise me something, and I'm not kidding," she said. "When you go see her, you tell me if she says anything—anything at all—that might help."

"Absolutely."

"And now you're done with this. Although I may not be done with you."

"Why not take me on as a consultant? No charge."

She gave a harsh laugh.

"I suppose you'll need a company car. How about the Aston Martin out back of the old pea-packing shed? Reese, I'm afraid finding Fred McInery's plane doesn't qualify you or Tireia to investigate a murder. Especially after removing evidence."

"We could still be of help."

"If you hear something, tell me. That's how you can help."

"Darlene, you'll have a new addition to your family sooner rather than later. You have a force of well-meaning people, none of whom has the ability to get this job done in your stead. And you have a federal agent sticking his nose into your jurisdiction."

"Your point?"

"My point is you know the kind of firepower Tireia brings, and you know what we did for McInery."

"Did you tell her you'd taken the statue?"

"She said I should give it to you."

"And when you ignored her advice, as you so often do, she didn't call me, did she?"

"Look, this crime occurred at Fabienne's place and I was the first one there. Those are big incentives for us to put effort into this—and, let's face it, you could use the help."

She sighed and placed a hand on her midsection.

"What do you propose to do?"

"Ask around and tell you what we hear."

"Ask and tell," she repeated with a thin smile. "You ask Tireia what she thinks about your plan and let her tell me. Then we'll see."

The A-frame portico upheld by river-rock columns made McCall's hospital look like a hotel from the outside, but Fabienne's starched bedclothes, color-coordinated with her bandages, dispelled any notion of vacations. Her head was trussed from chin to crown. Her left eye was bloodshot and bruised all around and the cheek hugely swollen. She was sitting up in bed, and her response to the sight of me proved she could communicate through clenched teeth.

"Asshole," she hissed.

"What?"

"They said there was a gun in my hand."

"That was the way I found you." I drew up a chair to the bedside. "I couldn't interfere."

She grabbed the little bouquet of chrysanthemums I offered and threw it on the floor. I picked up the flowers and laid them on the side table.

"We'll get a vase. So when are you out of here?"

"Probably today. No surgery but I've got a concussion, thank you very much."

"Did Davenport do this?

"You got it in one."

She smirked but it turned into a whimper and she clutched her jaw, eyes closed. A tear slid out of the corner of her good eye. My concern rose into a wave of anger that had nowhere to land.

"What was his reason?"

"He thought I knew where the falcon was."

"Why would he think that?"

"I don't know. Maybe he was working for someone. He could have been part of the scheme, for all I know."

"Why didn't you tell him you had it?"

"Why do you think, you dope? I was trying to help you." After a moment, she said, "What's the sheriff's take on all this?"

"Darlene knows I found the prop at your cabin. Why did you tell her?"

"What do you mean, why? Anyway, why didn't you tell her?"

"All right. Who was this man who called you?"

"I don't know. It came out of the blue."

"What did he look like?"

"I didn't see. He left it at the end of the driveway."

She gripped the edge of the bed, and then pressed a button to call the nurse.

"Was anybody else with Davenport?" I asked. "Did you see anybody else?"

"No. He was healthy as a mad bull when I went down."

She leaned back into the pillow propped behind her head, closed her eyes again, and took a couple of big breaths through her nose. Then she rolled her head sideways to look at me.

"How are Tireia and Minta doing? I haven't seen them for a while."

This was a surprise.

"They're fine. You know you're always welcome."

"I know. You should be living with them. Why aren't you living with them, Reese?"

I scratched a bicep, even though it didn't itch.

"Did I ever tell you about her sailors and farmers theory?"

Fabienne gave a minute shake of her head.

"She says most women think they want a farmer, who never goes away. But she prefers a sailor, who'll give her long stretches at sea."

This time, she executed a careful titter, which drew only a wince rather than a cry.

I put my hand on her shoulder for a second and she didn't resist. She let her head fall back and shut her eyes.

"Who do you think Davenport could have been working for?" I asked.

"I have no idea, Reese. He did not sit down and confide in me."

The nurse bustled in and asked if Fabienne was experiencing pain. She said hell yes and the nurse gave her something, which she said would make her sleepy. I thanked her and said I was about to go. After the nurse left, I stood, stretched my back, and took a few steps around the room while Fab watched drowsily.

"What were you supposed to do with the money after I gave it to you?"

When she looked at me, it took a second for her to regain focus.

"Where's the money?" she said.

"I returned it."

"Returned it?"

She closed her eyes again.

"Yeah, I gave it back to Geyer."

Her breathing deepened.

"Geyer ..." She tried to lift her head, but it sank back into the pillow. "Not my gun," she murmured.

"I know."

She didn't respond.

8

ireia's study ran the length of her east wall, its French doors providing a view of the lake beyond the cliff edge and then the pines of Ponderosa State Park. I left the truck out front and walked around to that side of the house, knowing she'd be there in the middle of the day with Minta at school. She looked up from a sprawl of papers on her big desk in the center of the room and motioned me in. She wore a kimono covered in a gray fractal pattern, which made her look like a necromancer, in a good way. I entered through the glass doors and she came over barefoot to give me a kiss that I took as a sign of at least partial forgiveness for making off with the bird.

"Still working on the San Jose thing?" I said with a glance at her desk.

"Just wrapping it up now."

I went around to peer at a jumble of graphs, tables, and equations.

"Anything with a variable in it, I hate."

She laughed as she moved to a kitchen counter in the corner to fill the coffee maker.

"What are you talking about? You deal with variables all the time in the air."

"But not in mathematical formulas." I sat in an armchair and pushed away the head of a standing lamp. "The whole idea of comparing San Jose's road network to a cardiovascular system boggles me."

"The concept's simple enough," she said. "To plan a road network properly, you have to consider how it connects people to where they go."

"What, road planners don't do that?"

"Not usually." She ground the coffee beans. After the noise stopped, she said, "They just look at the distribution of residents and their destinations."

"Sounds like the same thing to me."

She scooped the ground beans into their basket.

"You have to consider the properties of the transportation network. Just like a vascular system, roads distribute materials, they branch out to deliver their traffic, and they get smaller as they get farther away from the center."

She turned on the coffee maker and came toward me.

"In a well-planned metropolis you can minimize road congestion with mathematics. You base your calculations on how blood vessels and arteries branch to deliver materials to all parts of a body. The difference is that a city is more decentralized than an organism. Or you could say it's like an organism with multiple hearts."

"Anyway, calling it complexity science is apt."

"Ah, you've lost interest," she remarked, and perched on the edge of her desk.

"No, tell me more."

"Why don't you tell me what you've been doing?"

"But you're busy right now."

"Shut up," she said cordially. "Have you seen Fabienne?"

"Just came from the hospital. Her jaw's bandaged and she's mad as a hornet, but she'll recover."

"What did she say about Davenport?"

"He was trying to shake her down but didn't seem to realize she had the statue in the cabin."

"OK, he was involved somehow. And he figured hitting her was the best way to get information."

"His go-to tactic. Especially with people who couldn't hit back well."

She went back to the corner to pour the coffee.

"It's strange to think the thief would risk leaving the falcon with someone else," she said.

"He could have been watching the cabin."

"Who delivered it?"

"She claimed not to know."

"I wonder."

So did I, but it was painful to think Fab might not be a completely innocent victim. Tireia came over to give me the coffee, and then she sat in the swivel chair with her bare feet up on the desk. The coffee was very good, but I didn't say so, aware it was wiser to reserve praise for real skill.

"Fabienne should come visit when she's feeling better," she said. "Minta hasn't seen her for a while now."

It was kind of her to say, an expression of solidarity. It also was an implication that Fab had more to tell. But neither of these two truths cancelled out the other.

I described my visit to Darlene, and the news that a federal agent was in town. I said we couldn't figure out how or why someone had tipped off the FBI about the theft when the police didn't even know. I related my effort to convince Darlene we should help with the case.

"That is, if you want to help. She said if you do, you should talk to her about it."

"She thinks I'm the leader, that's sweet."

"You are the leader."

"I don't want to make a career out of this."

"God, no, me either."

"What are you going to do?"

"I'll drive down to Boise. Even though the bird was swiped after the exhibition, the museum's curator might know something."

"She'll tell you she knows nothing."

"She already did when I called to make the appointment. But I want to be in the room with her when we speak."

She rose and I made way for her to cuddle in the armchair. She always warmed to talk of me going away, even down the road. It was fun, if kind of befuddling. And now, given the way my decisions had dragged her into this fix, it was especially welcome.

"I think Fabienne's hiding something," I admitted. "It could be she was just groggy, but she seemed evasive. Maybe you could do some noodling and come up with another way to look at this situation. I know that's vague. If you have the time."

"I'll make the time. It'll be a good way to amuse myself while you're gone. But you're here now, and I don't have to pick up Minta for a while."

"A proposition?"

"I won't call it a command."

"But your command is my wish."

"And my wish is that a proposition, less than a command, should suffice to enliven your wish."

She was too good at this shit, she read Shakespeare. Anyway, she enjoyed having the last word.

It was cool and damp the next morning, but overcast was a long sight better than smoke, I reflected while cruising the straight stretch of Highway 55 through Long Valley. Pastureland edged in barbed wire and interrupted by an occasional house under trees went out green on either side to mountains bearded in tamaracks. The Linkin Park singer crooned lyrics that reaffirmed why I didn't often listen to the group. I came alongside the reservoir before entering Cascade. Soon, the road began to snake through the mountains, following the twists of the whitecapped Payette River below. It was always a letdown when the trees gave way to balding foothills and the vehicles accelerated during the slingshot ride down Horseshoe Bend Hill toward Boise. The traffic increased as I entered the city, yet it was easy compared to the freeway congestion around Philthy.

I found a parking spot in front of the Boise Art Museum's reflective glass entrance, framed in a square façade of cement, which felt like walking into a painting. The curator, Maggie Kornbluth, rose from her desk to cross an office hung with posters of the gallery's previous exhibitions. She was a stylish woman, mid-forties, in a pale green suit that overlapped itself inventively. Her straight black hair was in a bun, highlighting the round cheekbones and warm tones of tribal blood. Shoshone or Bannock, I guessed, if she came from these parts. She presented a manicured hand and a whiff of citrus. She motioned me into an armchair and sat in a love seat on the other side of the coffee table.

"What a shock to hear the statue was stolen," she said. "I'm so glad you recovered it. We had no trouble with its safety while it was here, so I'm really not sure what else to tell you."

"It's a routine visit, Ms. Kornbluth. A post-mortem, you might say."

"Would you like something to drink?"

"No, thanks, I've been drinking water. If you don't mind, tell me about the bird. How did you manage to get it for your exhibition?"

"Oh, that was Mr. Geyer's doing, or I should say he arranged it for the owner."

"Rowena Pascoe-Leyland."

"Yes, and I must say I never thought she'd be a detective film fan. But she has a vacation place in Sun Valley, you know, and when we were planning our 'American Noir' exhibition, Mr. Geyer approached me to ask if we might be interested in including her statue. Of course, I was thrilled by the offer. We had some lovely pieces from the studios and museums and so forth—I don't know if you saw the show?"

"Unfortunately, no."

"That's a shame, but as I was saying, even though we had wonderful costuming, storyboards, promotional materials, rushes, and so on, the Maltese Falcon was far and away the star."

"It hadn't been on display much, had it?"

"Hardly at all. I believe our exhibition was only the second time she had loaned it for public viewing."

"That showed faith in you."

"We're nationally accredited, you know. It's a distinction in the region."

"Is it?"

She laughed at herself. "Sorry, I guess leaving the girl in Idaho won't take the Idaho out of her."

I leaned back and said, "So the bird was the show's biggest drawcard, and yet it isn't even a particularly pretty thing."

"Hmm, that depends. We had many movie fans among the attendees, who were especially taken by the props and costumes. I think it's because they're after a feeling of direct connection to the stars. Cagney's firearms in *White Heat* were a big attraction, for example. The same with Gloria Grahame's black cocktail dress from *In a Lonely Place*, and the 1956 Chrysler New Yorker that blew up in the opening scene of *Touch of Evil*."

"But you managed to get that car anyway."

"What can I say? It was a great exhibition."

This with a straight face.

"Cassim took possession of the statue after the show, is that right?"

"Our security couriers brought it by armored van to his home in Sun Valley. Mrs. Pascoe-Leyland was at her London place and asked that Mr. Geyer handle it for her. He's well-connected with the rich and famous around the resort, you know."

"Oh, I know. But then it was stolen from his safe, and she asked him to retrieve it. Does that surprise you?"

She opened her dark eyes wide, which brought out faint lines on her forehead.

"No, I spoke to her on the phone after you called to say

it had been stolen and recovered. I needed to be sure she didn't think the museum was in any way at fault, you see. She told me she hadn't wanted to put the affair in the hands of the police. Outside of Scotland Yard's work in London, the chances of recovering stolen art are not strong, as you might know. And thanks to you, her strategy worked."

"I was good, wasn't I?"

That made her smile and fiddle with her wedding ring.

"Something I don't get is why anyone would steal the statue in the first place," I said. "Who would buy it?"

"I can't say. But as you might be aware, only drugs, arms, and human trafficking gross more illegal income than art crime."

"Is that right?"

"It's true, although some of it is fraud and forgery. Disposing of bona fide art on the black market can be more challenging, I think. To your point, an FBI agent remarked to me just the other day that in this sort of crime, the selling can be more difficult than the stealing."

"That wouldn't happen to be Graham Wheeler of the Art Crime Team?"

"Why, yes. It was the first time I'd ever spoken to an FBI agent, but I had to tell him the same thing I've said to you, that I'm afraid I don't have much of value to contribute."

"You're doing fine. What else did Agent Wheeler and you talk about?"

"Am I allowed to say? I mean, is it privileged? I suppose you're on the same side, though."

A little breathless. She was enjoying herself.

"Aside from what I've told you, let's see . . . he expressed concern—I won't say contempt—over the lack of education of the police when it comes to art theft. He felt they failed to fully appreciate that the art community itself can be, well, shady at times. That's how these stolen items get sold. The thieves locate people with money who are willing to overlook the legalities, although the exact how and who of it are beyond me. It's the provenance they're after, even though the documentation is often sketchy or absent. They're buying the story, you see."

"But the thieves aren't story lovers."

"I think not," she said, and gave the look of a night class instructor to a favorite student. "Most of the time, they're after a quick turnover, and they'll take a tiny percentage of what the object would be worth on the open market. Rarely, the thief will hold onto the art piece for a long time, until the notoriety fades, hoping to get a good price, perhaps from a gallery or museum buyer who will look the other way. Agent Wheeler pointed out there are more billionaires now than in the past, some of whom might be content to buy stolen art and keep it out of the public eye."

"Agent Wheeler was full of information."

"Do you know him?"

"Not yet, but I will."

"It's a closed case now, though, isn't it? Oh, no, I'm forgetting the poor man who lost his life."

"How did you know about that?"

"The agent mentioned it. I'm sorry, it was insensitive of me to overlook it."

I got up and took her hand, which again yielded its hint of citrus.

"Ms. Kornbluth, I doubt there's an insensitive bone in your body. You've been very helpful, thank you."

When I turned at the door, she stood in front of the desk, her lips set in a gentle crescent, a thumb and forefinger twisting her ring.

10

A nurse at the hospital told me Fabienne had been released. After entering Long Valley from Boise, I went straight to her cabin. She answered the door, her head still wrapped in white. She lifted her eyes in acknowledgment, shuffled aside to let me out of the mud room, and motioned toward the breakfast nook off the kitchen. To the right, a throw rug had been strategically placed over a section of the living room carpet. She poured coffees while I sat at the end of a window bench where the northern view was tamaracks and lodgepoles, interrupted only by the gravel scar of the access road. To one side was the tree that looked rickety from the work of bark beetles, but now was not to the time to mention it.

I noticed a package of muffins on the counter and asked for one, which drew a look that confirmed I was still in the doghouse, but she sliced the muffin and stuck it in the toaster. Her movements were deliberate and she kept her head still, her brown eyes downcast and hair pulled back, exposing her delicate neck. Her face appeared to be less swollen and the bruising had diminished a bit. Even jeans, a baggy T-shirt, and a Swedish cross of bandages couldn't counteract her elegance. Too bad about the attitude.

She glanced up and caught me looking. When she came toward me with the buttered muffin on a plate, her posture was exemplary and she did something with her hips, a second-nature signal of who was in control here.

"Do you have anybody looking after you while you're on the mend?"

"Helen from the pharmacy came over. She said she'll stop around again to keep an eye on me, but I don't need it."

I bit into the muffin.

"There's an FBI agent in town. Apparently, he doesn't like the looks of our roles in this, especially mine. It would help if I knew why the thief came to you with the bird."

Her lids went halfway down, and I assumed the set of her lips was meant to be a frown rather than a grimace.

"Fab, I'm on your side."

"That's what Jim used to say."

"Great. Davenport and I are the same to you."

"Don't be so sensitive." Her expression softened and she put her hand on mine. "You know you've always been my main guy. You and Stuart."

The mention of Stuart quieted us both. I took her fingers for a moment and then let go. She sat down across from me.

"I'm glad he was able to take care of you."

"He and his dad were always good at that, weren't they?"

We were silent.

"Who dropped off the statue?"

"He didn't leave a card." She touched her forehead. "He put it behind a bush, at the bend down there. I was told on the phone to get it immediately and call you, and you'd bring money for it. I asked what this had to do with me and the guy said nothing, just give the package to you, take the money, and await further instructions. He said do what you're told, right now, and keep your mouth shut if you want to stay healthy. I didn't like anything about this. I put on a pair of gloves, got the thing and stuck it in the linen closet. Then I called you, but Jim showed up. Where were you?"

"You haven't checked your voicemail since then? Car trouble. The delay gave somebody just enough time to knock off Davenport and get away."

"I'm the killer, dummy, or did you forget? I was the one caught with the gun."

I finished the muffin, chewing deliberately, drank some coffee, wiped my mouth.

"Yeah, nobody thinks you're a killer."

She stared.

"They found me with the weapon. No thanks to you."

"Darlene is no beginner. She knows you couldn't have grabbed a gun from somewhere and plugged him before you passed out from the beating."

She looked out the window, eyes hard. I drained the coffee.

"You're sure Davenport didn't bring the statue?"

She snorted. "I thought we established he wasn't roughing me up for kicks. At least not that time."

"Jesus," I said, pushing the plate away. "Is all this true, or are you painting yourself as the innocent?"

She raised her expressive eyes, which were now flinty with defiance.

"I'm tired of these questions, Reese. I didn't get much sleep."

"Well, that's just awful. I'll ask you an easier one. Who hired Davenport?"

"That's another question you asked me at the hospital and my answer is the same. I don't know. Did someone hire him?"

"Come on, Fabienne. Who are you going to trust if you can't

trust me?"

"Trust you?" she said angrily. "What about you forgetting to tell me until now that I don't have a murder rap hanging over me? Trust has to make good sense, mister."

I flicked the back of my hand in her direction.

"And good sense has never been your strong suit. Jim Davenport, for Chrissakes."

She stood slowly, summoning something bad, but her attention was diverted by movement beyond the window. I turned and glimpsed a dark-blue SUV as it disappeared from the end of the dirt-and-gravel path to her place.

"Who was that? Was that Wilber Arndt's rig? Don't tell me you're back with that knucklehead."

"He's not a knucklehead, he's a sweet guy, and I haven't seen him for months."

"He's not a sweet guy; are you nuts? He breaks into cars. He steals stuff from his neighbors' yards."

"Not all the time."

I went to the door, opened it, and looked at the empty drive. Even though it bent out of sight around the trees and her window was closed, I should have heard the vehicle coming. It must have been crawling up the road.

"Probably recognized my truck. He's not part of this mess, is he?"

"You scared Wilber," she responded from behind me. "Big man."

This made me think of Minta calling me little man. I remembered Tireia's invitation to Fabienne, and told myself to lighten up.

"Hey, listen," I said, turning to her. "Why don't you come over to Tireia's for lunch on Sunday? It's her birthday. Just us and Minta. For fun, no pressure."

She looked up with sudden warmth and for a moment the years fell away and there she was again, Stuart's gorgeous young bride. It was the same radiance she'd had throughout their wedding. I could see us all now at the Sedgeley Club on a bend of the Schuylkill River at the end of Boathouse Row. Fabienne with her three bridesmaids, one from the nightspot where she worked as a server and the other two Stuart's sisters, aged fifteen and twelve. Myself in a tux as best man. The celebrant strangely in black, her hair pulled back, her makeup white. Fab and Stuart kept their vows short, his about seizing the moment and hers about a love to transcend trouble and time. Her wedding ring was antique, its gold laced with diamonds and rubies. The cake was a pavlova, as delicate and ephemeral as a cloud. Stuart's school friends balanced little plates of immaculately catered hors d'oeuvres and coupes of expensive champagne while they jiggled in place to comply with the safety ban on dancing in the historic structure. His divorced parents arrived separately and kept a wary distance from one another. The mother gushed to whomever came near, while the father made a stiff show of engaging in banter with the young people. The celebrant raised a glass and then vanished. Circulating among the guests, the newlyweds stuck together all night, welded at the hip, and Stuart's bad lungs gave him a timely reprieve. All long ago now.

On the porch, Fabienne stretched forward and kissed my cheek, which caused me to back away and stumble on the step like a teenager. I quickly exaggerated it for a laugh and to cover up.

"I'd better get going."

At the truck, I turned and waved. Her smiling nod of response carried traces of triumph and contempt that made me less angry than sad, and most of all disappointed. On the other hand, I had my own ulterior motive for inviting her to the party, and she probably knew it.

55

11

Sometimes my work ethic nagged when I found myself in bed with Tireia in the middle of the day. Freud never actually said love and work are the main things but I think he believed it, which helped, because Tireia and I were in bed talking about work. She had taken my nudge about looking into Fabienne's role in this situation with the bird and had gone into flight. Darlene once said it reflected well on me to not be intimidated by a partner like Tireia, but really, it didn't have much to do with that. Her head was on the pillow next to me, she was looking at the ceiling and talking, and her mind was as immaculate as her uncovered body. My presence required no bravery.

She asked for a recap of what we knew. The way she put it was we needed to look at how roads connect people to where they go. I recounted that Fab claimed to have gotten a phone call from someone who left the falcon outside her place and told her to give it to me and take the cash for it, which the caller presumably would pick up later. She hid the statue, and then Jim Davenport burst in and tried to beat the whereabouts of the bird out of her, but she claimed ignorance because she wanted to help me. She passed out, someone came in, shot Davenport, and put the weapon in her hand, yet apparently did not look for the statue.

Laid out like that, it was a potholed route. But I wanted to believe Fab.

Tireia figured that starting with a hypothesis about what Fabienne might be hiding would be the wrongheaded method, akin to building a road without first considering the residents and their destinations. We should examine what we already knew about Fabienne and the situation, starting with when she met the man who would become her husband, my friend Stuart Sansverrou.

Tireia was aware we had been roommates in Mayer Hall at the University of Pennsylvania, a school to which I came a decade later than the average student and to which Stuart would not have been accepted without the intercession of his wealthy father. George Sansverrou was a New York City trader in high-end antiques and art who had a reputation for relentlessness in pursuit of what he wanted. His son was much different, a charmer who was disliked only by the sort of humorless prig nobody else likes. He occasionally was unreliable but his company was always a pleasure, and he could be counted on for splurges on food and drink whenever his father reloaded the coffers.

Stuart declared a communications major because someone told him it had the easiest classes, but he didn't do the reading and soon was in danger of flunking out. My bent was criminology, co-eds, and occasional flying for a Philadelphia charter outfit. From the start, our time together at Penn smelled as transitory as a pack of Camels.

I had told Tireia about the first time Stuart introduced me to Fabienne on Wynn Commons. I barely had a chance to say hello before she flapped and fluttered in alarm and escaped.

Stuart laughed, and I stood a tick too long with my mouth open. For a while, until she got used to me, she always seemed to be moving away with a little wave.

"I never did figure out why she was so skittish," I said to Tireia.

"If that's true, you didn't try very hard."

"No, it was never like that," I protested.

"Anyway, I have a question for you that came up from a little research I've been doing."

She said she had been attempting to find any prior connection between Fabienne and the bird. This had led her to collectibles in general and, from there, to Stuart and his father. Looking into the activities of George Sansverrou, Tireia came across a Victoria and Albert Museum display description of an enameled gold mourning ring that commemorated the death in battle of Vice-Admiral Horatio Nelson in 1805. The notation said the ring was donated by Sansverrou, who had purchased it from Anglophile Antiques in Philadelphia. She soon found a profile in the *Journal of Antiques and Collectibles* of the company's principal, Ellis Trask. The reporter asked what sort of merchandise Trask had moved lately, and among the examples he gave was sale of the ring.

"Do you recall anything about that ring?" she asked.

"No, but the little wooden box Stuart gave me had a Nelson connection, remember?"

"I do. Go over it again."

I reminded her it was the day Stuart hired student movers to bring his stuff from our apartment to a new place for Fabienne and himself. He plucked a small oaken box with silver inlay from among recent purchases and gave it to me. He said the wood was thought to be taken from the barrel of brandy in which Nelson's body was preserved during the long trip back to England from the Battle of Trafalgar, although he admitted to doubts about the provenance. He poured brandy and we toasted the future over the hero's blood.

"Fabienne was the one always scavenging for expensive trinkets with him," I said. "We should ask her about the stuff he collected."

Tireia also had discovered that the head of Anglophile Antiques made news a few years after the magazine profile, and not in a good way. Ellis Trask bought a collection of brooches designed by the artist Adrian van Geitel that had been burgled from a Seattle estate. He tried to sell them to a private collector, who realized they were hot, and reported Trask to the FBI. He was convicted of trafficking in stolen goods and spent eighteen months in a federal prison.

Less than a year after his release, five thieves in black masks drove an SUV into the metal security doors of a Neiman Marcus jewelry salon on Ala Moana Boulevard in Honolulu. They used sledgehammers to smash open a heavy glass case in which a statue called the Irwin Raptor was being displayed. Designed by jeweler Harold Irwin, it was a replica in gold of *The Maltese Falcon* prop, with ruby eyes and a huge diamond hanging from a platinum chain held in its beak. It cost eight million dollars to make and was considered to be worth much more than that. The theft took less than forty seconds.

"They showed it at the Academy Awards one year before the theft, remember?" she said.

"It rings a distant bell."

"Anyway, I got curious about it after I found out Trask had bought the van Geitel brooches. I knew the Irwin Raptor had been added to the FBI's top ten list of stolen art, so I put in a call to Red Davis."

I made a questioning face.

"An old friend of my dad," she said. "He works in incident-based reporting for the agency. So Red looked into it for me, and said the statue was thought to have gone to the East Coast. In the end, the agents couldn't pin down a culprit. But they were pretty sure the raptor was in Philadelphia."

I followed her gaze to a constellation of white vesicles plastered on the ceiling, like a negative of the stars. Once as we lay here she had marveled at the way goop troweled onto a ceiling could take on shapes that mimicked the points and swirls of a night sky. Now I thought of that whenever we were here.

"The FBI suspected Trask," she said. "During the investigation, their agents interviewed his regular customers as potential buyers of the Irwin statue. Red told me Stuart and Fabienne were on the list of interviewees, because Stuart bought stuff for his father from Trask, and Fab tagged along. I asked who signed the paperwork. It was the guy who's here now, Graham Wheeler."

"Hmm . . . I wonder what Stuart could have told us about any of this."

"I wonder, too."

She smoothed my hair, which had a tendency to dart up like bayonet rushes after our exertions.

"Spheres and triangles," she said, looking me over. "A cubist's dream."

"Isn't cubism kind of six-fingered and three-eyed?"

"It's a geometric conjugation of to be," she replied, slaying me with that smile.

She took my hand, and we looked up at the swirls.

"I don't trust Cassim Geyer," she said. "Still, would he set up a theft to extort money from his own client? Would he bite the hand?"

"I'd like to know why Fabienne's old boyfriend Wilber Arndt was hanging around her place the other day," I said. "Was he just mooning after her, or is he part of it?"

"Yes. And it interests me that Mrs. Pascoe-Leyland told Cassim Geyer and the museum lady, Maggie Kornbluth, that she didn't want the police involved. Why so untrusting?"

"A lot of parts are missing."

"They're there," she said, tracing a finger around the patterns above us. "Somewhere."

12

arlene told me on the phone she had spoken to Tireia and had decided to let us help, within limits. She didn't specify what the limits were. She said Davenport's widow had come to town and asked if I wanted to sit in on the interview. I arrived early at the sheriff's two-toned shoebox of an office and took a chair in front of her desk. Darlene didn't move. She looked worn and kept a hand on her swollen abdomen, which could have been an urge to comfort the fetus or maybe was more like holding your forehead when you have a migraine.

"You seem a little peaked. Can I get you anything?"

"I'm fine. Actually, there should be juice in there," she said, and pointed to a bar fridge in the corner. "And a bit of chocolate left, I think. See if you can find something for yourself, too."

I got up, went to the fridge, and extracted a small bottle of orange juice and a half-bar of chocolate. I passed over the Evian waters and glanced at the other contents, the artichoke hearts, a jar of pickled asparagus, an unpeeled kiwi, a decimated wedge of Gorgonzola. No sardines and peanut butter, though. I closed the door and brought Darlene her goodies.

She unwrapped the chocolate with the absorption of a child, an effect heightened by the freckling on her round face above a bob haircut that as usual looked unfamiliar with a brush. She chewed, seeming to have forgotten me for a moment as she stared at a small framed picture on her desk, which showed Hank and their two kids near a corral on the ranch. Tireia and I had gone with Minta to their place for dinner a few times. Darlene was good at preparing stereotypical western fare but her affable, stay-at-home husband gave Tireia the willies. Hank enjoyed chatting with me about stuff I never did, like green chopping or herding. Tireia usually wore something western, a denim skirt or checked shirt with mother-of-pearl snaps, and drank more wine than normal. Minta got along great with the Carmody kids.

Darlene roused herself and said, "OK, if we're asking and telling, you go first."

"Right. Fabienne insists the gun isn't hers and she doesn't know where it came from. She said some guy called, she didn't know who, and told her he'd left the package at the end of her driveway. Davenport was trying to beat information out of her."

"How would he know anything about it?"

"You got me. Maybe Mrs. Davenport will tell us."

"All right. What else?"

"I saw Wilber Arndt lurking around Fabienne's cabin. He raced off when he spotted my rig out front."

She looked up dreamily, suffused by a sugar rush.

"You wouldn't want to leave your change on the bar next to Wilber, but he's not violent."

"Don't let that goofy kid style fool you. I've seen him when he feels like somebody isn't treating him right, and it's not pleasant. Listen, could you do me a favor and check out what he's up to these days?"

"Call out the troops? Deploy a garrison? All right, I'll send someone, now that you've fetched an orange juice for me. Will that make us even?"

"Just barely. And I've got other news for you."

I told her what Tireia had discovered about the art collector Ellis Trask, who was suspected of possessing a stolen replica in gold of the Maltese Falcon called the Irwin Raptor. When I said Trask had been interrogated in the past by the same FBI agent who was in town now, and both Agent Wheeler and Trask probably had met Fabienne, she looked sharply at me.

"Good information."

Derek the deputy knocked on the open door and bent his upper half around the frame.

"Mrs. Davenport's here."

"Give her a coffee and put her in the interview room. We'll be there in a sec."

She made an effort to rise and I hurried around the desk to put a hand under her elbow.

"I'm OK. Here we go," she said, patting my arm.

"How long is she here for?"

"She's taking the ashes back to L.A. tomorrow."

Sondra Davenport sat in a plastic chair, smoking over a cup of coffee that sat on the bolted-down table in the interview room. A raveled blonde in her early thirties, she peered at us through glasses so big they looked like a disguise. This sparse room with its video camera in the recess of a wall seemed like the wrong place to be getting information from her, but I kept silent.

"Mrs. Davenport, I'm Sheriff Carmody and this is Reese Mencari. Thank you for coming in to talk with us. I know it must be a difficult time for you."

The guest drew on her cigarette and blew smoke in my general direction but said nothing. Darlene had done well with the quick introduction that avoided giving me any descriptor, which simultaneously put me in it and kept me out of it. Did Sondra Davenport recognize my name? Hard to tell behind those big lenses. Her hand trembled, which revealed little.

Darlene was in no hurry. She sat quietly, hands intertwined on her inflated stomach, her bob cocked in sympathy. More time ticked by in silence.

At last, Sondra said, "So have you put that woman in jail? The one who did this?"

"Fabienne Sansverrou is a suspect."

We watched closely but she made no response.

"Do you know her?" Darlene prodded.

"I knew her first name. Never met her, of course. Jim was coming back to me, though. She distracted him for a while but we have kids, and he was a responsible man. Difficult sometimes. Very difficult."

"He told you he was coming back to the family?"

"It was never in question. Have you taken her in?"

Darlene placed her hands on the arms of the chair and straightened up carefully.

"At this point, we're still gathering information, Mrs. Davenport. We're making progress but there's a lot of investigating left to do."

"You go ahead and gather as much evidence as you want. In the end, it's her. She's the one with the motive."

"Why's that? Do you think she knew your husband was going to leave her?"

Wearily, Sondra stubbed out her cigarette and lapsed into silence again.

Darlene flinched and shifted in the plastic chair.

"You all right, sheriff?" I asked.

"The little one's kicking up a fuss is all. How about if we move to my office? It's a bit more comfortable there."

Darlene hoisted herself up, stepped past me around the little table and took the elbow of Sondra Davenport, whose surprise showed in her stiffness as they moved toward the door. Darlene let go to cross the threshold but once in the hall, she took Sondra's arm again as if it were expected. Behind them, I caught enough of their murmured conversation to be impressed. Darlene confided that she had expected this third pregnancy to be easy but it had turned out to be the hardest, which prompted the other woman to offer that in her experience it never was easy. By the end of the short walk to the office, they had fallen into the companionable reminiscence of veterans, with all the shared sacrifice and hardheaded duty it implied.

When they reached the office, the two settled themselves on the couch as Sondra continued an account of the birth of her second one in a van parked in the driveway, attended by a midwife because Jim was out of work at the time and it was cheaper that way, plus she never had much faith in hospitals anyway. To me, sitting gingerly at a distance from the sofa, it looked like any second now the two women would be holding hands. Sondra probably didn't get much chance to do this sort of thing. I found it hard to imagine her hobnobbing with other parents outside the grammar school. And then Jim lost his investigative license, she said, which was why he came to Idaho, one of the only places where he didn't have to have one. It was hard being on her own, even though it wasn't the first time, but then he took up with that woman, who got mixed up in the theft of the statue. That was her motive. Because Jim was hired to get it back.

Darlene wondered aloud who had hired him. Sondra replied that she didn't know who it was. She took a drag on her cigarette and said Jim was after something else, too. He didn't give any details, just said it was really expensive. It would have been a big payday to find it and he would have done so, too, but …

Darlene asked if this was the same person who hired Jim to locate the falcon but the widow only shrugged. Darlene asked about the funeral. Sondra said she was bringing the ashes back for a ceremony with the kids but nobody else would be there because Jim was out of touch with his own family and her parents didn't care much for him and he didn't have any friends, not that she would count as friends, anyway. Her tone had gone flat again. Everyone in the room knew it was the end of the interview. Darlene asked again if she had any notion of who might have hired him to locate the statue or the other object, but she replied wearily she had no idea.

After she left, I remarked that the other valuable thing could be the Irwin Raptor.

Darlene nodded and said, "I had a session with the FBI guy, Wheeler, who made a vague mention of interstate crime. I'll have to tell him Sondra Davenport is here, but I wanted to give us first crack. He's already clamoring to talk to you. Don't make that face, I don't like it either, especially because he's a bad listener and insists on regarding you as his main suspect. He kept going on about you and Fabienne. You won't like this, but I decided it was in your best interests that I give him the history of you two."

"For Christ's sake, Darlene."

"For your sake, buddy. I knew you wouldn't tell him, and I didn't want you reacting badly under what he likes to call his interrogation."

She blinked and put a hand on her stomach.

"You sure you're feeling all right?"

"Yeah, fine. I made a call to a guy I went to school with who's at the agency. He heard Wheeler's not in the department's best graces. He shot and seriously wounded a suspect, supposedly in self-defense, but it turned out the man was unarmed and innocent. Wheeler got through the hearing but not without damage."

"So our agent's hoping to clear his name by focusing on me."

"What can I say, a slow learner. But he likes to hear himself talk, which might be useful."

"A suggestion, Darlene: check with California on who shows up at Davenport's funeral."

"We can do that."

"Good. And now, if you will, tell me about your meeting with Wheeler."

13

Darlene's ability to reconstruct anything she witnessed was marked by an investigator's eye for detail and a meticulous memory. She delivered a nuanced description of her encounter with the FBI's Graham Wheeler. He looked like a cop's imitation of a college professor, she said, in his deck shoes, wrinkled slacks, and Greek fisherman's cap. She gaped at his pocket protector. Sandy-haired and bearded, Wheeler stood with hands behind his back as if to compensate for his slight under-sizing. She found it weirdly comical the way he leaned forward and produced one hand to shake with her, but kept the other behind him. When she motioned him toward the beat-up armchair in her office, for a moment it looked as though he would brush it, she said, but he withdrew his hovering fingers, spun around, and plopped down with a sigh of satisfaction. He looked like he'd ask for a cup of coffee, so she offered one.

"No, thanks, I never drink the stuff," he said. "Bad for the blood pressure."

"You're too young to have blood pressure problems."

"I don't," he replied. "Because I don't drink coffee."

Darlene gave him water. Then she steered her amplitude

around the corner of her desk and settled, with far less pleasure than that of her guest, into her whimpering chair.

"When's the happy day?" he said. "If you don't mind my asking."

"Too soon," she replied. "And not soon enough by a damn sight."

A stupefied look came upon him and disappeared, as if he had remembered not to wear that expression. His upper body bent forward like a joystick.

"Excuse me for getting right down to business, but I'm anxious to gather the basics from you before interrogating people myself."

"Talking to them won't suffice?"

The stunned expression bloomed again, held, and withered.

"It's a term of trade, Sheriff Carmody, as you know. Doesn't matter, I want to start with this pilot who picked up the object for delivery, Reese Mencari. Now, I know from your report he was working for Cassim Geyer and he returned Rowena Pascoe-Leyland's statuette to Ketchum. I also understand he found said statuette in the home of a young woman named Fabienne Sansverrou, who apparently was armed and unconscious, lying beside the corpse of a private investigator, Jim Davenport, with whom she was romantically involved. Mrs. Sansverrou had bodily injuries inflicted by the deceased. I'm here to untangle all this, and, frankly, I'd be surprised if Reese Mencari isn't the right thread to pull."

"Well, regardless of which threads you pull, I can't say I understand why the FBI is getting involved in this homicide. You just pointed out the falcon was returned. Nor do I understand how you found out about the theft. It wasn't reported."

When Wheeler leaned back and put his hands behind his

head, he revealed patches of perspiration as big as elbow pads, although it wasn't hot in the office.

"I can't tell you how we knew, that's privileged. But I can say the homicide was committed in connection with the theft of an art object."

"We don't know that for sure."

He ignored this.

"Of course, the statuette didn't travel across state lines, so our involvement wouldn't normally be warranted."

"Why is it warranted, then?"

He put his arms down. She saw something at work on his soft, furry face—a struggle of some kind, a decision to be made. He wanted to tell her something and didn't know if he should. It was as if several strings, his tangled threads, were being pulled inside his head, drawing his lips and eyebrows tight.

"You have another motive for being here," she prompted.

"That's right, you're right, I have another motive. We have reason to believe state borders were crossed in this case, I can tell you that much. Does that bring any ideas to your mind?"

Darlene recalled that around this time she fidgeted, not at his question but at a thump from her internal passenger. She reached for the glass on her desk and took a drink of water.

"I can't say it does," she replied. "Should it?"

"You're sure?" He peered at her, waiting. "In that case, let's just say it's a federal matter. No, don't interrupt." He held up his hand as if to stop her from talking, although she had made no attempt to speak. "I realize you're a colleague, but this is a question of jurisdiction and need to know."

"Did you say need to know?"

"I did, yes."

"OK. First time I heard anyone actually use the term, is all."

Wheeler put his palm on the top of his cap and left it there for a second; another gesture she considered noteworthy.

"Let's continue. What can you tell me about the nature of the relationship between the deceased and Fabienne Sansverrou?"

Darlene folded her arms and said, "Davenport was the latest of a dubious bunch of admirers since the death of her husband. I would describe their relationship as mutually abusive. She harangued him and he cuffed her around."

"How long had they been together?"

"I don't know, a few months. Fabienne doesn't have a lot of staying power. Or maybe she just suffers fools temporarily."

"I see." Wheeler pulled out his phone and started poking and scrolling. "And this late husband, ah, Stuart Sansverrou. He and Reese Mencari were friends?"

"Yep, they went to college together back East. All three of them met there."

"This intrigues me," Wheeler said, and looked up from the screen. "According to your report, Mencari received a call from Mrs. Sansverrou, who said she had the statue. The thief had left it with her and told her to call Mencari. He arrived with money for the exchange, but instead he found two bodies on the floor. He reported the homicide to you. Later you discovered that Mencari had taken the statue and returned it and the money to his client in Ketchum."

Wheeler put away his phone and rubbed his hands thoroughly, as if applying moisturizer.

"Mrs. Sansverrou's unconscious state makes it unlikely she would be the killer, whether or not in self-defense. If someone else got there before Mencari, why would this other person shoot Davenport, unless he wanted the statuette? Yet as we know, it wasn't taken, and it wasn't well-hidden."

Wheeler leaned back and gazed at her.

"This is where Mr. Mencari's long association with Mrs. Sansverrou gets interesting."

Darlene listened silently as the FBI agent laid out his logic.

"I find it fascinating that Mrs. Sansverrou was the wife of Mencari's best friend, and that these two have kept a close relationship long after Stuart Sansverrou's death. They even live in the same town, far from where they first met. This suggests a connection likely to be romantic. Maybe Mencari had wanted to marry her. Maybe he'd been in love with her all along. It could be Mencari came upon Davenport attacking Mrs. Sansverrou, which might have been related to the prop in some way or completely unrelated to it; you've just confirmed that the couple had a violent relationship."

"Fabienne says he was roughing her up because he thought she knew where it was."

"I see. I'll talk to her next. But Davenport's motive doesn't alter my theory of his death. Mencari could have shot him, which Mrs. Sansverrou didn't witness because she was unconscious by then. Realizing what he'd done, he could have wiped the gun and put it in her hand, knowing she wouldn't be suspected of the shooting because of her condition. And even if she were accused, it obviously would be self-defense."

"Interesting," Darlene said when he was done. "And you intend to confront Reese with this deduction?"

"You don't think I should?"

"It's just that he can be a little moody. Especially if you accuse him of gunning down a private detective and framing Fabienne for it."

Wheeler's teddy-like visage fostered another double-take and then wiped itself back to the blank slate.

"I don't see it as a stretch," he said. "Mencari has a history of assault against Davenport, doesn't he? You didn't put that in your report but, you see, I did my own backgrounding."

"It was a scuffle. He wasn't charged."

"He's my chief suspect, sheriff. He has an unhealthy fixation on the woman, and we both know what can come from that frame of mind. What's more, Mrs. Sansverrou isn't guilt-free. Somehow, the two of them are in this together, and I'm going to get to the bottom of it."

She let this sit for a moment, and then said, "Look, you're missing something about Reese and Fabienne. Not many people are aware of this, and he wouldn't want me blabbing it to a stranger, but I'm going to anyway. It's need to know."

Darlene was our friend; she knew the whole story. And she was right: I wasn't thrilled that she blabbed it to a stranger.

At my place, I called Anglophile Antiques in Philadelphia and spoke briefly to the boss, Ellis Trask. The East Coast was beyond my aircraft's range without refueling, so I got on the computer and booked the soonest flight achievable. On the drive through Long Valley, I called Tireia to tell her Sondra Davenport had said her husband was after both the bird and another valuable object.

"There you go," she responded. "The other object was the golden statue made by Harold Irwin."

"That possibility crossed my mind." I kept an eye on several Red Angus that had gotten through the wire and were grazing on the verge. "But what does the Irwin Raptor have to do with the prop? Aside from being a fancy tribute, I mean."

"I don't know, although I imagine a fancy tribute should be enough to put you in the air going east."

"Heading out of town now."

"How exciting. You should stop by and I'll bid you a fond farewell."

"That would be a delight," I said. "Unfortunately, I have to hustle to catch the flight. My love to Minta. Tell her I'll see her Sunday."

As I drove down the steep and winding gorge to Boise, my mind struggled to identify a connection between the Maltese Falcon and the Irwin Raptor.

If Jim Davenport had been chasing both statues, why? Had the Irwin crossed state lines and, if so, for what purpose? The strain of trying to puzzle it out made my head feel heavy. Maybe answers could be extracted from Ellis Trask, if he had any to yield.

Seven hours later, after an hour layover in Denver, I took my carry-on through the gates at Philadelphia International, stepped onto the regional train, and in twenty-five minutes got off at Jefferson Station downtown. It was about midnight. On my way to the Marriott, I passed a couple of guys arguing over rights to a blanket in the dark underpass on Filbert between the transit hub and the Reading Terminal Market.

In the morning after coffee, I emerged into pleasant weather and the sight of a man diving headfirst into a trash bin. He surfaced and sucked down a drink through a straw. I strolled down Twelfth Street past a jewelry store, a patisserie, a kitchenware shop. A trio of office women in their spring dresses expertly ignored a panhandler. The beggars on the streets of Philthy were like toll collectors at spectral bridges spanning the gulf between worlds. I gave a dollar to an old lady on crutches, her ankles swollen, dressing gown askew.

"Thanks, I'll drink it," she rasped. "You don't like me so much now, do you?"

Not far from a stunning mural on the back of a sandstone building, a sour little fellow occupied a corner of sidewalk on Locust, silent beside his planks pinned with scores of cardboard squares that were covered in a scrawl I felt disinclined to read. I passed a coffee shop, a barber, a tavern. A guy on Spruce Street ranted about black men and white women. At Cypress

Street, a man ran down the alley screaming, "And I mean, *that's it!*"

From behind the plastic window of a newspaper vending machine, a *Philadelphia Inquirer* headline announced the police department had started a gun control task force. It reminded me of the city's gun violence epidemic when I first came here a dozen years ago. I bent down and read a few paragraphs of the report. The task force appeared to be a replica of the one the D.A.'s office had started back then, trying to quell so-called straw purchases of weapons by people who sold the guns to convicted felons.

In my college years, I'd joined other student activists marching on city hall and clamoring for tougher gun control laws, even though the local government was prohibited by state law from creating its own such statutes. I smiled at the memory of how the city council had amazed us by defying that limitation to pass a raft of laws aimed at licensing, multiple gun purchases, assault weapons, ammunition sales. It looked like we'd made a difference, until the state took the city to court and the new laws were struck down within a year.

The brick-fronted Anglophile Antiques was in a good spot amid Pine Street's hip dishevelment, a democratic mix of high- and low-end arts endeavors. In the shop, I told the young woman behind a counter that Mr. Trask was expecting me. She went through a door in the back wall between shelves filled with crystal ware, silver cups and bowls, amulets and bracelets. Tables were crammed with lamps, clocks, and statues. Paintings and mirrors hung between shelves on the side walls. The attendant emerged quickly and held the door open. Trask stood in front of a bureau-style desk with a writing surface that folded down on hinges, which didn't look practical, but the oaken sides were covered in scrollwork of astonishing craftsmanship. In a perfectly cut suit, his eyes underlain by purplish vales, he looked like a banker with a drug habit. He offered a firm handshake and motioned me into a chair with a high rounded back that was like fitting myself inside a cobra's hood. My host sat behind the desk in an upholstered swivel chair with carved armrests of oak.

"You've come a long way," he said. "I hope it won't be in vain. Like I said on the phone, there isn't much I can tell you about the mourning ring given out at Admiral Nelson's funeral. It wasn't exceptional. Maybe fifty of them were made for family and friends who attended. Really, that's all I can say."

He reached for his in-basket and pulled out a copy of the *Journal of Antiques and Collectibles*. "I looked this up and read it again after you called." He flicked to the start of an article about him. "It refreshed my memory concerning a few things but unfortunately I still can't come up with the answer to your question over the phone about who sold the ring to me."

He was lying. It wasn't something a collector with an Admiral Nelson fetish would forget. Never tell more than you have to.

"Can't recall, huh," I said. "What about your records?"

"I'm afraid I haven't kept anything from that far back."

"Maybe I can help. You also sold a small wooden box with silver inlay to Stuart Sansverrou that day. Remember? The little box made from the wood of the brandy barrel Nelson's men put him in after he was killed? Stuart gave it to me."

I pulled the box out of my pocket and put it on the desk. He picked it up.

"Ah, yes, I remember this. The Nelson box. I don't know if Stuart told you, but its provenance is uncertain, not to say dubious. Sorry if that's a surprise. I didn't even mention the box to the antiques journal writer. And where I got the mourning ring or this little box continues to elude me."

"Let's talk then about someone we both know. Fabienne Sansverrou."

"I thought she might be a reason you wanted to see me."

"Why is that? How did you know I'd ask about her?"

Trask showed vibrantly yellow teeth. "I didn't see it in any news report, if that's what you mean."

So he knew about the theft. And he was letting me know he knew. This was a surprise, after his stonewalling about the mourning ring. I paused a moment, and considered Tireia's discovery that the FBI had questioned him years ago over the Irwin Raptor. I took a guess.

"Graham Wheeler would have told you about her."

His hooded glance was sharp. "Yes, Wheeler stopped by. I'm impressed you know that."

"He's talkative."

Trask's laugh was appreciative. I had no problem with him being under the impression I had already met the government man. He wasn't the only one who could play the game of not telling more than you have to. I leaned forward in an attempt to get clear of the cobra's hood.

"How was Wheeler aware you knew Fabienne?"

"Can't say. Did you tell him? You're friends with her, aren't you? Live in the same town and all?"

I flared up inside at his attempt to imply he knew all about me, but kept cool on the outside. "It's interesting you know I live in the same town as Fabienne. You've been paying attention."

"I always pay attention, Mencari. It's one of my gifts."

"Like trafficking in stolen jewelry? Is that another of your gifts?"

Trask selected a pencil from a leather cup, held it at both

ends for a moment, and then tossed it onto the writing table.

"Receiving the van Geitel brooches was a mistake," he said. "I served the time, and my standing in the business was damaged beyond repair. This place is just for walk-in trade. I'm a pariah now among serious collectors."

"Gee, that's too bad. But you'll be a featured speaker at a collectors' convention in San Francisco pretty soon, isn't that right? So your reputation can't be too damaged."

"I'm surprised you know about it."

"It's a gift."

He touched a fingertip to his tongue and drew a mark in the air.

"San Francisco is the first public invitation I've gotten since my legal troubles. We'll see how it goes."

"Let's get back to Fabienne. Did Wheeler tell you why he was interested in her?"

"He said he got a tip about a theft, and she was involved. He was digging for background on her. But I couldn't help. I barely knew the gal."

"When was the last time you spoke to her?"

He let this question hover, and then said, "Like I told the agent, the last time I saw her was almost a decade ago, when Stuart was in college. She came along sometimes when he bought stuff from me on behalf of his father. I wouldn't even have remembered her if she hadn't been with him."

"What do you know about the falcon?"

"Only what I saw in the movies and read in the collectors' journals. And what Wheeler said . . . that it was missing."
"It's interesting he identified it."

"Like you say, he's talkative."

Trask displayed his teeth again, as strong and uniform as the Yellow Brick Road. I receded into the hood and put my hands behind my head.

"The thing is, it doesn't make much sense the FBI would contact you about a woman you barely even knew. But I can think of a better reason for Wheeler's interest in you. It has to do with the theft of a statue in Honolulu. That would have been, oh, not even a year after you got out of the slammer."

Trask stood and smoothed his immaculate suit. He turned his back and stepped toward a small painting of a valley sunlit through storm clouds.

"You mean the Irwin Raptor," he said to the painting.

"That's what I mean. They traced it to Philly, but they couldn't pin you down, could they?"

The collector turned.

"I told you, I paid for my one error of judgment with the van Geitel jewelry. Ask yourself if you really think I would have been foolish enough to fence an item as hot as that statue."

"Maybe not. But you might have bought it for yourself with some of the dough you stashed from years of fencing stolen goods before you got caught."

"Please. What's any of this got to do with Wheeler coming to see me?"

"For one, he says the Irwin Raptor is involved in all this." There was no percentage in telling Trask that Agent Wheeler had merely hinted at it to Darlene. "Two, it was made in the likeness of the film prop, which Fabienne was mixed up with. Three, you know Fabienne."

"Oh, my God!" Trask mimed casting a line and reeling it in. "It's a monster!"

I stood and stretched, and then moved about the office, tracing a finger along clutter that looked as though it had made its way here from the shop floor. I picked up a sandstone whistle in the shape of a peacock and tried to make a sound from it, but failed. I kept holding it.

"You're just the person to know how those two statues are linked," I said. "And you're right that I'm friends with Fabienne. She's in a tight spot and if I can help her, I will."

Trask folded his arms and peered, his eyes almost obscured by the darkness underneath them, as if he were watching me from a glade.

"It's an interesting situation," he allowed. "From a professional viewpoint, I think you have to ask yourself what do people do with a famous stolen item? One answer is they hang onto it, enjoy owning it, and wait until it's safe to find a buyer and make a profit. But the Irwin Raptor's provenance is no tangled web. It proceeds directly from the maker to the thief. Anybody who recognizes it—a golden statue with a diamond pendant, one of a kind—knows it was stolen."

"So how does a person get rid of it?"

"They could take it apart, sell the rock, melt the gold. If they weren't philistine enough to do that, it would be difficult." He paused. "I can offer a hypothetical. I'd say anyone who did have the Irwin Raptor might be tempted to trade it for the Maltese Falcon, if that opportunity arose. Of course, you can argue it's a bad deal, trading lead for precious materials. The characters in the movie sure wouldn't have done it."

The peacock went back in its place atop a low bookshelf.

"A trade. But why would Rowena Pascoe-Leyland, who owns the falcon legitimately, trade it for the stolen Irwin?"

"Why, indeed? You'd have to ask her, I guess. In my own opinion, possession is an illusion."

"A philosopher thief. I love it."

"I'm neither of those things. But you came all this way, so I'm happy to see you're entertained. The truth is, I've never laid eyes on either one of the statues except in photos."

I returned to the cobra chair.

"Even if you did, there'd be no reason for you to tell me about it."

"No, that wouldn't make sense." He went back to his chair as well, and folded his hands over his flat stomach. "If I were the Irwin's owner, there'd be no point in telling you any of this. Unless, I suppose, the idea of some bastard cheating me out of it was just too annoying."

"Cheating you out of it? Let me get this straight. You're saying maybe there was a trade of the two birds, but it fell through when the prop was swiped." I crossed my arms. "Let's say you were the one who had the Irwin, and you were trading it for the falcon. But let's say you didn't get either one of those statues back. You were cheated. What that tells me is both birds were stolen."

"I agree … hypothetically. Both statues would have been snatched sometime during the trade. And clearly, the owner of the Irwin, whoever he was, would do just about whatever it took to get it back."

"What exactly would you be likely to do in that scenario?" I asked.

"I'd likely offer a large fee for its return."

"Large, huh? Just out of curiosity, what kind of figure do you think would qualify as large in a situation like that?"

"I have no idea. But considering the Irwin's worth, it would have to be nothing less than, say, fifty grand."

"In that case, someone investigating the matter, someone like me, would be nuts not to accept such an offer … if it were made."

"I can't see why it wouldn't be." Trask sat up straight, and his lined face went still. "I guess Fabienne would be a prime suspect in all this. Or maybe there was someone even closer to the trade than she was."

"Yeah, both those ideas make sense theoretically."

"They do, and I'll go further. They make sense in the real world, too."

After leaving Ellis Trask's shop, I phoned Tireia to tell her it looked like a trade had been set up for the two birds, and both had been stolen. Then I had a sandwich in a café on Chestnut Street and walked back to Pine, where I picked out a doll in colonial dress from a toy store in Antique Row. At a nearby dealer, I found a silver brooch of an osprey stooping toward its meal—Tireia probably would envision the fish as a trout in Payette Lake. Back at the hotel, I packed the gifts, and took the train to the airport.

The layover in Salt Lake City was long and boring, except for the delight on the face of every fourth person in the terminal, a signal no less plain than a badge that read, "Saint." I was surprised and pleased to find a copy of Albert Camus' *The Stranger* at a newsstand to skim for the next few hours. It was precisely what I needed. I slowed down at parts that had captivated me the first time, yet all the while endured the low-grade anxiety of not getting something done.

We deplaned in Boise after 11 p.m. Feeling muzzy from the trip, I didn't look forward to the switchbacks rising into the mountains but consoled myself that at least the road would be dry. I trudged with my carry-on down the single flight of stairs from the arrival area to the concourse and walked outside across the street to my vehicle on the ground floor of the parking structure. I unlocked the truck and reached in to put the bag on the floor of the passenger side. As I straightened up, something made ferocious contact with the back of my head. The shock and force were worse than the pain, which didn't have a chance to kick in before I went out.

The first sensation when I came to was the hardness of cement all along the side of my face, and then someone talking. And then the pain, which at first stabbed hot, but quickly encircled my head from the back and haloed outward. The voice was a woman's, and then a man joined in. Hands on my waist and underneath my arms, they lifted me to a sitting position, propped against the truck. I helped to push myself upright even as the woman said, "Let's not move him anymore."

"He'll be OK," the man said.

I tried to agree but wasn't sure the words were comprehensible. I touched the back of my head, sat still, and closed my eyes. A moment later, I unstuck them upon a middle-aged couple and smiled weakly at the expressions of concern on their open faces, shadowed by winged things that were recognizable as their fear of involvement.

"I'm feeling all right now, thanks. Must have passed out."

"No, no, there's blood," the woman replied worriedly. "Something hit you."

"Or someone," the man added.

"Just the pavement. What time is it?"

"It's 11:25," said the woman. "I'll go to the terminal and get help."

"Don't do that," I said with as much authority as possible. "Otherwise you'll be here answering questions the rest of the night. Did you see anyone around me?"

"Nobody," the man said. "I figured it was a heart attack when we spotted you on the ground."

Leaning a little on my helper, I got to my feet. The pain was woolly yet hard at the center. My hand explored the back of my head more thoroughly than the first touch and came away with blood, but not a lot. Probably a baton.

"I get blackouts once in a while," I lied. "I'll have someone take a look at me."

As I made a move toward the exit, the man looked skeptical.

"We better come with you."

"No, you go on home."

"Sure?"

"Absolutely. And thank you."

"Come on, Joe," the woman said. And then to me, "You take care now."

"I will. Thanks again."

They walked away, clinging to one another as if they were the injured party.

I went around to the passenger side of the truck to get my bag, locked up, and limped to the terminal. In a men's room, I cleaned my head with wet paper towels and washed my arms and face. I took a small first aid kit from the bag and taped gauze over the wound. In the bag was a plain brown baseball cap, which I put on gingerly to cover the gauze. At a kiosk in the terminal, I bought a little packet of aspirin and a bottle of water for an enormous price. I swallowed half the aspirin and returned to the pickup.

In the driver's seat, I sat for a moment to make sure this was a workable idea. My vision seemed OK, so I started the engine. I paid the parking fee at the booth, got on the road, stopped at a red, and took a right into the first hotel lot beyond the light. That night, I tried to sleep on my side. In the morning, the roughness against my cheek of the towel I'd placed over the pillow reminded me of the grit on the cement.

When I sat up, my head screamed mutely, making me cradle it with spread fingers. I groped for the bottle of water on the bedside table and took the rest of the aspirin. I shuffled to the bathroom with the empty coffee pot, filled it with water, and shuffled back to the machine. The gauze wasn't in bad shape when I removed it. I kept the shower cool and patted the wound with a soapy washcloth. The mirrors didn't allow me to see the back of my head, but renewed bleeding from the shower wasn't heavy and the swelling was no more than a fair-sized lump. I patched myself up again with the used piece of gauze. As I packed the shirt from last night in my bag, I felt a folded bit of paper in the pocket. On it was a typed note:

If you value your kid and her fake mom, back off.

I drove through Boise and took the twisty, rising highway to McCall in a daze: no music, staying to the right, pulling into the turnouts on inclines like a trucker or an octogenarian.

At the cabin, I made a cheese sandwich and had just taken a bite when Derek the deputy showed up at the door, saying Sheriff Carmody and that FBI guy, Wheeler, wanted to see me, right now. I let out a sigh, changed into my Phillies cap, and took the rest of the sandwich along.

"You look pale," Darlene said as soon as I entered her office, even before she introduced me to Wheeler, who stood up.

"*You* look pale," I said to her.

"I have an excuse. What's yours?"

"One Scotch too many, I guess."

"Graham Wheeler," the agent said as we shook hands. "I assume you know the cure for a hangover."

"I'm aware of conflicting theories, yes."

"Eat something healthy," Wheeler said as he sat. He motioned me into a chair, as if it were his office. "Lots of water, exercise."

"That isn't my camp," I said, and sat. "Thanks for the chair."

"Not a hair of the dog man, I hope?"

"I favor sleeping it off. Which is what I'd be doing right now if Derek hadn't come knocking."

Darlene gave me the slit eye.

I turned stiffly from her to Wheeler. "Speaking of theories, I hear you have one about me."

"Right to the point."

Wheeler nodded in approval, as if he were a debate instructor. He extracted a rubber-tipped stylus from the little army of implements that festooned his pocket protector and took his phone from a vest pocket to commence poking and dragging. He recited what had occurred on the day of Davenport's death, just as he done for Darlene, who looked distressed. When Wheeler was finished with his lecture-cum-accusation, I thanked him for his imaginative interpretation of events, which visibly annoyed him.

"I can understand why you would lose control," he retorted, "and gun down the man who had attacked the mother of your child."

This prompted me to fire a glare at Darlene, who responded by upbraiding him for a half-truth and a cheap shot, but her voice was weak. Wheeler seemed oblivious of her.

"Something major is missing in your theory," I said, raising a forefinger. "What about the Irwin Raptor?"

Wheeler's soft beard couldn't disguise his surprise, a reaction that caused me to drop any benefit of the doubt about his skills I may have carried to this encounter.

"What makes you think the Irwin Raptor has anything

to do with this?" he said. "Did you talk to . . . did you talk to someone?"

"I did talk to someone, yes, and so did you if I'm not wrong."

Darlene moaned, and we both looked over.

"I'm having contractions. Get Derek for me, will you? It's time to go."

Derek rushed in at my call, a female officer with him. I announced I'd follow the police van to the hospital. Wheeler tried to object.

"But I have to go, Wheeler, don't you see? She's carrying my child."

The agent's eyes went wide and I turned away to hide a villainous grin.

"Oh, shut up, Reese," Darlene muttered.

I tagged along while Derek and the other officer guided her to the vehicle. On the way, she set the ground rules.

"Reese and Tireia will take the lead in the Davenport investigation for the time being. Derek, give all the help you can. And report to me. I expect to be back on the job before long."

The police van blazed away in a show of sound and light. I took off after it. Wheeler dithered in the doorway. When the van turned off the highway at the hospital, I kept going straight. I called Darlene's land line at her house and left a message for Hank that his wife was in labor. At my cabin, I took an ice pack to the couch, turned off the phone, and watched three movies on Netflix, half of them bad, meanwhile subsisting on soup and cheese sandwiches. By the time I went to bed, which was still early, I felt recovered enough to be thinking about a drink.

16

For Tireia's birthday lunch the next day, I wore my Phillies cap to cover the bump and the gauze. When I drove up, Minta was showing a calligrapha beetle to Fabienne, who sat at a picnic table near the garden on one side of the meadow. Her hair fell below the bandages and she wore her favorite ensemble of a light cardigan over a shift with deck shoes. As I watched her stroke Minta's arm, I reflected a bit desperately that the situation had been workable so far. The kid didn't remember any other setup and liked the way it was. She'd never asked to live with her real mom and never had been asked to do it. Everything was fine, so far.

Minta showed me her bug and then ran to set it free. We watched her go.

"It's strange to think she's ours," Fabienne said.

"You think of her as ours?"

"Not really."

"Then that's why it's strange."

Tireia came out of the cabin and put a bowl of fruit salad on the table, which was covered with an oilcloth.

"Watermelon and the like," she told Fabienne. "Easy to chew."

Her guest gave a little nod. I kissed Tireia and wished her a happy birthday, and she went back indoors.

"What I meant was she seems more like Tireia's kid than anybody else's," she said.

"Tireia the sailor-lover. But she's good to that little girl."

"I know. It's just . . ."

"Don't worry about it right now. You need to concentrate on recovering."

Tireia, who had insisted on cooking, brought out miso soup with little squares of tofu floating in it, sprinkled with chopped spring onions. Fabienne would have to forego the homemade bread, but she looked pleased by the pinot grigio. Minta ran to the table. As the dishes were passed around, she declared with delight that she could eat like a bastard, which made Fabienne laugh and then wince.

"I doubt she means it in the legal sense," Tireia said with a sly glance at us other adults.

After lunch, Tireia opened her presents. She pretended surprise at the sight of the book and was pleased by the osprey brooch, which I'd kept back when I gave Minta the doll. The child sat in proud silence as we exclaimed over her present to Tireia, a drawing with colored pencils of a moose amid wildflowers on a mountainside. It was a nine-year-old's vision that most adults lose along with their vivid dreams, and Tireia was touched. She got up and hugged the little girl and then came around and gave me a kiss as soft and welcome as the early summer sun. Fab presented her with a silk scarf and then went indoors for the cake she'd brought, which bore four lit candles, one for each of us, she said. Minta and I sang a lusty *Happy Birthday*, Fab mumbled along gamely, and then Tireia blew out the candles.

After we ate our cake and ice cream, the child ran off to

greet the neighbor's golden retriever, who had wandered into the meadow for one of her regular visits. We rested for a moment in the high-country stillness and then I asked Fab if she was thinking of getting back together with Wilber. She professed astonishment that anyone could imagine such a thing. "Getting back together" was a misnomer, anyway, she claimed. Their past lacked sufficient content to qualify as history. A bad dream was more like it. When I told her Darlene was checking on his whereabouts, she responded by pouring herself another glass of wine. She allowed it was unwise to drink too much because of the ibuprofen for her jaw but then again, maybe the drugs would keep the booze from giving her a headache.

Once she seemed to relax again, I said, "I met with Ellis Trask in Philthy the other day. He said he knew you."

This drew an almost subliminal flash of apprehension.

"Vaguely," she admitted. "He was one of those guys Stuart dealt with, mostly for his father."

"I talked to him about the Irwin Raptor."

"The Irwin Raptor." Her voice was full of caution.

"It appears a swap was planned, the Irwin for the falcon."

She reached for the bottle again.

"I don't know what you're talking about." Pouring, she splashed a little wine on the oilcloth. "What's the Irwin Raptor?"

"Fabienne, it's too late for that," Tireia said.

"If we're going to keep you in the clear," I added, "what we need to know is who stole them."

She drank, her hand unsteady.

"I have no idea," she said.

"Look, you were in the middle of the deal," I said with a finality that didn't brook debate, "and that's dangerous. The

Irwin's a hot item and worth millions."

She finished her wine, sighed, and shrugged.

"Ellis Trask called me. He said he had a job for me that would be easy and would pay well. He wanted me to make what he called an exchange."

She took a moment to refill her glass and we waited.

"I asked him why he was calling me after all these years and he said because I was a known quantity." She snorted. "A known quantity. We barely even knew each other. But he also said it was because the so-called exchange would happen here, in Idaho."

"I assume you asked him what would be exchanged," Tireia said.

"Of course. He said two small statutes. He said they were both valuable and it would be a trade. He had one of the statues."

"The Irwin Raptor," I put in.

"Yes, but I didn't know what it was at the time. He didn't give me any details. He just said he didn't want to send it by courier. He said he'd feel safer if I came to Philadelphia and got it."

"You, the known quantity," I said.

"Exactly. Trask said my job was to get the statue from him and bring it to a guy in Sun Valley named Cassim Geyer, who had the other statue."

"The Maltese Falcon."

"Yeah, but again, I didn't know what it was until later. Anyway, I was supposed to make the trade and bring the new statue to Trask."

Tireia shook her head. "This didn't strike you as weird, Fabienne? This guy enlisting you as his mule?"

"I wouldn't say weird, but risky, yes." She picked at a little square of watermelon. "It certainly wasn't lost on me that he didn't want to do the trade personally. But the money . . . I figured it was worth the risk."

The first time she saw what she had been carrying was at Cassim Geyer's house in Sun Valley, when they looked at the two pieces.

"Did you recognize the statues?" Tireia asked.

"I realized they were similar birds, one of them apparently in gold and with the biggest diamond around its neck I'd ever seen. You'd think the black one was a model for the golden one—which it was, in a way, when Geyer explained them to me."

Cassim offered dinner and after they finished, it was pretty late, and he had someone show her to her room. Trask had warned her not to leave the package out of her sight until the exchange was completed but Geyer put both birds in a safe, which seemed a lot better to her than keeping one in her room. The break-in happened while they slept, and the thief made off with both of them.

"That struck me as very strange," she said. "The house was Fort Knox. Plus how could anybody know where the statues were that one night? Swear to God, I didn't tell anyone. It had to be Geyer."

"Looks like him, although there are other possibilities," I said.

"Like who?"

"Maybe one of his toadies got greedy."

"Geyer arranged the whole thing," she insisted. "He frightens me."

"He is kind of creepy," I acknowledged. "So after all this you came back to McCall without the Maltese Falcon you were supposed to bring to Ellis Trask. And then some stranger phoned you out of the blue and said go get a package they were leaving in the bushes outside your place, call me, and I would come to take it."

"That's right."

"And I'd give you money for it."

"Yes, well . . ."

"And then, presumably, they'd get the money from you."

"Correct."

Tireia and I turned our faces toward each other and just sat there, expressionless.

"So you stash it in the linen closet," Tireia said. "Your boyfriend Davenport comes in and whacks you around but you don't tell him where it is because you're helping Reese. You black out, somebody shoots Jim, and that's all you know."

Fabienne tilted her half-glass of wine, which disappeared seemingly without so much as a swallow. She put down the glass with authority and challenged us with a look that bizarrely suggested anybody who could drink like that must be telling the truth.

Tireia apparently decided this was enough on her birthday, because she refrained from what I feared, that she would bring down the hammer on Fabienne. Even I didn't believe she was telling the whole story.

After lunch, Fab gave Minta a hug and promised to come again soon. She thanked Tireia and got in her car, sober enough to make it home, I figured. She rolled down the window and fixed me with a glare that would have been bruised even without the beating.

"You said a nice no-pressure birthday lunch. I'd say pants on fire."

I kissed my fingers and pressed them to her arm.

"I'll take care of you."

She backed the car out. "That's what they all say," she called, as she turned the vehicle to leave. "Have a look at me now."

When she was gone, Tireia asked who had cracked me on the head. I adjusted the bill of the cap, which had been snugly in place all afternoon. She said I was stiff-necked, moved like a zombie, and had looked at my hand after touching my skull. I glanced across the meadow at the child, who was brushing the dog's coat with a pinecone, and then described what had happened at the Boise Airport. When I told her about the written threat, I said she'd better keep an extra-close eye on Minta, especially going to and from school.

Her face remained still, but the black light of alarm went on in her eyes. She took two steps and stopped with a finality I'd seen before, when she was thinking hard and movement became a distraction. She turned to me, her green eyes still darkened, and it pained me to realize she was trembling on this warm day. I moved quickly to embrace her.

"You do what you want," she said into my shoulder. "I'm going to take shooting lessons."

This surprised me, but I recognized the motivation: the same rage, fear, and sense of helplessness I'd felt when my friend Belinda died from a gunshot years earlier. When I objected, Tireia had her logic ready, as if she had been thinking about it. She swept through the turn-the-other-cheek versus eye-for-an-eye arguments and rendered the conclusion that lying down in front of a tank will work only if the tank driver isn't a sociopath or a brainwashed soldier, which are the same thing. I saw no use in pointing out it was an argument from emotion or that to participate in the problem was hardly its solution, so I said self-defense made sense. You don't have to choose passive resistance, but why not take up martial arts? People don't die in numbers at the hands of Krav Maga. She said my Krav Maga might work at close quarters but what about beyond arm's reach? I told her skill, self-assurance, and focus will win out. She flicked this away, assuring me all the chutzpah in the world won't stop a bullet.

17

The hospital people said everything had gone fine for Darlene, who had returned home with her new arrival, a boy. I stopped by the florist in McCall and had a bouquet delivered with a congratulations note.

At the sheriff's department in Cascade, Derek eagerly shepherded me into the tiny gap between filing cabinets and the desk in his cubby.

"Big news," he said. "The Blaine County office is unable to locate Cassim Geyer. And he never delivered the statue to its owner."

This was strange. The original theft of both statues from Cassim's safe was very suspicious, just as Fabienne said. But then he hired me to get the falcon back for Rowena Pascoe-Leyland. I did that, and now it looked like he had taken off with the bird. If he was going to steal the statues, why didn't he just do it the first time?

"What did the staff have to say?"

"The house is closed up. They located a maid in Ketchum, who said everybody was let go."

"Jonathan's his main guy," I said. "Don't know his last name."

"It's Evers. Jonathan Evers. Burglary and assault, a decade

ago, when he was just of age. Clean since then. We haven't been able to locate him yet."

"Does the owner know the prop is missing again?"

"Yeah, she's coming to Sun Valley day after tomorrow. Alerts are out on the perp, Wheeler's on it for the feds. I wouldn't want to be in Geyer's boots."

"They're barefoot shoes, generally. Any leads on where he might have jogged off to?"

One of Derek's laughs was a kind of masked chortle, a snuffle he emitted with a fist under his nose as if to suppress a cough. He did that and then answered.

"No leads. His people haven't seen him for two days. We're checking passenger manifests, but for all we know he could be in the Caymans by now."

The way Derek looked at me was often a little disconcerting. He had adopted an almost floppy-eared alertness ever since Tireia and I recovered Fred McInery's prized plane. The old pilot was Derek's great-uncle and a worthy hero to the younger man. For years, Fred had carried mail and supplies to ranches and mining camps scattered along the rivers and creeks deep in the mountains. Like most career backcountry fliers, he left his bits of wreckage strewn along the drainages, but he walked away from those scrapes. Later in the same year that Tireia and I located his airplane, which had been co-opted for transporting drugs over the border with Mexico, Derek joined the police force. He claimed we were his inspiration.

There was no reason for this to bother me, as Derek was a friendly and decent man, a father of two, who liked to watch football and eat potato chips with sugary iced tea. Every holiday, he flew his oversized flag from a big pole in his yard between a double-wide for his father-in-law and a '65 Shelby GT 350 on blocks that he had been restoring forever with no visible results. He knew a lot about tools, though, and could talk engines with the best if you let your guard down. His eagerness and unflappable morality were probably what prompted Darlene to make him her chief deputy. She had a couple of detectives who were deep into cruise control and a dozen incurious patrolmen, most of whom had more experience than he did. But Derek appeared to be the arrow in her quiver with the best combination of sturdiness and straightness, even if he wasn't exactly heat-sensitive when it came to finding the target.

Now he sat at attention, watching … as if I should throw a stick. I told him about Ellis Trask and the golden bird called the Irwin Raptor. I said it looked like Trask had wanted to secretly trade the stolen Irwin Raptor for the Maltese Falcon, but now both statues were missing. I described the attack on me at the airport, and the note in my pocket. He looked concerned about the threat and said he'd have a man keep an eye on Minta when she was at her summer school activities. I thanked him.

"You'll let Darlene know about all this, right?" I said.

"Yessir."

I considered not mentioning Fabienne to him, but changed my mind.

"Fabienne Sansverrou met Ellis Trask when she was younger. He recruited her to handle the trade of the Irwin Raptor for the falcon."

Derek whistled and asked whether I thought he should bring her in. I killed a smile and advised it was best to leave her in place for now, at which he nodded uncertainly. I asked whether he had followed up on the activities of Fabienne's former boyfriend, Wilber Arndt, and he said Wilber's truck had been seen parked outside his cousin's place in Warren. Derek figured it was better to leave him be rather than to send a sheriff's vehicle way the hell out there. Wilber was an odd one, he allowed. Friendly enough, but there was something squirrely about him. He figured it wouldn't hurt if Wilber stayed in Warren because he'd fit right in there, and short of lighting a forest fire, he probably couldn't cause much trouble out in the boonies. He made an inquisitive face and I nodded.

"What about Agent Wheeler?" I asked. "What's he working on?"

"No idea. He has the feds' holier-than-thou routine down pat. It's all need to know, and I guess there's nothing we need, far as he's concerned. I told him the same thing I told you, that Wilber is out in Warren. Oh, yeah, and we know Agent Wheeler showed up at Jim Davenport's funeral in California. Would have been hard to miss him, apparently. The room wasn't exactly packed."

"Did he talk to anybody?"

"There wasn't really anybody to talk to. Word was he offered condolences to the widow and her kiddies. He followed her home, so they had a conversation."

We chewed on this a minute. Derek was all perked up, ready to bolt if I so much as scratched my head.

"What I'm thinking," he remarked, "is Geyer plans to fence the Maltese Falcon."

"Maybe."

"And maybe the golden statue, too."

"Also possible."

"What do you think we should do now?"

"You'd better report all this to the sheriff and see if she has any orders."

"What will you do?"

"I'll go see Mrs. Pascoe-Leyland when she gets back to

Ketchum. In the meantime, I'll have a chat with Wilber in Warren."

"So you think he's involved in this?"

"I don't know, but Fabienne said she hadn't seen him in months and then he seemed to be shadowing her. The timing's fishy. It's worth a trip out there to have a chat."

"Good idea," he said, which made me think of Jesus, the Republican Party, and the Boise State Broncos: all the things that couldn't be wrong in these parts, like the guy who got back your great-uncle's favorite airplane.

"What's Tireia gonna do?" he asked.

The question indirectly affirmed Darlene's opinion of who was the brains in the outfit, which didn't bother me, beyond maybe an initial flinch.

"For one, she's learning how to use a gun."

I said it with annoyance, but Derek gave a vigorous nod. This made me realize I had contained my opinions about guns around him, just as I had around others in town. Darlene was one of the few exceptions. Her husband Hank, who politely listened to my angst about shooting deaths, just as politely stopped listening when I got onto universal background checks and buy-backs. He equated control with absence, a prospect that alarmed him, because a rancher without a rifle would be like a plumber without pliers. And now even Tireia seemed to believe that an adult without a gun wasn't much help to a threatened child.

18

It was bright and balmy on the cruise up Warren Wagon Road past cabins planted in the woods along the lake's western shoreline. I drove past Tireia's place on the cliff, past the potato baron's numbly acquisitive swimming pool beside a blue inlet, past a gaggle of tourists renting kayaks and canoes near North Beach for a paddle on the river that drifted down from Upper Payette Lake. And then the pavement stopped and the dirt track continued into the enfolding national forest. Nature's wall of tamaracks and undergrowth went along for a long while, and I played Aldous Harding's first album and didn't test the fading cell signal by calling anybody.

The track ended forty-five miles deep into the mountains at Warren, an 1860s gold mining boom town. Back then, it got regular hauls of wagon-drawn supplies to provide for two thousand people, although now the village would be lucky to harbor thirty residents during the warm months. It had an airstrip but I wasn't keen on flying. Wilber's cousin's cabin was near Slaughter Creek at the far end of the settlement, and I wanted to avoid the conspicuousness of strolling there from the Husky. It was wiser to blend in, and I had the rig for it, down to the V license plate for Valley County to differentiate me from 1A-plate yokels out of Boise and surrounds.

After almost an hour of driving, it was tempting to turn off at Burgdorf for a peek at the log-lined hot springs below a smattering of cabins in the meadow, but that was unnecessary nostalgia about good times with Tireia, plus there would be tourists and today I was the woodsman. Awhile later, I did have a beer at the Secesh Stage Stop. I commandeered a pleather-topped tree stump at the bar next to a guy in spiffy camo and his burly wife, both of them ostentatiously armed. This reminded me of Tireia's new affinity for weapons, a thought I pushed away.

In Long Gulch, the giant matchsticks of a burn were scattered grayly on both sides of the trail. I took a low gear over rocks and potholes in the dirt track that switched back through the high country. Eventually, I crossed Warren Creek and passed the airstrip, which lay in wide-open reproof of my land transit. In town, a man sat under Old Glory in a metal folding chair against the tiny post office as the Dodge puttered by. Several motorcycles were parked in front of the bar, and outside the ranger station, a family inspected the mining equipment display, but mostly the mixture of nineteenth-century cabins and newer ones along the dirt road was undisturbed. The cousin's place, the last one on the Slaughter Creek turnoff and separated from its nearest neighbor by a hundred yards, was the familiar roofed rectangle of a modular unit, its narrow end facing the road.

I pulled up next to Wilber's SUV, the only rig parked outside. Nobody came out. It was quiet all around. I stepped up to the cement-slab porch, banged on the door, and called for Wilber. No answer. A dog's bark arrived along the wind in the trees over the faint rustle of the creek behind the house. The throaty hum of a generator began at the cabin down the road, followed by the whine of a table saw. I turned the doorknob and stuck my head inside, calling Wilber's name again. In a small kitchen, an open overhead cupboard revealed boxes of cereals and other dry goods. A door beyond it was probably for the bathroom. Past a little wooden table with a couple of chairs, I entered the only other room. I froze.

Wilber was sprawled face-down on the floor between two bunk beds, one of them unmade. He lay in his underwear, the hair on the back of his head matted and awry. Everything inside my chest and stomach felt like it was lit up and racing around but I made myself lift his T-shirt for a better look at the gunshot wound in his back. It was round, signifying an entrance wound, and the margin of abrasion was concentric, which I remembered from college meant he was shot straight-on. It looked like he'd been surprised in bed, made to stand up and turn around, and then executed. By the smell, he'd been dead for a while. Houseflies were busy.

I used a handkerchief to open the drawer of the night table and found a loaded Glock. Stepping carefully, I checked the rest of the room, the kitchen, and the bathroom of the tiny place but found nothing. The front door and windows looked secure. Not a single blood spot was visible on the cement porch.

The neighbor was running the table saw off a gasoline-powered generator in his little back area near the creek. He stopped when I came around, took off his protective glasses, and shook hands when I introduced myself and said I knew Wilber. The man was in his sixties, beer gut, red patches on his palms. He said his name was Bill Atman. He pulled two brewskis out of an ice chest, handed me one, and motioned to a camp chair. After a long draught, Bill exhaled an ahh, and sat down with me.

Wilber should be at the cabin, he said, that was his vehicle outside, unless he went for a walk or something.

Bill was up here every year, mostly summers, and had met Wilber a couple times. He knew Ollie, who owned the cabin. Ollie's place used to be a miner's cabin back in the day, when Bill's dad worked a placer claim right up here on Slaughter Creek. His dad made a lot of money but he stopped the dredger in its tracks to join the war and the vein was still rich and Bill owned the claim now and he was gonna get that gold out of there if the damn government and the Indians and the greenies would climb off his back long enough to let America be America. 'Course, he couldn't blame the tribe much, seeing how the discovery of gold was what got their land taken away in the first place, but still the process was taking him years and years, even though he owned the claim, he owned the damn thing. He was gonna get a bulk test done pretty soon, it'd be a step toward a permit, but he'd still have to negotiate EPA, NOAA, the Nez Perce Tribe, the U.S. Forest Service, the possibility of bull trout in Warren Creek, which were listed as threatened, the watershed, steelhead, creek fords, biological opinions, reviews, analyses, restoration plans, it went on and on, it'd take forever, his wife wouldn't even come with him to Warren anymore and why should she, they had practically a mansion in Boise, pretty much a palace, she had everything she needed and this was just a base.

I was so slapped silly by this onslaught that I had forgotten my beer, and he wasn't done yet. He pointed to the shelves he was making, declared he'd fix the place up, there was a generator now so she'd have lights and a fridge and she'd probably come back later this summer he bet. After Bill had knocked off his second beer and I had taken a sip of my first, we made it back to Wilber. I told him his corpse was in the cabin and added what he wanted to hear, that I was on a case. Amazed and excited, Bill grabbed another beer to get the skinny.

Holy shit, he didn't hear a gunshot but he'd been creating his own noise with the saw. He did notice a vehicle passing his cabin a couple of days ago, which he knew must be going to Ollie's place, because it didn't look like the kind of rig that would be heading up the trail for firewood or anything; it was too new and shiny, a flatlander toy, a Hyundai SUV. It had Washington plates, maybe a rental. No, he didn't notice anybody else coming through; the SUV was it. A couple of guys flew in yesterday, apparently. People said they walked around a while and then left, likely just tourists.

Anyway, Bill had a good bottle of whiskey and remembered a fun time once drinking whiskey with Wilber and Ollie, so when he saw the SUV arrive he decided to go offer a drink. It was mid-afternoon. He walked over with the bottle and his dog. The Hyundai was there next to Wilber's rig, all right, but when he hammered on the door nobody answered. He had a feeling someone was in there, you know, the feeling that everybody inside a place has stopped moving all of a sudden, and his dog was getting excitable, but he couldn't be sure they hadn't just gone into the woods and anyway they weren't coming to the door. To be honest, he started wondering if maybe Wilber was light in the boots and he'd arrived at a bad time. This thought freaked him out a bit, so he left. Not long after, the Hyundai passed his place and headed on back to Yellow Pine.

I asked if the vehicle might have turned toward town. No, he insisted, it went down towards the South Fork, same way he'd seen the guy coming from. It was strange, he thought, because that drive's a hassle, but maybe the dude saw himself as adventurous. Did Bill get a look at him? Nah, he was here out back and only saw the vehicle turn at the corner through that break in the trees there, same as when the guy arrived. Never laid eyes on him.

He told me to come around to the front, where he opened the trunk of his Chrysler (low-slung, 1A plates) to show off his rifle and handguns. The Idaho County sheriff was cool about a vigilante posse and Bill could muster the boys quick-smart. We should load up and check out Ollie's. I was a detective, right, so I must be packing.

I thanked him but said I'd already checked it out. No need for a posse right now. I knew he'd be pleased if I said the perp had been careful not to leave obvious clues, so I did. The Forest Service station will radio it in, I said. His job was to make sure nobody went in there. Protect the scene for forensics, OK?

As I drove away, he transferred the bolt-action Weatherby Vanguard to one hand so he could raise the other in a wave that was part salute.

19

The Sun Valley vacation home of Rowena Pascoe-Leyland was a bit surprising for someone who could pay four million for a lump of lead. It was a beauty in a nouveau-rustic way, but hardly the many-headed monster I was expecting. Even though it was the last place on a road that dead-ended at a bend in the Big Wood River under the cornrowed pines of Bald Mountain, she had nearby neighbors, for God's sake. She had given me the gate combination over the phone and after I went through it and parked on the flagstone drive, she came out to greet me, moving with the liquid grace of a woman used to being admired, although she was pushing sixty and her cheeks had that cemented look. She was in a knit tunic and tights, her blonde hair piled up, rubbery lips red.

She led me straight into the main room, between two wide wooden stairways. I took a seat at one end of a sofa. The view was big. Past a stone verandah and a low hedge, over a creek that must have been diverted from the river a few feet beyond it, the ski hill loomed above an aspen grove. Inside, huge railroad ties held up the room, classic Sun Valley repurposing, and the high arch of a corrugated tin ceiling was finished in burnt umber. Rowena went past the double-sided stone fireplace to the bar and came out from behind it with a couple of Manhattans.

"Beautiful cabin," I said as she placed my drink on a chessboard that also was the surface of a large coffee table. "Although I wouldn't have guessed it would be on the edge of town."

She gave a throaty laugh.

"Actually, when my late husband Vic bought this place for me as a wedding gift, he asked if I'd prefer a ranch but I made it clear I'm a town girl."

Her tone was aerated and high-pitched, a laryngitic child's voice.

"I've been coming alone here for years now, no help, do everything myself. But it's nice being close to the restaurants and shops, and I do enjoy living amidst the hoi polloi. My neighbor John is an accountant, and Evangeline across the road sells real estate. Lovely people. I'll always keep this cabin; three bedroom suites and a cottage for the caretaker in winter are more than enough, although I can tell you if I ever did want to let it go, it wouldn't be on the market for years like Carole King's place out in the valley."

Clearly, she had the skills to keep up this patter, and even though parts of it could be inadvertently revealing, enough was already enough. A terrifying image flew into my brain of Bill Atman transported here from Warren and both of them talking to me at once.

"We should discuss your bird statue."

"Yes, let's do. I assume you want to offer your services in retrieving it for me. The idea is appealing, especially given how quickly you returned it after the first theft. Of course, the authorities have been alerted but I'm hoping your dealings with Cassim Geyer have given you a notion of where he might be."

Her cocktail beat the daylights out of Cassim's weak tea. I gave her a little test, and put down my glass on the chess table at white pawn to e4.

"I haven't a clue where Cassim is and I didn't come for a job, although it's a thought."

"No? Then why, may I ask, are you here?"

"To talk about the trade."

Her hand stopped halfway in lifting the cocktail glass to her lips. She set it down on the face-to-face confrontation of black pawn to e5.

"What sort of trade might that be?"

"I had a chat with Ellis Trask. He wants his bird back, too."

I took a sip and went with my bishop to c4, which exposed her pawn at f7.

Her veneer of sociability melted. She picked up her drink to recoup.

"I see." She put the glass to her lips and maybe got them wet. Hard to tell. "I shouldn't have listened to Cassim Geyer. It was poor judgment."

"Oh? What did he tell you?"

Her sigh had a long tone in it, like an orchestral tuning note.

"He kept talking about how beautiful Mr. Trask's statue was, and how it had been missing for such a long while that everyone had given up looking for it. I said his idea was out of the question but he insisted I could display the Irwin Raptor privately, and my friends and acquaintances could be trusted not to raise a fuss. Actually, they'd be impressed, he said. People did this sort of thing all the time in the art world; blind eyes were turned. As a collector, I knew he was right about that. It's a game, really."

Her glass went to c5. Another face-off, this one with the bishops. Or maybe she thought it was cute to cozy-up our glasses.

One reason Geyer's argument wore down her resistance, she said, was that she never had cared much for the Maltese Falcon. Her husband bought it at an auction right before his heart attack. She did develop a taste for American film noir through him, but even so, the prop wasn't a pretty thing. It rarely wowed anybody in London, not like the Irwin Raptor would do, as surely as gold and diamonds can. Another reason she finally capitulated to the idea of the trade was Geyer claimed the worse thing that might happen if someone complained would be she'd have to give the Irwin back to its maker, Mr. Irwin. Rowena said she was telling me all this because it was a moot point, now that both birds were missing. Anyway, she felt certain I was the man most likely to retrieve the falcon for her, if I would consider taking the assignment. She could promise the reward would be handsome.

"I wonder what the definition of handsome would be," I said, and observed the echo in my head.

"It would be defined somewhat less in the sense of attractive than of generous," she replied.

We picked up our glasses at the same time.

"Do you think Cassim has the Irwin Raptor as well as your falcon?"

"I would think that's obvious," she said.

"Why?"

"Because he told me both statues had been stolen from his safe."

She seemed about to put her glass down but held it.

"I was immediately suspicious when he said the thief would return my falcon for a price. But it clearly was lost for good if I didn't take the initiative."

"You're saying he didn't run off with the statues the first time because he wanted to get ransom money from you as well."

"Traveling funds, perhaps."

It was my move. Queen to h5. I watched her put down her glass and said to myself don't, don't, but she broke out her knight to f6. Maybe she really had been dumb enough to get talked into this by Geyer.

She tried to defend the idiocy of it, going on about the uncertainties in judging character and in deciding when to cut losses versus taking a calculated risk, but there was no way out of her having been a bonehead, and the more she blathered the tighter her trebly tone got toward Geyer. She seemed less angry than contemptuous, perhaps a class thing, how certain people react when they can afford to let the principle be more important than the cash. Or maybe it was just ego. The rich were prone to delusion.

I suppressed a sigh and pushed my glass, queen takes pawn at f7. Checkmate in four moves. I waited for her to say, "I let you win," but she didn't react. I lifted the hapless maraschino by its tail and then on second thought, let it go.

"Do you play chess?"

"What? Oh, this was my husband's table. I never learned."

20

On the drive back to Hailey's airport, I called Derek to check on the recovery of Wilber's body. He said it was taken care of, no problem. To make sure Derek had noticed, I pointed out that Wilber's condition suggested he was caught asleep by the gunman. The neighbor said he'd seen the probable killer come the long way from the direction of Yellow Pine and go back that way, no doubt in an attempt to avoid detection by staying on Warren's southeastern outskirts. Before I could continue, the deputy said something else had happened.

"I'm at Tireia's place right now. A couple of agents from the state's Child and Family Services were here. They got a tip that Tireia wasn't Minta's mother and then talked to the school principal. He thought she was Minta's legal guardian."

A flush went through me, hot and cold. I asked him to put Tireia on the line.

"They're going to take Minta away," she said, her voice stripped thin. "I was reckless to take her in the first place."

"They won't take her away." This sounded more irritated than I'd intended. "Just hang on. I'll be back in town shortly and we'll work this out. In the meantime, you'd better call Ornice Fullerton as soon as you can."

During the flight over the mountains to McCall, my mind seemed willing to function only well enough to do the task. It had been stupid of us, lax. We'd let ourselves believe nobody cared, because fixing the situation seemed too hard, especially when Fabienne showed no desire to cooperate with the legalities. But it was pointless to worry about what would happen now without having all the info.

By the time I got to Tireia's cabin, the CFS ghouls were gone. They said an anonymous complaint had been called in, and handed her a notice to appear in family court. She had set up a late-afternoon meeting with Ornice Fullerton, the county's public defender and the only lawyer with an office in town. Ornice had a reputation for earnest thoroughness. Like most rural attorneys, she handled all kinds of law, family issues prominent among them, mostly domestic violence. She had said this initial interview could take a while and I suggested that Minta and I might wait at the cabin, but Tireia was having none of it.

"The time for me to take responsibility for everything is gone," she said. Her customary coolness had turned to ice.

I knew not to argue. Besides, it wasn't that much of an overstatement.

I couldn't tell what Minta had absorbed of all this. She didn't look upset, although her usual speedy speech and movement might have slowed a tad. We grabbed some of her books, put her in the back seat of Tireia's car, and drove alongside the lake through slanting light to Ornice's downtown office. It was on the main drag, a shingled cabin rimmed in decorative tiles with a white picket verandah, across the alley from a candy store. We left Minta with her books in the waiting room under the secretary's eye and went into Ornice's office.

Everyone around town had seen Ornice so frequently in

the gray suit she was wearing today that the question was how many of them did she have? It was well cut but couldn't conceal the wearer's dramatic thinness, exacerbated by a slight stoop unusual for a woman of average height and on the younger side of thirty. She shook hands with us, a gesture that seemed partly a symbol of the gravity of our business and partly just hand-holding. We took chairs in front of her desk and she offered water, which we declined.

We knew Ornice only casually, not well enough that she'd be familiar with the details of our lives. She sat down, entwined her elegant fingers on the desktop, and told us she'd made inquiries about the concerns of the CFS officials.

"The problem is you're not the child's legal guardian," she said in that beautiful speaking voice of hers, a voice the word *mellifluous* was made to define. "Tell me, why is she in your care, Tireia, instead of with Fabienne?"

"Because Fabienne's a crackpot."

"It's a long story," I put in. "At the time, getting the law involved seemed superfluous and potentially a big hassle."

"I was supposed to be helping out," Tireia said, "not taking over."

I put my hand on the back of her chair and slipped it around to her upper arm. Ornice managed to hold a professional expression even while a shade of sympathy edged into her eyes and mouth.

"Who is the father?"

I looked at Tireia but she didn't look at me.

"That's another part of the long story," I said.

"It would be good if you could tell some of it to me."

"His name was Stuart Sansverrou. We were college roommates. I was ten years older, and he became kind of a little brother to me. He had health problems, a genetic disorder that interfered with the movement of the cilia on the surface of cells. He couldn't keep his airway clear of mucus, among other problems. He'd had several operations but there was no cure. He was always huffing and coughing, and I helped him with the physical therapy. Simple stuff: tapping, applying pressure to help shake loose mucus."

"It sounds like you were fond of him."

"Stuart was a great guy. He was witty, he had excellent taste, and he loved fun. In fact, I think he chased the good life harder than most, because he knew his odds for a long life were poor."

"And then he met Fabienne?"

"He did."

This mention of their early happiness cheered me up, and Ornice looked gratified, or maybe relieved, by my response. I told her about the first time I saw them together, on Locust Walk near the Department of Criminology.

"I could tell immediately it wasn't casual, by the way their arms were entwined, and how she tucked her head into her shoulder to look at me. And then she suddenly announced she was going to be late for her shift at the bar and left us staring after her."

"Left *you* staring," Tireia murmured.

"No, both of us," I said, and stroked her arm. "She had that impact on everyone."

"And they got married, and Minta came along," Ornice said.

"Not exactly," I replied. "They got married, yes, but Minta coming along wasn't so easy."

"Stuart's disease had made him sterile," Tireia explained.

"Ah," said Ornice.

I put my hands in my lap. "By then, I was in my senior year," I said. "It took me by surprise when they asked me to be the donor. I hadn't known about Stuart's problem. I hesitated, and I think they saw my uncertainty, so they tried to take it back and of course that made me insist on helping."

"I see," Ornice said. "But legally—"

"I relinquished all rights. It was by mutual agreement. I didn't think much about what it might mean if Stuart died young. His dad was rich and I assumed Fab and Minta would be well taken care of. And they were, financially. I guess I had some denial going on."

That was putting it mildly, but Ornice needed the legal background, not the rest of it. She wouldn't be helped to know that although I admired both of them, it bothered me that little Minta would be mine and not mine. Or that although I saw them occasionally during Fabienne's pregnancy, Stuart seemed to feel as awkward as I did, and only Fabienne was relaxed. Or that when I visited her at the hospital after the birth and had a look at the infant, it made me both happy and anxious. Ornice didn't need to hear it was difficult for me to see Minta—that even though I was pleased for my friends, it was hard to even think about the child.

Nor did I tell the lawyer that Stuart and I seldom saw each other during the time I finished my Master's, which I think suited both of us. I gradually had become impatient with his conviction that his life would be short. It's true he wasn't fooling himself but neither was he open to hope, and that bothered me.

As for Fabienne, her beauty had captivated the two of us, but I was skeptical of her motives. I never much liked the way she cooed over the latest expensive gift from the auctions and estate sales they went to all the time. Later, I saw she loved him. But that wouldn't matter in court. None of this would. I kept it to myself.

21

It was past dinnertime when we got back to the cabin, and Minta was grumpy. I had suggested we go out to eat, but Tireia was adamant about going home, as if she were compelled to demonstrate that the kid would be staying put. She didn't seem angry with me at the moment for getting her into this jam so much as disturbingly determined. Her focus put my own attention on a single insistent track, like when a smoke alarm goes off and nothing else can be done until it's fixed—except there was no easy way to deactivate this situation and eliminate the noise.

In the living room, Minta read a story aloud, with aggression, about an unhappy pie that had lost a slice of itself. As Tireia preheated the stove, I approached her from behind and put my hands on her shoulders, at which she dropped her head. She patted one of my hands and moved to the freezer to get a pizza. At the counter, she fumbled with the packaging and I realized with a start she was crying. It was so seldom she shed tears that the sight filled me with an odd combination of panic and directionless rage, followed by a sense of helplessness so deadening that I didn't even reach out to her. She wiped her eyes with the back of her hand, shoved the pizza in the oven, and announced we had a lot of work to do.

"The game's become serious," she said. I took a step toward her but she folded her arms. "We have to get you and Fabienne in the clear, right now."

I resisted the urge to point out this was what we'd been trying to do.

"Luckily, Graham Wheeler's the only one dopey enough to think I shot Davenport."

Her laugh held no delight, which was OK except for the tinge of scorn that darkened it, which I took as a reminder of how dumb I'd been to leave the scene with the statue.

"I thought of Maggie Kornbluth telling you how hard it is to unload stolen art," she said. "I asked myself, who would buy an item as hot as the Irwin Raptor? It occurred to me that one person who might want it was the guy who made it, Harold Irwin. I called him, and he said he had been approached over the phone by someone who claimed to have the statue and offered to sell it back to him. It was a woman."

I stood motionless.

"My bet is it was Fabienne," she continued. "I asked Darlene to run a check on her calls but she said state law allows it only for sex offenses or computer crime. She said she'd ask Wheeler to get it done."

"She was in on the double steal? I can't believe that. Next you'll be saying she shot Jim Davenport."

The look she gave me was coldly defiant yet somehow warmer at the edges, an icicle in the sun. She turned away and fiddled with utensils at the counter.

"Fabienne's alibi for the shooting of Jim Davenport rests on the question of how, in the midst of being beaten, she could produce a pistol before passing out," she said. "But it is possible to imagine that sequence. And if you grant the possibility, then the main reason to believe she didn't do it is faith in her. And if she did do it, then it's feasible nobody else was there aside from you three."

"Somebody had to deliver the falcon."

She took a few things from the refrigerator and started to make a salad.

"Yes, but that was before Davenport showed up, if we believe Fabienne's account that she already had the falcon but wouldn't tell him."

"I think it's still a long stretch to explain how and where she got the gun."

"I agree it's highly unlikely she did it. My point is we haven't established anything about the shooting. All we know is the bullet matched the weapon in her hand."

We were silent, and then she started up again.

"I know what you think. You're guessing Wilber came by, and when he saw Davenport smacking Fabienne around, he shot him. But how can you be positive she didn't have a pistol in the pocket of her shift or nearby?"

"Because she has never owned a gun that I'm aware of and she's not a killer. And because there was no stippling on the victim's head, which could indicate he was shot at fairly close range. And because the abrasion collar on the forehead, the blood spatter on the rug, and the position of the body indicated he had turned toward the door and was shot between the eyes. Plus, Davenport was a lot taller than Fabienne, so the exit wound should have shown an upward trajectory unless she fired when he was sitting, kneeling, or lying down, which might be possible only if he was taking a break from pounding on her."

"You didn't tell me any of this."

"It didn't seem necessary. We agreed right off she couldn't have been the shooter. It never occurred to me until now you would even consider the possibility."

"For God's sakes, Reese. You had information that helps Fabienne and you didn't tell me? Why not? Because you're so certain we should think no ill of her that it *didn't seem necessary*. You need to get out of the clouds."

She turned away to take glasses from the cupboard. And maybe to hide whatever showed on her face.

"Wheeler's suspicious of her role," she said, and turned back to me. "We know what he thinks of you. And now a judge will come into it. We have to clear this up for Minta's sake."

She stepped around the corner and glanced into the living room, where the child had stopped reading and now dangled a piece of twine over Sasha the cat, who lay on her back swatting at it.

"One thing's for sure," I said quietly. "Minta's not going anywhere."

She grabbed me by the shirt, yanked me up against her, and glared into my face. Then she punched me in the chest, not really hard but not lightly, either. She went into a bear hug, squeezing the air out of me, and it would have taken a rough move to get free, so I just wheezed for a while. She pushed off, turned her back, and I knew from the rare previous instances when she got worked up like this it was best to do nothing.

After she'd clattered a few dishes and started pouring drinks, she turned around again.

With a note of sadness in her voice, she said, "If Fabienne was more than an innocent victim, it probably meant she had wanted you to be the one to bring the ransom money to her. She knew you'd be worried about her safety, and she knew you wouldn't involve the police."

"Maybe Wilber was working for Cassim," I said. "It's too much coincidence that he was lurking around her place and then turned up dead with all this happening. He could have dragged her into it. Anyway, we have no proof yet that she was the woman who called Harold Irwin."

My defense of her sounded lame even to me. Tireia said she wanted to take a deeper look into Cassim Geyer than she had done before I first met him. I announced my intention to go to California to talk with Sondra Davenport. After Darlene and I had spoken to her in McCall, Agent Wheeler took his turn, but then he went to the funeral in California to question her again. This made me curious.

When the pizza was ready, I ate a piece with them and then announced a retreat to my place. At the door, I hugged Minta a little too hard and Tireia maybe not hard enough. But at the moment her resolve seemed a delicate sculpture too easily shattered.

22

On a SkyWest flight to L.A. the next morning, I gazed out the window and endured an uncomfortable daydream of moving Minta into a foster home. We were at Tireia's place, explaining and promising we'd visit often, but Minta didn't see the logic. If we were taking her away from Tireia because she wasn't her real mother, why were we giving her to someone who wasn't her real mother either? Why couldn't she live with Fabienne? Or why not with me? The kid probably would ask exactly those questions, unless maybe she'd prefer to be with a foster parent than with Fabienne. Was that possible? And would it even occur to her she might live with me? Lousy thoughts. I turned away from them and the window.

Sondra Davenport lived in Cypress Park, a mostly Latino neighborhood a couple miles north of downtown L.A. Under blue skies, I drove the slopes of cracked and worn streets to her place, a gray adobe on a corner behind a cyclone fence. The plastic blinds on her front window were bent. New terracotta roofing was being laid but nobody was up there putting the rest of the stacked pieces in place. An analog TV sat in the dead yard like retro art. She was expecting me and flung the door wide, waving me in through a cigarette haze. A toddler regarded me with knit brow from behind her mother's pant leg and in the living room a boy glanced up before returning to his plastic dump truck.

Doors on either side of the living area apparently opened to bedrooms. She told the boy to watch after his sister and walked straight back to the kitchen and dining room, where she collected papers and a laptop from the table and put them atop a battered sideboard. She worked at home as a bookkeeper for several small businesses, I remembered. I sat at the table while she poured coffees. I clarified right away I was not a member of the county sheriff's department. She already knew.

"Jim said you were a friend of that woman."

"Then you probably know he and I weren't on the best of terms."

"He hated your guts is more like it," she replied, as she put the mugs on the table. "But I guess you didn't like him being with her, so maybe in a way you were my ally."

"Is that why you agreed to talk to me?"

Through those huge eyeglasses, her regard of me was like a botanist inspecting a specimen. I couldn't tell if her messy blonde locks were a statement or evidence that she hadn't worried about a visitor. The little girl came into the room and Sondra pulled her up onto her lap.

"You don't think that woman did it," she said. "But at least you're trying to find out what happened."

"I'm not the only one still at it. Graham Wheeler, for instance. I understand he attended the funeral."

She put down the child, who wandered away.

"If you could call it a funeral," she scoffed. "Wheeler was just about the only one there, except for the kids and me. And he was on the job."

"I suppose he questioned you. Anything interesting come up?"

She sighed.

"It was more like him telling me stuff than the other way around. He said he'd spoken to Jim's client. It was a collector back East. His name was Trask. Is that what you want to know?"

"Why do you think Wheeler told you Trask's name?"

"He wanted to know if I'd heard it before—if Jim had said anything."

"And?"

She picked up a package of cigarettes from the table and offered me one. I declined. She lit hers, inhaled, blew out the smoke.

"I didn't know any names but like I told you before, Jim said his client had lost something valuable. The FBI man, Wheeler, said it was a statue called the Irwin Raptor. You've heard of it?"

"Yes. How did your husband find out about it?"

"From your friend, that Fabienne woman."

"She told him?"

"Hell no. Jim got hold of her phone and read texts she'd been exchanging with this Trask guy. So he contacted Trask. The only thing Jim told me was he'd been hired by an antiques dealer in Philadelphia to find a couple of things that had been stolen and were worth a bundle."

"Two things?"

"That's right. Wheeler told me Trask wanted to trade the Irwin Raptor for the Maltese Falcon, which I assume you know. Trask hired that woman friend of yours to bring the Irwin Raptor to Idaho and make the trade. After the statues were stolen, that's when Trask hired Jim. He wanted his raptor back but he wanted the falcon, too."

"You say you didn't know any of these details at the time," I said, "but it must have worried you that your husband was chasing around after expensive stolen merchandise."

She cocked her head and admitted, "I was concerned. I asked him if the job was dangerous, and if it was on the up and up. He just said don't worry. And his client was offering good money, which we sure as hell could have used."

"How are things for you? I mean, financially?"

"What, you're going to make a contribution?"

She glared. We drank coffee in silence as she made a visible effort to collect herself.

Then she said, "Jim and me were a team. We had our troubles but we were there for each other. I was his sounding board, he always told me everything, or not everything but most things. He thought it was safer to keep some stuff to himself. Not that it did him any good. And now you and the FBI have the facts. Let's see you do something with them."

The little boy came in carrying his dump truck and she ruffled his hair.

"This is Jim Junior," she said. "He wants to be a private investigator, like his dad."

"Or a garbage man," Jim Junior said.

I stayed a while longer with Sondra Davenport but there was little more to be had. She was the kind of woman who made you wonder if her choice of a man like Davenport was just bad luck or a sign of some flaw in her. But that was for a psychiatrist. She'd made it clear my commiseration was unwelcome. On the way out, I put a penny in the back of the kid's truck and he dumped it on the rug. She told him to give it back and I said he could keep it.

"For my thoughts?" she said, and lasered a squint at me through the goggles.

23

In the car on the way back to Los Angeles International, I called Tireia, who immediately said the CFS people had come again. This time they'd inspected the cabin, including Minta's room. Afterwards, she called Health and Welfare to complain about their intrusiveness but got only the verbal shrugs of it's hard, yes, but it's the law. They'd already made up their minds, she figured, and nothing they saw or heard would change their conviction that the state knew best, although of course they knew nothing, they were a bureaucracy, it was like something out of Kafka.

"I knew it was a mistake for me to take her in the first place."

"Don't be silly. You two are great for each other."

"But I was supposed to take her only for a while, if you recall that delusion. As if I were feeding someone's pet."

Maybe she interpreted my silence or maybe she was appalled by her own complaints, but in any case she changed her tone and the topic, asking about my visit with Sondra. I said she told me Davenport had found out about the plan to trade the two statues when he read texts between Fab and Ellis Trask.

"Davenport never gave her the details but Graham Wheeler

did. He told her that Trask had hired her husband to get the Irwin Raptor for him. And Trask also wanted the falcon."

Sounding tired and distracted, Tireia reported she'd done further checking on Cassim Geyer and found out the glister wasn't gold. He had inherited money but was an unwise investor with a penchant for backing startups whose promise proved to be confined to the gloss of their prospectuses and the hyperbole of their founders. He went through an expensive divorce, took out a second mortgage on his house, and all the while kept throwing lavish parties for the jet set and making purchases that would give pause to all but those with the deepest pockets. And he was a gambler, well known in Las Vegas, particularly fond of sports betting. He patronized several bookies but the main one was a man named Lou Faulkner. Turning to Darlene for help with Faulkner's police record, Tireia had learned he was the head of an illegal offshore operation and loan sharking business. Apparently, Geyer had been borrowing from him at usurious rates for years, and was into him for a huge sum.

"Cassim, Cassim. Living beyond our means, are we?"

"What means?"

"See what else you can find out about Lou Faulkner, will you?"

"I've already started."

Early that evening, my flight arrived at Boise Airport. I was vigilant on the way to my truck in the parking lot, even though common sense said the message had been delivered. The back of my head was still a bit sensitive but not bad. I got behind the wheel and put on my Phillies cap.

Boise is a foliated upper lip between the teeth of the desert and the nose of the foothills. The hundred-mile transition to McCall, amid the arrowing pines of the mountains, the thunderous river, and the lakes, went by mostly under the receding light of summer hours before night. I slowed into turns around the mountain face without braking and played the game of trying to keep nobody in sight between the bends in the road before and after me. Frank Ocean streamed from the phone through the truck's CD player and speakers, which weren't the best but served the purpose of combining song and scenery as a respite from the threat of injury to my most important people. I rolled down the window to smell the tamaracks and hear the Payette River crash like a brown bear emerging from the woods.

Tireia wanted me to come straight over, so I bypassed my place in town and drove up Warren Wagon Road alongside the lake to her cabin. It had gotten dark and Minta was asleep. We went to Tireia's office, where she poured Scotches. I sat in my customary armchair and pushed the head of the lamp out of my face, as usual. It was like the damn thing was alive, always moving back from where I put it the last time, but I couldn't sit elsewhere, because this was where I sat.

"This loan shark, Lou Faulkner, has turned out to be an interesting character," she said.

Her intensity was evident in the way she paced, yet her voice was collected and efficient, all emotions tamped down and sealed in. She'd put on her armor for the little girl.

"Darlene had a source in Las Vegas. He told me Faulkner was reputed to be a major collector of film noir memorabilia. He knew a woman Faulkner apparently had been trying to impress. I got hold of her, and she said he had bragged about a prize purchase, a jewel-encrusted statue of a bird."

"Jewel-encrusted?"

"Diamonds and emeralds. Sapphires, garnets, amethysts, you name it."

"She got a look at this statue?"

"No. He said it wasn't for public viewing, even for her. But it had a name. He called it the Ottoman Osprey."

She hadn't stopped pacing back and forth between her work table and the kitchen area behind it. Now she went to the table and picked up a sheet of paper.

"This statue has quite the pedigree. I found a copy of the inscription on it." She read aloud: "Presented to the Right Honorable Rear Admiral Horatio Nelson, by Sultan Selim III, high sovereign of the Ottoman Empire and overlord of the Levant Seas, in commemoration of the glorious victory at the mouth of the Nile on the 1st of August 1798."

"Admiral Nelson surfaces again," I said. "First it was that little box Stuart gave me, and then the mourning ring Ellis Trask sold to Stuart for his father's collection. And now this."

She handed me the printout, which showed a photo of the bird, its body covered in jewels. It stood on a base shaped like a curled snake or an eel, dominated by what appeared to be diamonds with beads of turquoise and onyx. The osprey's expression was baleful, regal. Its ruffled wings were slightly arched, as if about to spread.

"What's with the fancy birds?"

"What, indeed?"

"Did you find out anything else about this one?"

"A lot. The Ottoman sultans liked to present a diamond plume to their military commanders for outstanding service. After Nelson saved Egypt from invasion by Napoleon, he got the whole bird."

Tireia's research showed Nelson had willed the Ottoman Osprey to his brother, William Nelson, who apparently set it on a shelf in his study amid a raft of other bling. After William's death, the bird went to his daughter, the wife of a baron, and then to their son, a general and viscount. He made bad investments and auctioned the statue, which was bought by the wife of Admiral Nelson's great-great nephew. The Great Depression forced her to put it up for sale but the purchase was made through a shell company. There the provenance trail submerged. Tireia had found suggestions that the statue changed hands several more times over the years, most likely through inheritance.

"Did Faulkner say where he got it from?"

"That's something to find out."

"OK, but here's the hard question. What does any of this have to do with our investigation?"

She came over and put her hand in my hair, the most affectionate thing she'd done since the state started chasing after Minta.

"We've been chasing a prop made of lead from a famous movie and a golden statue inspired by it," she said. "But get this: in Dashiell Hammett's novel, he spun a story that the Maltese Falcon was created by the Knights of Rhodes. Hammett's fiction was mixed up with a little history. Those knights really existed and they were driven off Rhodes by the Ottomans in the 1530s. The Holy Roman Emperor Charles V then gave them the island of Malta. So in Hammett's novel, the knights made the falcon as a gift of thanks to Charles V."

"And?"

"I'm getting there. Two hundred and seventy years later, Napoleon began a campaign to conquer Egypt by establishing a naval base on Malta. The knights were still there, and he took the island from them. Then Admiral Nelson saved Egypt in the big naval battle and was given the Ottoman Osprey as a reward. Not long after that, the Brits took Malta from Napoleon."

"So you're saying the inspiration for Hammett's imaginary Maltese Falcon was this statue the sultan gave to Nelson for protecting Egypt."

She grabbed a handful of my hair and pulled it lightly. "That's right. The Ottoman Osprey."

I reached up to take her hand.

"That raises another question," she said.

"What does the connection mean, if anything?"

"Precisely. And we better find out fast."

I went in to see Minta, who lay on her side, one hand curled beside her face. I kissed her and left quietly. Tireia had given signals that she wanted to be alone tonight. Nothing obvious, just gestures or postures I'd learned to interpret: the way she'd place one hand over another, a slightly up-tilted chin, something polite in her smile. It was OK. Even though I felt the need to spend time with both her and Minta, it would have to wait. There was dirty work overdue in Sun Valley.

24

I got up early. As the Husky flew southeast, the sun rose over Jughandle Mountain. Visibility was bell-clear but I wasn't singing through the air these days. Instead I listened to the engine's motorized mantra beneath the drone of my looping attempts to make sense of what we did and didn't know.

From the Hailey airport, the drive in the rented Toyota Tacoma to Cassim Geyer's place went along a quiet road through the foothills east of the highway. The cheatgrass going brown and the blue-water sky were bisected by blacktop well-oiled for the wealthy. Only a few houses appeared along the way, marked by stands of trees, gray-green bitterbrush, white picket fences, and startling swaths of lawn. I turned into a lane several hundred yards long that held just one estate, where the recycling and garbage bins had been wheeled up from the driveway for emptying. But at the end of the lane, where the road curved to Geyer's place, the gates were locked and no bins had been deposited.

I swung around the cul de sac to position the pickup for a straight drive out, and parked. My call at the intercom got no response. I regarded the wrought iron fence, which had sharp tips that curved down toward me. It was about my height, six feet, but there was a crossbar that would help my footing. At least there was no barbed wire at the top, probably because it wouldn't have looked pretty. What a pain this was. I deliberated for a tick longer, and then stepped and pulled myself over the fence, struggling to keep clear of the iron prongs.

On the other side, the road approached a copse of fir and aspen within a draw that sheltered the timber-and-stone manor. Aware of Geyer's cameras, I kicked a rock and gazed around at the foothills stubbled in low sage. Not a breath of movement on the property, no vehicles, no animals. Derek had said Geyer let everyone go. Even so, there might be a caretaker in the cottage that crouched behind the main house. I kept an eye on the small dwelling, barely visible amid the trees.

At the double doors of the big house, I pressed the bell. No response. Another try got the same result. I jiggled the door handle. Locked. I'd seen his cameras and alarms and knew better than to break in. At the cottage, which also was locked, again nobody answered the bell. An ax leaned against a tree by the woodpile and a wheelbarrow lay on its side. In a shed between the cottage and the main house, I found the wheelie bins. The garbage was wrapped in two bags, so I carried them and dragged the recycling bin behind me. All the way down the gravel path, I felt like the apotheosis of two-bit burglary and hoped not to get shot, because what an embarrassing way to croak. At the security gate, I heaved the garbage to the other side and climbed over, which was easier this time because the prongs were facing away from me. I threw the bags in the bed of the truck and backed it up against the fence. The wheelie bin that held the unbagged recycling materials was still on the other side. I climbed the fence again. It was a devil of an effort to lift and push the bin over the barrier, where it landed in the truck's bed.

In a far slot of the almost empty parking lot at Hailey's Airport Inn, I dumped all the recycling out of the bin into the bed. The day was balmy and windless, a garbage-picker's nirvana. After the cereal boxes, cardboard inserts, shredded paper and other chaff went back into the bin, I sat down cross-legged to do the piecemeal work. Nothing.

I certainly didn't have sufficient expectations to bother with the shredded stuff, so I looked at the white orbs of the garbage bags, which looked back at me. When I untied one and dumped it, a sensory assault of neglected omelets, unclean bones, and soft fruit established that composting wasn't a priority at Geyer's place. I put on latex gloves and fingered through the acrid mess to no avail, put it back, and tied up the bag. In the midst of stirring through the second bag, I brushed coffee grounds and mustard off a slip of paper that had been ripped out of a small, spiral-bound notepad and obviously had missed the shredder. An image popped into my head of Jonathan, Geyer's big right-hand man, who was always at the mansion door when I came to visit, scribbling in a little notepad as if it were pre-cellphone days. The numbers written on the scrap in ballpoint pen were cryptic, but what got my attention was the scrawl at the top, "RPL."

I sealed the paper in a plastic bag and pocketed it. There was nothing of interest in the rest of the garbage, which I put back where it belonged. I dropped the gloves in after it, set the bin beside the hotel's big receptacle and drove to the airport.

25

Ornice asked us to visit her office. We left Minta with friends who had a kid her age and drove downtown. Once we were settled in front of her desk, she asked about Minta's grandparents and we assured her they weren't an issue. Stuart's folks were back East and wouldn't take Minta in, although his father—George Sansverrou—remained a regular source of monetary support. Fabienne's parents had never been in the picture, we told her, and might not even be alive.

"Legally, there's always the presumption that a natural parent should have custody of a child," she said. "Even so, the Idaho Code says there are conditions under which a third party can have custody."

We asked for a summary of those conditions and I held Tireia's hand as we listened. I took in what Ornice said, could parrot it back if need be, but my attention was on autopilot. Part of me—alarmed and angered by the situation we were in—observed the attorney from a distance. The rest of my mind was occupied with the deaths of Jim Davenport and Wilber Arndt. The P.I. had been in pursuit of both statues, which would explain why someone would want him dead, even if we didn't know who that someone was. But why would anyone drive out to the sticks to execute Wilber? Was his killing related to any of this? My thoughts shifted to the note I'd found in Geyer's trash, which I'd given to Tireia, and then to a meeting I'd set up in Las Vegas with Lou Faulkner. Beside me, Tireia's mask was in deep freeze, but undoubtedly the workings were ablaze under the surface.

"An appreciable period of time," was the phrase Ornice used that leapt out and smacked me on the focus node. That was how long a kid had to be under a non-parent's custody to overcome the parental rights. It was either that or abandonment, or if the parent was unfit. But what did "unfit" mean in Fabienne's case? And did we even want to "overcome" her rights? How would "abandonment" be defined by the judge? How long was "appreciable?" Ornice didn't scrutinize these key words upon which the finessing would turn. She said the judge would determine what was in the "best interest" of Minta, which made me smile grimly. As if we didn't know.

It looked like everything would be run through the public grinder now. For my own part, that would be no big deal, but Tireia and Minta deserved better, and the assault on their privacy pissed me off. Somebody had called Health and Welfare, had set the CFS dogs on us. Could it be this was what the threatening note meant that my assailant at the airport had stuffed in my pocket? Or had it merely been some anonymous malcontent on the phone? Ornice had pointed out that plenty of folks could have known or found out easily enough that we weren't Minta's parents. Maybe she was right, maybe I was being paranoid. Or maybe I preferred a legal threat to kidnapping.

I asked what she thought of the magistrate, John J. Totorica.

Lots of us in Valley County were aware of him as a clean-cut and lean man of about fifty who had been a magistrate for a decade, and seemed to have donned an imperious manner along with the robes. We knew his great-grandfather had arrived as a Basque sheepherder at the turn of the century to found what became a prosperous family business. We knew this because Totorica told everybody. Like too many people who got a lift from hardworking forebears, he was big on bootstraps.

Ornice answered my question by saying Totorica handled any case in the valley that didn't involve big crimes, which were under the purview of the district court judge. Mostly, he dealt with family and juvenile law, but he also ruled on small claims, civil cases, and petty crime. She said he liked to set the "rules" of a hearing at the outset, which amounted to announcing his biases. She warned he leaned heavily toward natural parents' rights in custody matters, even to the point of being hard to convince whenever abuse had occurred.

"So he's going to try to put Minta in Fabienne's custody," Tireia said.

"To do that, he'd first have to determine she was a fit parent, which could take time."

"A psychological evaluation?"

"We're getting pretty far ahead of ourselves," she said, "but it's a possibility."

"What would happen to Minta while that was going on?" Tireia asked.

"I can't be sure. It's likely he would leave her with you, but he also might want her placed with a foster family for a while."

Tireia didn't even blink. She seemed to stare right through Ornice, who tried to reassure her this was all just hypothetical talk. I rested my hand lightly on Tireia's back for a moment.

Ornice might have thought she was in shock, but I knew it was more likely a blend of anger, determination, and the internal gears churning.

"You have the right to a full custody trial but it could take months, and it would be expensive. And emotionally excruciating," the lawyer said. "Another option is an informal trial. You'd give testimony from the counsel's table and the rules of evidence wouldn't apply, so you'd get to say pretty much whatever you wanted."

"Either way, rather than helping Fabienne, we could end up formally taking the kid away from her," I said. "Or the judge taking Minta away from us."

"In an ideal world, you'd all probably get along fine without the courts," Ornice said. "But there's no choice now. The judge might well appoint a guardian *ad litem* to represent Minta's best interests, especially because you aren't the parents, and Fabienne doesn't have legal representation, at least not yet. A law guardian would submit a confidential report that would recommend what was best for Minta."

"Someone else prying into our affairs," I muttered.

Ornice said she wanted to hear the story of how Minta came to be under our care. We exchanged a glance that confirmed Tireia should start.

"Reese was badly shaken when Fabienne called to say Stuart had died." She put a hand on my arm. "He'd been bow hunting from a tree stand in eastern Pennsylvania, waiting for whitetail deer, when he fell twenty feet to the ground. His bones were weakened by all the steroids he had to take for his condition. They snapped, and the doctor said even if Stuart had the strength, he couldn't have moved from the foot of the tree, where his hunting partner found him an hour later. He wasn't wearing a restraint harness."

"I went to the funeral," I said. "Fabienne seemed so stunned she was barely even there. Stuart's parents, sisters, and a big crowd of friends attended. The sight of little Minta in a tan suit, clinging to her mother . . ."

I had to stop for a second. I hadn't talked about this for a while, and hadn't realized it would still hit hard. I cleared my throat.

"After that, I kept in regular touch with Fabienne. She seemed increasingly less able to cope with what had happened and I didn't think she was getting any emotional support from Stuart's family. I knew she was drinking and taking prescription meds—you could tell from the slurring, and she admitted it, anyway. Whenever I asked about Minta, it was like the question had reawakened her awareness that she had a daughter. It seemed the only thing to do was get them to Idaho, where I could keep an eye on them. She wasn't against the move, but she couldn't get herself organized. Finally, I went over there. I visited George Sansverrou, who approved of the plan. He had two daughters of his own at home and his ex-wife had been traveling in Europe for months. He wasn't exactly preoccupied with Minta."

"But you say he has kept up the financial help?" Ornice asked.

"He has. Stuart had bought a townhouse in Philadelphia, so I arranged for it to be sublet. I sold some of Stuart's collectibles to his father on Fabienne's behalf, and hired a moving company. Tireia rented a condo on the town side of the lake for them, and I put them on a flight."

"So the two of them lived together when they arrived."

"For a while," Tireia said. "But it became apparent pretty quickly that Minta wasn't in capable hands." She laughed ruefully. "Fabienne looked like a femme fatale right out of central casting. That woman is too blessed by loveliness to get into as much trouble as she does. But especially when she first got here, there was something disordered about her. She had just enough incentive to get to the bars, where she didn't stand a chance."

"And then she surprised us," I said. "She got George to handle the sale of her townhouse and bought herself a cabin in the woods. It helped her to keep away from McCall's darker recesses."

"Although she kept a stock of first-rate booze and pills at home," Tireia added. "And the denizens, who already had her number, didn't mind house calls."

"This was about when Minta was starting school," I said. "I went by the cabin a lot but I couldn't keep a constant eye on them. Tireia started filling in when I wasn't around. She'd bring them cooked meals, watch after them. Fab realized she'd become useless and was grateful for the help, at least whenever she was sober enough to think about it. She was always fond of drinking but it wasn't like this before—she spun out after Stuart died."

"And you didn't mind helping?" Ornice said to Tireia.

"No. Which surprised me a little, to be honest. I guess at first when Reese became preoccupied by the two of them, I was a bit miffed. But after I got roped into contributing, I started to like it. I started taking her to school. Fabienne said it was OK for Minta to visit at my place, and the visits turned into overnight stays. I set up a separate room for her, the overnights became a few days, a week. Eventually, it was a matter of visiting Fabienne rather than the other way around."

"Another good thing about it was Fabienne started to improve," I said.

"Maybe it was just a function of time," said Tireia. "But for whatever reason, she seemed to be sober a little more often, and she replaced the revolving door of male visitors with somewhat longer-term serial mistakes."

"Did she ask to take Minta back?" Ornice wanted to know.

"She might have broached it once, but the arrangement actually suited everyone," I said. "So we left things as they were. It wasn't premeditated. It just worked out that way."

26

Las Vegas was about as far as I cared to take the Husky in terms of range. It was a good thing Rowena Pascoe-Leyland had paid well for the delivery job, but the truth didn't escape me that the expense of this venture was both small penance for sticking Tireia with the kid and a small price to keep her.

I flew south, straight across the dead heart of Nevada. On the way, I considered what Tireia's research and inquiries had uncovered about Lou Faulkner's loan-sharking operation. At first, it had been encouraging to hear that the broken bodies and cement boots for welchers had mostly been abandoned except in the movies and on TV, and maybe in a few diehard neighborhoods of Chicago or New York. At the high end, when a Joe or Judy with a desperate need for cash at any price was trapped nowadays, the threats of retribution for failure to keep up the repayments took the form of extortion. Cassim Geyer would have been a perfect mark, because he had attachable assets. But we figured that whatever goodies he had given up probably wouldn't come anywhere near settling his debts with Faulkner. Something else would have to happen. The question was what?

With help from Darlene, Tireia had discovered that loan sharking was far from all Faulkner was up to. His people were suspected of laundering drug money in casinos by buying chips and then cashing them in, always under the ten-thousand-dollar limit that required a federal form, but the grift never had been traced to him. He also was suspected of running illegal offshore sports betting operations that trapped its victims in loan sharking, again without incriminating evidence. Worst of all, word on the street was that Lou Faulkner wasn't above using Chicago methods on those in whom he lost faith.

My objective was to find out more about this bejeweled statue he had, the prize called the Ottoman Osprey that had been bestowed on Admiral Nelson. Did it have anything to do with the other two bird statues, aside from being the prototype for them? Was Lou Faulkner's possession of the osprey in any way related to his grip on Cassim Geyer?

From North Las Vegas Airport, I drove downtown and parked in a structure on Fourth Street next to Faulkner's building, a monstrous curve of glass and concrete on a corner block. His fancy business name, the Capital Transactions Group, was engraved on a monument-like chunk of granite embedded in the garden out front. I had to use an intercom to get into the foyer, where a young woman behind the receptionist's desk looked like she'd been brushed up and placed there along with the carefully positioned oil paintings of pastoral landscapes, the chrysanthemums in the vase, the crystal bowlful of wrapped candies. It all looked clean and removable, like a front for a con, which was maybe my projection and maybe not.

The receptionist pointed to the elevators, outside of which a plaque identified the floors that held the gym and weight room, sauna, swimming pool, café, library, lounge, conference rooms, something called the Balzac Club, and the penthouse garden. Almost lost amid all this fun was the company that had its name in stone outside: Capital Transactions Group, fifth floor. Inside the elevator, a card reader and keypad indicated controlled access to parts of the building, but I had no trouble zooming up to Faulkner's offices.

They had the foyer's same neat-to-a-fault appearance, which belied permanency or real work being done, and here the sky views were huge. His secretary sported a viridian silk blouse, ironed red hair, and white eye shadow. She had a multi-line touchscreen phone on her desk, a MacBook, and nothing else. When I introduced myself, she picked up the phone and announced my arrival. As I entered his office, Faulkner was pulling a curtain across a painting on the wall. From the glimpse I caught, it appeared to be the same one of Katherine March that had been at Cassim Geyer's place. Next to it hung another painting, also curtained, which I'd lay odds was Geyer's noir portrait of Lady Caroline de Winter.

Faulkner's handshake was hard and his Dick Tracy jaw looked like it required twice-a-day shaving. The suit was cut too fully for his blocky physique, which made me smirk at the memory of a salesman once saying an overlarge jacket would give me room to move on the dance floor. He saw the smile, and his bushy eyebrows jerked in readiness.

I went serious and took a mesh chair held together by chrome tubes, which was unexpectedly comfortable. He sat behind his L-shaped desk, also empty, his back to a picture window through which the city lay low, rimmed on the horizon by a crust of mountains in royal blue. To his left, the other picture window in the corner office gave upon the high-rises of the Arts and Gateway Districts and the needlepoint of the Strat Hotel. The sky ascended over all this, scarred only by reflections on the glass from fluorescent light panels and a few ragged rips of clouds.

He knew I was investigating Geyer and had told Tireia he had no problem talking, although he doubted it would be of any help. Now he came straight to the point, asking what in particular I wanted to know about Geyer.

"I understand he's deeply in debt to you."

"He was, yes, not anymore. And it was to the corporation, not to me personally."

"The Capital Transactions Group. Nice name. Nowadays, is the actual business still called loan sharking?"

The strategy was to skip past the usual left jabs as we circled and catch him with a right cross to that lantern jaw, but he didn't even blink, which tweaked my self-esteem.

"Consumer lending, small business loans, those are the preferred terms," he said in a relaxed baritone. "Aside from licensing considerations, I'd say loan sharking is difficult to define, and its meaning has changed over the decades. Many lending practices—most, in fact—that you might label loan sharking are not only legal but dominated by reputable financial institutions. For example, Nevada has no legal cap on interest rates in contracts. Is this what you came to discuss?"

I backpedaled, looking for another opening.

"So Geyer paid off his debt, did he? Or maybe you forgave it?"

"We never forgive debt. That would be bad business."

"He had a big win?"

"Not at all. It was a secured transaction. Mr. Geyer was in possession of certain artifacts and works of art."

I glanced at the covered paintings on the wall and said if they were what I thought they were, Geyer had told me his versions of them at the house were fakes and he had been forced to get rid of the real ones. Faulkner blinked lazily and said the curtains were to keep them from fading in the bright sunlight.

"My associate told you on the phone Geyer has disappeared. Did she mention he took a valuable object with him that should have been returned to its owner?"

"She didn't have to tell me. We have our own channels of communication."

I wondered if he knew about the Irwin Raptor's disappearance as well. Could he somehow be aware that a trade of the two birds had been planned? I couldn't think how to ask without giving too much away, and decided to let it go for now.

"You say his debts to you are resolved."

Faulkner adjusted his big suit.

"To my company, yes. And now you want to know if Rowena Pascoe-Leyland's statue was part of that settlement. Do you really think I have a need to accept stolen goods as repayment for debt, Mr. Mencari?"

"I doubt need has anything to do with it."

He screwed up his mouth.

"That sort of behavior comes from lack of discipline."

"I would have thought it came from lack of honesty."

His unflinching expression made it obvious he considered the comment unworthy of response. Even though I had slipped inside his reach and was body punching, the shots just ricocheted off him. I broke the clinch and circled.

"You're a bird fan, and it appears you're a fan of film noir, too."

Faulkner lifted his chin and regarded me with the most interest I'd seen since entering the room.

"I do enjoy a good detective movie," he acknowledged. "But birds? Are you talking about *The Maltese Falcon*? Or Hitchcock's *The Birds*, maybe?"

If he was aware of the Irwin Raptor trade for the falcon, he wasn't letting on. I shifted the attack.

"I was thinking of the Ottoman Osprey."

The left hook tagged him, and he closed up.

"It's interesting you own it," I pressed, "given that it was the inspiration for the fictional statue."

"You're well-informed. That was a private transaction but, in any case, you're quite right. It was a personal purchase, unconnected with the business."

It immediately was evident he didn't feel good about offering that last bit of info. Sloppy, unnecessary.

"But not unconnected with Geyer," I chipped away at the wound.

"Only in that we both appreciate fine works of art."

"Like the film noir portraits?"

"Like the portraits, yes."

"And the Ottoman Osprey?"

"He wasn't even here at that point," he said dismissively.

Another stumble. What exactly did he mean by *here*?

"You mean among the members of the Balzac Club."

It was a roundhouse, but it connected. His curt nod was like recognition of my prowess; approval of one puncher to another. He admitted Geyer had seemed like a good sort when he first joined, and he did have a collection, and the two of them had the film noir in common. But he turned out to be a bad businessman and a gambling addict. When his financial straits became a burden to lenders, it didn't suit the club at all, and he was drummed out.

"His lenders meaning *you*," I prodded.

Faulkner realized he was in trouble and went back into a defensive crouch. He probably sensed I didn't know as much about the Balzac Club as he had thought. He wouldn't say who he got the Ottoman Osprey from. It was in safekeeping, he said, and unfortunately wasn't available for me to view.

I didn't care. I'd found gaps in his defense.

"Those two paintings." I waved at the curtains on the wall. "I'm sure they're nice but they wouldn't cover what Geyer owed you. What else did he do? Did he help you to get your hands on the osprey?"

Faulkner gave me a pitying look, like a boxer who just been staggered and wants to know is that all you've got?

"I can't imagine how Cassim Geyer could have anything to do with such a work of art," he said. "It's out of his league."

He had stepped back and covered up. It wouldn't be a clean knockout. When we shook hands at parting, it seemed for a second the bastard was going to hug me. He liked putting on the gloves and wasn't even that concerned about getting thumped, if it was a fair fight. Privately, I weighed up my reaction to this as equal parts admiration and scorn. It's a confounding thing, a moral code for the amoral.

27

At Tireia's place, she handed me a drink in the study and then wanted a report on the Vegas trip. Her tone was abrupt, as if I were procrastinating or intended to withhold information. Her stress was understandable but I gave her a warning look anyway.

I talked about the Balzac Club and gazed out the window at Minta, who was enjoying the last rays of daylight in the meadow with the retriever.

"Practically the whole high-rise was devoted to leisure. The company was like an afterthought. There was a listing for the club at the elevator."

"A private members' club," she mused. "My folks have friends who paid a deposit of three hundred grand to join one."

This made me whistle.

"These groups are secretive," she said. "They like to keep a low profile. They're supposed to be about socializing and recreation, but wherever the rich get together, you can bet business is being done. I'll check it out."

We talked about how Lou Faulkner had let Geyer join the Balzac Club. I told her I'd seen his paintings at Faulkner's office. I said he'd admitted to having the Ottoman Osprey but wouldn't say who he got it from or let me see it. And he showed no sign of knowledge about the Irwin Raptor.

"We know Geyer's deeply involved with the falcon and raptor statues," I said. "He has to have something to do with the osprey as well."

"Add another supposition to the list."

Cranky. I poured another Scotch and went back to the window, where the afterglow was all that remained of daylight. Minta looked in the direction of the cabin as the dog snuffled in the grass. I waved and caught her attention. She waved back eagerly and then gazed at the retriever, no doubt trying to decide if there was any fun left to wring out of the moment before surrendering to the interior.

Behind me, Tireia said she had spoken with Ornice again and once more the attorney had pointed out the case's unusual nature, as it was neither the normal parental squabble over visitation rights nor about the child's living conditions. Plus, there was the complicating involvement of Fabienne and us in the theft and murder case. Tireia told her our involvement was irrelevant, to which Ornice replied that Graham Wheeler's take on my role made it trickier. As if we didn't know.

We heard Minta bang indoors and took it as a signal to start getting dinner ready. We went to join the child. On the way, I asked Tireia if she had any progress to report.

"It's hard to get anything done while waging rearguard skirmishes against people trying to take the child away," she said.

She made a show of good humor at dinner for the sake of Minta—who chatted away about a friend, the dog, and a song she liked—either oblivious to the pressures all around or, more likely, ignoring them—and Tireia's mood slowly improved. By the time we retired, she was pretty much back to her old self.

It was our first night together since the threat arose of Minta being taken from us. When we were alone and she moved in for a hug that signaled a need for comfort, I had trouble responding at first, still feeling the sting of her snappishness. She sensed my reluctance and apologized for her behavior, kissing me on the neck and cheek. That was the end of being aloof, especially with my partner looking winsome in her favorite pajamas printed with Droop-a-Long, the purple coyote sidekick of detective Ricochet Rabbit. It really wasn't Droop-a-Long she liked so much as Ricochet, who shared his name with the secure service she used for online chat. It wasn't either character I liked so much as the drape of the silk, which worked well on the back of a chair, too.

After matters of dress had been put aside and the present tense had been conjugated, so to speak, we lay facing each other in the new breaths of stillness and she shifted again, from coquettish to brooding. Turning onto my back, I regarded the wing-like shadows on the ceiling in the candlelight, and thought again of the observation she'd often made about patterns repeating everywhere in Nature. She interpreted my silence to say she'd again been thinking about the case in terms of her discipline of complexity science.

"I'd begin with the three birds," I said. "They're a pattern, and the value of them keeps rising. That could mean something."

"Yes, and how their value is differently assessed by the people who want them."

"But they're all greedy in their own ways."

She was quiet for a moment and then said, "What annoys me is I don't see the overview. I still can't arrange things in a way that makes sense."

We both knew this wasn't unusual. Her work often involved trying to construct explanatory patterns, which never failed to be frustrating at first. My skills were more mundane, but in the case of finding Fred McInery's airplane, our different approaches had combined to produce quick results. Now that we needed quickness most of all, it eluded us. What I wouldn't have given for a clean path through this thicket of collectors, plotters, thieves, usurers, and hirelings.

"I think you're right," she said. "Cassim Geyer was involved in some way with the Ottoman Osprey. The three birds are interconnected, I'm sure of it. What I have to do is trace the provenance of the osprey. Find out how it came into Faulkner's hands."

Her vivid gaze was intent on the shadows above us. Not for the first time, I considered bringing up the marriage option as a parry of the threat to Minta. But I never could get out the words. It wasn't fear of the probable response, her sympathetic and maybe even thankful rejection. The strategy itself rankled: being forced by malignant circumstances to do something which, above all else, had to be chosen freely. I would have married her in a second but not at the price of her independence. She'd be a falcon in anklets and jesses.

"We need to go see Fabienne," she said. "The sooner the better."

"OK, but I have to meet with Darlene first."

"Is she back in the office already?"

"Yeah, and all over me for a report on what we've been up to."

We both smiled grimly at the ceiling's stucco galaxy.

"How's Fabienne faring?" I asked.

"Hard to be certain over the phone but my guess is she's

barely holding up."

"Let's wait until later to go over what we'll say to her. I don't think I have it in me to strategize just now."

"Agreed," she said, and turned toward me. "Now's the time for you to abandon strategy and embrace the free form."

28

No sooner had I climbed into the Dodge the next morning and headed toward the meeting with Darlene than the phone rang. It was Ornice Fullerton.

"I just now heard Judge Totorica has cleared a spot on his schedule."

She asked us to come by right away if possible. I said I'd come alone, as I was already in the truck and Tireia was busy doing research on the case. That was true, but what I didn't tell Ornice was that another discussion with our lawyer was probably not the best thing for Tireia's frame of mind right now.

I soon swung into one of the few slots in front of our lawyer's repurposed cottage on the main drag. Her receptionist said Ornice was with a client, so I sat and picked up a magazine but hadn't settled on anything to read before her office door opened and a middle-aged woman in jeans and a checked shirt emerged. Behind her, Ornice waved me in.

I took a seat in front of her desk and fidgeted at its warmth, a disconcerting connection to its previous occupant. Ornice, who was wearing one of her gray suits again, regarded me gravely.

"This is happening pretty fast, isn't it?" I said.

"It is. I don't want you to worry, but the rush could be because the state is eager to get Minta into a foster home."

"The CFS has been all over Tireia's place. They can't possibly think it's a bad setup for the kid."

"No, but as you realize, the issue is she doesn't have formal guardianship. The state could take Minta away right now. No doubt, her stable home conditions made a convincing case to leave her there until we get the hearing."

She kneaded the edge of the desktop with her long fingers and then made eye contact.

"Look, I'm not saying if or when Minta might be placed in foster care, but it's best to think ahead. In a normal custody case, when parents are still around, they often get to participate in the choice of a foster family. Your situation is complicated, and I don't know whether either of you would be given that chance."

"And so?"

"And so it would be good to have a name I can offer, if necessary. A solid family nearby that would take her in for you."

"Christ. OK, I'll think about it."

"Try to identify a family for me as soon as possible."

I thanked her and we made a time to meet again before the court date. Outside, I drove south past the airport. Despite everything going on, I couldn't help craning like a truck driver at a cafe window to spot my Husky on the tarmac. As I headed toward Cascade, I put on a Kendrick Lamar album. Reflexively, I checked out Jughandle Mountain to the east, whose ridgeline always seemed to me more like a stretched-out reptile than its namesake. In the mountains to the west were the far scars of the ski runs at Tamarack Resort, and soon

Lake Cascade revealed glimpses of its plate-like face from the highway.

At the police station, Darlene looked hale for a recent survivor of childbirth, and we talked about the new arrival for a while, weights and measures, that sort of thing. I was happy for her but didn't have it in me at the moment to summon much beyond the expected palaver. She probably sensed this and pretty quickly switched to business. She said striations on the bullet that killed Wilber Arndt showed it came from a Beretta M9. I took this in and then told her about the court date, it being foremost in my mind, and Ornice's warning about the possibility of a foster family taking Minta. She sat quietly, smoothing down the front of her loose-fitting dress, as if checking out her changed shape. For the first time, I noticed a wisp or two of premature gray in her rusty hair.

"We could take in Minta, if it came to that."

"What?"

"I mean, if you and Tireia wanted me to. My children love her, and we have plenty of room."

"Darlene, with a brand new kid—"

"My cousin's daughter is staying with us for a time to keep an eye on the baby while I'm at work. It would be no problem, and I know Hank would be supportive. If Ornice needs a name, you should put ours out there."

"Thank you, but it's too much to ask."

"It's the least I can do."

This struck me as an odd comment. "What does that mean?" I asked.

"Nothing," she said, and patted down her dress again. "It's just what you say when somebody needs a hand."

I didn't point out the obvious, that it's something you say when you feel indebted. I was way too relieved by her offer to get into a debate about word use.

"And Reese, I appreciate the work you and Tireia have been doing while I was otherwise occupied."

No doubt this was true, but we had our own motives for what we were doing. Darlene was putting out a weird vibe. It wasn't as if she had to feel guilty about taking a few days off to have a baby. Odd … but anyway, what mattered was her offer. If we were forced to park Minta somewhere, there was no better place in the valley than hers.

She'd heard from Derek about me being clobbered at the airport and the threatening note left in my pocket. She asked if he still had a man posted outside summer school for Minta and I said yes.

"Even though Derek has been reporting your progress, it would be good if you'd catch me up as well."

I didn't know exactly what she'd learned from him, so I began with the news that Rowena Pascoe-Leyland had hired Cassim Geyer to oversee the secret trade of her falcon for the Irwin Raptor. I said Agent Wheeler told Sondra Davenport that her husband had been hired by the antiques dealer Ellis Trask, so Davenport was working when he went over to Fabienne's cabin and got plugged. Trask knew Fabienne through her late husband and hired her as the Irwin's courier. But both birds were stolen from Cassim Geyer's safe before the trade was completed. The thief demanded money I was supposed to deliver for the Maltese Falcon's return. Then Jim Davenport stuck his nose in.

I told her Rowena Pascoe-Leyland contended that Cassim had set up the double steal of the statues. And then he got Rowena to pay for the return of the falcon so he could make off with her ransom money as well. I said we thought the shooting of Wilber Arndt was no coincidence. And I filled her in on the bejeweled statue owned by Cassim's shady acquaintance, Lou Faulkner.

"But there's no known connection between the two missing statues and this Ottoman Osprey, right?" she said. "Other than the fancy bird was what inspired *The Maltese Falcon*."

"Right, so far. Tireia is working on it."

"Let's go back to the cabin," she said. "Somebody shoots the P.I. and frames Fabienne by putting the gun in her hand. Then the shooter goes all magnanimous and leaves the bird where Fabienne hid it. Why would anybody do that?"

"I'd say either they panicked or they didn't know the bird was there."

We sat still for a while.

"Tireia thinks Fabienne might have been involved in the theft," I admitted. "If Wilber Arndt was in on it as well, he could have tried to frame Fab out of revenge for her dropping him as her beau. Don't forget, I saw him lurking around her place."

"Wilber wasn't clever or daring enough to have gotten the statues out of Geyer's safe by himself."

"Agreed," I said. "We figure if he did it, he would have had help from someone on the inside. Odds are it was Geyer's man Jonathan Evers. Your deputy says Jonathan is nowhere to be found."

"You think Wilber was working for Geyer, and he took both statues," she said. "He delivered the falcon to Fabienne's place and he was supposed to come back and get the ransom cash from her. Meanwhile, you brought the falcon to Geyer. And the plan was that Wilber would give the money and the Irwin Raptor to Geyer, who would then have everything."

"That's the theory."

She asked me to fetch a cup of chocolate pudding from her bar fridge.

"Presumably, Wilber was shot because he had the Irwin Raptor," she said. "But if he was going to deliver it to Geyer, who would shoot him for it?"

"Good question."

I delivered her treat with a warning that the privileges of convalescence have a use-by date. She dismissed this with the assurance that good training has no shelf life.

I told her about Bill Atman, the neighbor in Warren.

"Atman said the car out front was a Hyundai SUV that might have been a rental, with Washington plates. Do you think you could put someone onto tracking down where that vehicle came from?"

"We'll give it a try. What interests me most right now is Cassim Geyer's disappearance. I'd like to know if he set up the whole thing."

"Do you have any leads on his whereabouts?"

"Not yet, but a lot of people are on it. We'll find him."

She scooped out the last spoonful of her pudding.

"Tell me more about your visit with Ellis Trask."

"He sees himself as a smooth operator who got duped by Geyer. And now, whatever else happens, he can't let his opponent get away with the goods. Or at least that's what he wanted my takeaway message to be."

"You don't believe it?"

"As far as it goes, I believe it. He did imply he would pay me to get it back for him."

"Oh, my, a low opinion of your integrity. How did you respond?"

"He thinks I'm on board. Or at least he acted like he thought I was."

Darlene leaned back in her chair, her freckled expression sated, even a little blissful, from the sugar. I hadn't told her about the note I'd found when rifling Cassim Geyer's trash, but we didn't know if it meant anything and I wasn't keen on revealing to her that I'd been trespassing. I decided to keep it under my vest.

"Graham Wheeler was in touch with Derek while I was laid up," she said. "He's still big on his theory that you killed Davenport."

"Christ."

"How's Tireia taking all this? The situation with Minta, I mean."

"She's reeling at the moment. We both are. But she'll make a comeback. I have no doubt she'll come storming back."

"Reese, although I want like mad for this custody hearing to work out for everybody, you have to understand that right now Fabienne is still on my list of suspects in this business with the statues. The shootings look like somebody else and I'm not saying she was involved in theft but it sure seems possible."

"Understood."

"Well, my offer stands. If need be …"

"Thanks. But first, I guess, we'll see you in court."

I drove to Tireia's cabin and read my cell phone on the porch until she returned from picking up Minta. The school year had ended and she was in a summer school class. It was a small triumph—and, as Tireia would say, a Kafkaesque development—that nobody had challenged her about ferrying the kid there and back.

When Tireia's car arrived, Minta bolted out of it and crashed into my stomach with her head by way of greeting. I lifted her by her hips and turned her upside down, keeping my head back to make sure she didn't catch me with an errant foot. I let her down on her palms, slid my grip to her ankles, and wheelbarrowed her around the meadow. Tireia went inside. Minta and I set to tackling each other, although our main objective was to roll around on the grass while the neighbor's golden retriever, who appeared on cue, contributed a percussive bark to the kid's squeals over my hoots. After a while, I achieved the feat of making myself superfluous to the other two and followed Tireia, who had gone to her study.

I squared up and told her about the foster family thing. Immediately, it got arctic in the room. How she managed to achieve such an effect without doing much of anything always amazed me. It was like a magic trick: watch carefully, and by no more than the lowering of eyebrows and a hardened line of mouth, I shall dispel all warmth. And it won't return until you give me good news.

"It was a surprise when Darlene offered to take her," I ventured.

"We can't farm her out to anyone who isn't family," she said quickly. "If she has to go anywhere, Fabienne's stable enough."

The other day, Tireia had warned me not to dismiss the possibility that Fabienne had killed her boyfriend and today Darlene had done the same thing. Even if it was in self-defense, this did not exactly qualify Fab's life as stable. The contradiction was unlike Tireia. It showed just how tight the corner was that we were in.

"Did you tell Darlene about this?" She pointed at the food-stained note from Geyer's garbage, which lay on her work table.

"I thought it might be better to keep it to ourselves for the time being."

"You'll have to trust her more than that if she's going to be Minta's foster mother."

I had no idea how to take this reversal of what she'd just said.

She bent over the slip of paper, her face partially obscured by the undone latticework of her hair. She examined the note in silence for a moment and then straightened up.

"I take it we're agreed that 'RPL' is Rowena Pascoe-Leyland."

"Definitely."

"I haven't seen anything of significance on the paper aside from the numbers. What do you make of them?" She looked down and read aloud: "75, 142, 71042, 70249, 7324."

"There's repetition in them—two, four, seven—but I can't make out any obvious pattern," I said. "Something mathematical I'm missing?"

"I haven't had time yet to work on it but I'm going to start now."

I said we'd meet tomorrow for the visit with Fabienne but she just nodded and stared at the scrap of paper. Her reaction was understandable but nevertheless deflating. It made me worry about the prospect of long-term damage to us, to the three of us, that could result from all this. Rather than indifference, I much preferred her bursts of fondness when I left her presence. That might have started as a kind of joke— something that happened once and that she'd kept up over the years for fun—but even so, such pretense was way better than disinterest. I stretched and said it was time for me to go. She nodded again, lost in the numbers. I kissed her cheek through the soft screen of her hair and left. Minta was coming in the front door as I went out. She patted me on the stomach as we passed and said not to worry.

"Worry about what, sweetie?"

"Reese, you know. That I tackle better."

29

On the way to Fabienne's cabin the next day, a Saturday, I noticed the last of the ice had burned off the lake, which brought to mind the local joke that it meant winter would be here any day now. Minta sat between us in the truck, absorbed in a children's *manga*. We adults each had an elbow out an open window, trying to soak up the good stuff from the lake and pines. We cast a benevolent eye on the occasional cyclist or jogger on the quiet road and attempted to ignore a tailgater, who most likely would soon conform to type and defy the solid double lines in his rush to reach whatever would be the next stimulus to his flat-screen mentality.

Assuming Fabienne would be on her defensive game, we'd prepped for it with a discussion of what to say and when but we weren't looking forward to the confrontation. Ornice had tried to interview her, hoping she'd make a good witness for us, but Fabienne's answers to her questions had been so vague and evasive that nobody knew where she stood. We told Ornice we'd see if she was more forthcoming with us.

At midmorning, the weekend traffic downtown would be pretty heavy as people came up from Boise to enjoy the warm weather, but we avoided most of it when we got to the bottom of the lake by taking Boydstun Street, which curved into Deinhard Lane and hooked up again with the highway at the southern end of town. We kept going across the highway and turned down South Samson Trail to reach Elo Road. When we came around the curve in her drive, I noticed again the sick pine near the window and resolved to do something about it but this time decided that instead of taxing my imperfect skills with a chainsaw, especially working so close to the house, it made better sense to hire a faller.

Fab must have seen us come around the bend because she stepped out onto the porch and held up a hand in greeting, a good sign. We stopped and Minta got out quickly, trotting up to give her a hug, which was so fortuitous I hoped it didn't look rehearsed. She got down on a knee to receive the child and as we walked up it was evident the damage to her face was healing. She was still young, had strong recuperative powers, and the overall effect was much improved now that the bandages were gone. But when she looked up at us and said hello, it became obvious she was either boozy or on opiates, maybe both.

In the living room, the throw rug was gone and the wall-to-wall rug had been replaced by one similar to its predecessor. Minta stayed with us for a while but soon wanted to go outside, which made Fabienne nervous and then we got nervous, too. We tried to convince her to go up to the mezzanine, where there still were playthings in her old room from when she was "a little girl." This made her consider, and then Fabienne said she had left a present up there for her, at which both of us tried to suppress our surprise. The kid raced away and her mother confided it was a remote-controlled car that could talk. Would she like it?

"Hell, yeah," I said.

"Well, hell on wheels," said Fabienne, "who wants a drink?"

Neither of us wanted a drink but we both accepted, and at the bar she poured a well-aged amontillado. She was wearing a blue sundress, close to the same color as the one she was wearing on that day not long ago when I found her unconscious on this very floor and reacted by calling the cops and leaving the gun in her hand. Yep, it was fraught between us but in this tough spot she'd be on our side or at least I hoped so. Nobody knew how to start as we sipped the sherry, uncertain of where our alliance stood. Tireia ventured that she looked good, considering, and Fabienne finished the phrase with "for someone who had her brains beaten out."

Upstairs, Minta squealed, which lightened our mood.

"I put the batteries in," Fab said, still speaking carefully because of her jaw. "She just needs to find the switch."

"In another ten minutes, she'll probably have the thing reprogrammed," Tireia said.

Fabienne put down the glass and announced, "Look, I don't want you to think I'm ungrateful. You guys have been great. Taking care of my little girl without help … I don't know. But I don't want to lose her."

"Right. Nobody wants to lose her."

"Yeah, but you never really had her, did you?" Fab's tone had gone suddenly surly. "I'm the one who did the work, I'm not just the mule here. People forget that."

We didn't know where this outburst came from or how to react to it. Tireia tried a reassuring approach. She reminded Fabienne that the child knew who her real mother was.

"I never gave you permission to take her."

"Fabienne, that's a dangerous thing to say," Tireia warned, a hard edge in her voice. "Don't you realize if you were to tell that to the court, you could expose us to charges of kidnapping?"

"I'm not saying you took her away. I brought her over there. You just kind of forgot to bring her back."

Tireia retorted that in the case of the Irwin Raptor, a mule was exactly what Fabienne was. Transporting stolen property is a crime and who knew what else she was tangled up in? This was way off script. Fab squawked that she hadn't known what she was carrying and I leaped in with an appeal to our friendship, saying Stuart would want me to do everything possible to protect his wife and child and I hadn't wavered from that commitment.

"Two men are dead," I said, "both of whom once meant something to Fabienne. And whoever did it might well be behind this effort to take Minta away from us all. We have a mutual enemy who would like nothing better than to divide and conquer."

At this, the women became less fiery, although plenty of heat and smoke remained. We returned to our planned examination of events and Tireia's face relaxed as she regained control. We asked Fabienne to think back to when she and Stuart used to go hunting for collectibles. One time, when he was working on behalf of his father, he bought a ring from Ellis Trask. Did she remember?

"The mourning ring," she said and looked relieved at the change of subject. "It was for Horatio Nelson's funeral, which was quite the spectacle in London. Trask knew all about it; he told us the story. He's an oily dude, I never liked him, but at least he's full of stories about the things he collects. He loves the history, he studies it, and there's something appealing about that, although I wouldn't go so far as to say it's a saving grace."

Instantly, she'd gone from combative to loquacious.

"Stuart had done his homework on the ring, so he knew what it was worth," she continued. "He was usually pretty conscientious when it came to buying for George but less so for his own purchases. Not that he threw money away, exactly. He made some great finds, especially when he knew more about a thing than the seller did, but once in a while he just splurged, overpaid, didn't care whether he'd make a profit later."

"Yeah," I put in, "I always figured dealers like Trask must have lived for times when Stuart lost interest in bargaining."

"The same day he bought the mourning ring, he got ripped off by Trask for that box he gave you, Reese, the one that was supposed to be made from the wine barrel they pickled Nelson in. Stuart tried to convince himself he could resell it for big bucks but the provenance was shaky. He just got charmed by Trask's story. I was impressed when he gave it to you, though. I mean, it was not cheap. But that was Stuart, right?"

"That was Stuart," I agreed, glad we were off the topics of Fabienne's legal situation and Minta's future. "Did Trask say where he got the box and the ring from?"

"Oh, sure. Like I say, he was full of info. He got them from the Pascoe family … some relative of Rowena."

30

"I thought of the Nelson box and the mourning ring when Trask told me Rowena was the owner of the Maltese Falcon prop I'd be picking up in exchange for what I was carrying," Fabienne sailed on. "But he didn't say it was the Irwin Raptor, Tireia. I had no idea the thing was made of gold until I got there. It was boxed and tied up pretty good and I left it like that driving all the way across from Philly. He said I couldn't fly because he didn't want security people messing with it, which maybe should have set off alarm bells, but I just wanted it to be an easy job, so driving seemed less of a hassle to me, too."

Whatever combination of intoxicants she'd taken was working in our favor. She babbled on without prompting, just the opposite of the closed-mouth response Ornice had received.

"When I got to Sun Valley, Cassim Geyer showed me the falcon. Trask had told me what to look for on the statue, particularly the bent tail feather where it had been dropped, and it seemed legit to me. Geyer unwrapped the Irwin Raptor and my mouth fell open. Solid gold, ruby eyes, with a chain fixed to its beak that held a diamond as big as your thumb.

Why anyone would trade it for that black thing was hard to imagine but I knew Trask was fascinated by the falcon. He said a bunch of statues were made out of different materials as props for the film, and there was controversy over which one came first, but this one had been the leading contender for decades. I don't remember all the details but he was full of yarns about the props and the infighting over who had the real goods. There's a little cult of those guys, rich collectors vying for the best noirish stuff. I wouldn't be surprised if he had found a buyer among them. Of course, I didn't know the Irwin was hot, so to get rid of it obviously sweetened the deal for Trask."

"That's not quite true, is it?" Tireia interrupted. "You did know the Irwin was hot. After Trask received it from the people who first stole it, you and Stuart were interviewed by the FBI."

She looked startled and confused.

"We were, yes, I'd forgotten. But I didn't know Trask had the Irwin. He didn't say what I'd be carrying."

"I wonder why he didn't tell you. Was he worried you might make off with it?"

She laughed sourly.

"We weren't in it out of friendship. But listen, Geyer was responsible for Jim's death—I mean, just look, he took off with the falcon."

Tireia kept to our agenda. She avoided the question of who was guilty of what and asked instead about Fabienne's struggle with Jim Davenport on the day of his death. Fab let go of her concerns about Geyer and shifted into how Davenport had burst into the place already full of fury, which of course was not the first time she'd seen him like that. He rushed up and cracked her without saying a word, and it was only after she got back on her feet that she realized what he was after. This made her even more worried than if he was just in a foul mood. Not that she hadn't had a taste of his penchant for beating up women, as she said I would remember.

She gave me a winning smile at this and proceeded to recount the story we all knew about my encounter with Davenport the day after he came over drunk several weeks earlier, accused her of sleeping around, and gave her a split lip. I confronted him downtown at Foresters, she reminded Tireia, and Jim was apparently a little nonchalant, not to say dismissive. Guys at the bar who saw it told her later I lost my usual cool, which she thought would have been fascinating to witness. Anyway, she said, I apparently made short work of Jim and it was a good thing I was buddies with Sheriff Carmody or there might have been a charge of disturbing the peace or whatever. Fabienne appreciated the strong-arm tactic, though, and would have thumped the sonofabitch herself if she had more heft and experience in such things.

In truth, he was half-tanked as usual, and he threw a right that came at me with all the speed and power of a playground swing set. I stepped under it, drove a left into his gut that made him say "oof" and then a right cross put him down. It seemed insufficient for what he'd done to her but would have to do and I walked out.

Tireia steered Fab back to the day Davenport was shot. Well, she said, after he made it obvious what we wanted, she tried to bluff ignorance. He just sneered. He kept working her over and she tried to defend herself but good luck with that. She kept yelling that she didn't know anything and he kept clobbering her. She got woozy and tried a new tactic, told him the delivery hadn't come yet. He smacked her again and said delivery from who? She wasn't sure if she even answered before she blacked out. That's all she remembered. There were no firearms involved. Somebody must have come in, shot him, and left the gun in her hand.

Minta came downstairs and requested again to go outside. Fabienne asked if she liked the car and she said yes, but she wanted to go outside now. Tireia suggested it would probably be all right if she promised to stay in the back yard where the adults could see her from the picture window. Nobody disagreed as the kid dove for the door.

Tireia stuck to our plan and said we should talk about Wilber. She said she didn't know much about the arc of Fabienne's relationship with him, which left her wide open to Fab's rejoinder that it was less an arc than a flatline. She'd met him at Foresters, her hangout when she was living at the condo on the lakefront. She wasn't particularly a fan of dive bars but it was an easy walk, which was preferable to driving, even in the relative absence of traffic cops. What could she say, she was civic-minded. Anyway, it was obvious from the start Wilber was a rodent but she met him at a vulnerable time and it didn't really so much develop as just lingered for a while. She had no regrets about what she was up to in those days. It was a phase, not a good place to be in, of course, but she was beyond that now.

She should have regrets, I thought, and knew Tireia would agree. Fabienne used to leave Minta unattended in the condo at night during her drinking bouts and no doubt brought back all kinds of chaos. Our realization of what was happening had prompted Tireia to intervene. But right now, we kept quiet. Fab said Wilber was unreliable and usually drunk and he was a petty thief with a bad attitude, so when she bought the cabin and moved out of the condo, she left him behind, too. The problem was he didn't want to be left behind. When they bumped into each other once or twice, he tried to turn on the charm but it came across as smarmy and made her feel bad for him.

"He knew I was seeing Davenport by then," she said. "He probably was sneaking around the place, just like you thought he was, Reese, when you spotted Wilber's rig outside my cabin that day. All up, he was pathetic but pretty harmless. I knew he had a weapon but everybody has guns up here. It didn't make sense that he shot Jim, because he couldn't have stolen those birds from Geyer's house. Wilber didn't have the brains or the balls to pull off a heist like that. He was useless but he wasn't a killer."

Tireia was handling the interview now, which we all knew was an interview but pretended was a conversation among friends. She moved at last onto the primary question, the one we had come to get an answer for. She said the court hearing was coming up and we weren't exactly positive where Fabienne stood in terms of the whole custody thing. We figured she'd back the current setup but after what she had said, Tireia wasn't sure. Fabienne went for the sherry but we put our hands over our glasses. She poured a tastelessly large one for herself. In front of us beyond the window, Minta ran in erratic circles, arms outstretched, no chance of catching a butterfly that seemed to be toying with her.

"I realize I could get into trouble over the Irwin," she said, "even though I did nothing wrong. And I know it won't look good that I left Minta with you for a long time, Tireia, although it was the responsible thing to do under the circumstances, don't you think? I mean, let's face it, I wasn't in a great frame of mind. And Reese is the biological father, so it's not like you're strangers, for Chrissakes. But I don't think that will wash with the judge. Maybe he'll say I'm incompetent or unfit and he'll take my baby away from me, even though I'm much better now and could do a better job. Do I want to be a full-time mother? That's kind of a big jump right now. I'd probably rather keep things the way they are and sort of gradually move in that direction, see how it works out over time. But I'm worried the judge won't let us do that. What if he makes it black-and-white, says take my girl back or give her up? What do I do then? I've had a fantasy I could take her and then we could slip back into what we were doing and who would know? But they would know, wouldn't they? I doubt they'd keep their snouts out of our business."

She paused and worked on her sherry. We didn't say anything, aware from her manner she wasn't done yet. On the grass, Minta attempted cartwheels that looked more like sideways hops on her hands and feet.

"I haven't gotten a lawyer," Fabienne said. "I don't like them and I haven't been charged with anything, so call me crazy but I'm not getting one until I have to. My plan is to see how this court case goes. I won't ask to be given custody but if the judge puts the question to me, I'll answer honestly. The trouble is I don't know what the honest answer is, because I'm not sure how I feel, OK? I'm not against how things are now, Tireia, I think it's worked out pretty well. But if the judge puts me on the spot—and I assume he will—I'll say what's in my heart, whatever that may be. I wish I knew. I'll have to trust that my response will be what I truly feel."

31

Mindful of Minta seated between us during the drive back to Tireia's cabin, we tried to speak cautiously about Fabienne and her evasions. No doubt it was a real condition to not know what you'd say until you said it but it also was convenient, I pointed out. Like admitting upfront to alcoholism, Tireia said, which allows you to go ahead and indulge. Minta leaned her head against Tireia's arm and hummed quietly. The outdoors exercise had relaxed her. She petted the talking car parked in her lap, a dopey grin on its grill. The way to unite our stance would be if Ornice represented all of us, I suggested. Tireia said she'd already asked about that and Ornice confirmed it could be a conflict of interest. At least we had some info to pass on, she added. But how like our errant friend it was to go into court unprepared.

We crossed the highway and once more cut through the quiet streets away from downtown. Tireia, speaking in calm tones, asked if I believed that Fab didn't know the contents of the package she'd transported for Trask.

"He might have said nothing because he didn't trust her," I replied.

"On the other hand, interstate transport of property worth more than five grand is a felony only if you know it's stolen," she said. "Trask might have told Fabienne she'd be carrying the Irwin Falcon to implicate her as an accomplice. That would put her under his thumb."

We passed the pizza joint, and then the road that went to the smokejumper base, which made me long for the relative simplicity of wildfires.

Tireia glanced down at Minta leaning against her. I shook my head in reassurance that the kid couldn't be following all this; it was hard enough for me to keep up.

We arrived back at the highway and turned onto it for the short jaunt to Warren Wagon Road. Tireia stroked the child's hair, which set her to humming again. It wasn't late in the day but the mountains already had begun to shoulder out the sun. She mused that Lou Faulkner's Balzac Club wasn't the only thing she had to research now. She also needed to find out more about this relative of Rowena who apparently had sold my little box and the mourning ring to Trask.

We agreed it was still vaguely possible that Wilber had knocked off Davenport because of jealousy or protectiveness. But if that was the motive—if Wilber had been lurking around Fabienne's cabin but had no part in the theft of the statues— then why would anyone go all the way out to Warren to eliminate him? No, we liked our theory that Wilber had been killed because he had the Irwin Raptor. But Darlene's question lingered: if the plan was for Wilber to give the ransom money and the raptor to Cassim Geyer, then who shot him?

The occasional car passed us on the way to town. Its occupants probably had spent the day swimming off North Beach or boating at the top end of the lake, but it was pretty quiet for a midsummer weekend. Tireia pointed out a hawk as I turned off Warren Wagon onto the access road and began the short climb to her cabin. The lake's glimmer through the trees was temporarily obscured by the incline. We stopped and let out Minta, who took a moment to shake off her grogginess from the ride, like a mountain bluebird that had bumped into a window. Tireia took my arm and leaned in, which gave me a chance to inhale the familiar fragrance of her hair.

"I remember after Fabienne got out of the hospital, she told you someone had phoned and instructed her to pick up the package at the end of her driveway," she said.

"Yeah, that's right."

"If Wilber was working the con for Cassim Geyer, he would have been the one who dropped off the falcon. She would have recognized his voice on the phone."

"Yeah."

"But you didn't ask her about that," Tireia said. "Was it because you were afraid she was shielding Wilber? Were you worried about finding evidence that she was involved in a crime?"

"Why didn't you ask her?"

Tireia turned around and touched the side of my face. "I felt like the question had to come from you."

"It didn't seem strategic to bring it up," I said, flustered. "We can't be sure yet of how Wilber fit in."

"You want to protect her."

"That, too, but we need her on our side. We can't let them take our girl away."

Her arrestingly mismatched features went still.

"Whoever's behind this," she said, "we'll get them."

Minta yelled at us to watch her do a somersault. We watched. It wasn't too bad, and we clapped.

"I'm going to fix something to eat," Tireia announced.

"Hooray," Minta said, "I'm starved as hell."

After we got the little cuss fed and to bed, Tireia powered up her browser to see what she could find out about the Balzac Club.

Aware that my presence was unneeded, I went home.

The next morning, she called to say she had gotten on a darknet microblogging platform and found a link to a forum about private members' clubs where someone had posted information about the Balzac. Of course the post was pseudonymous and unverifiable but it had a ring of authenticity, she said, like a consumer's product review, full of detail and deep background. The man who wrote it—claiming to be a former member of the Balzac Club— said Lou Faulkner had founded it himself, intending it as an alternative to the stuffiness, hypocritical probity, and celebrity obsession of other such clubs. Membership required two recommendations, one of which had to be from an existing member, followed by a secretive selection process by committee. Musts for approval were a demonstrated talent in "creative deal-making" and "daring innovation in trade," which translated into big-time shady dealings, according to the informer. The initial membership fee was a quarter-million. No weapons were allowed in the club, no cameras, and women were as scarce as minorities.

The club's official motto was a quote from Balzac, "Glory is the sun of the dead." The snitch figured they misinterpreted this as advice from the long-dead French author to stay out of the limelight while alive. The members saw themselves as dauntless privateers, according to the post, and they met at their luxurious club in Vegas to network and exchange ideas in sanctuary from any form of publicity. The informer wrote it was easy enough for people to find out Faulkner was the club's founder. But beyond that, the writer wasn't willing to name members, on the grounds that even the darknet could prove to be insufficient protection from these people if they got annoyed and determined.

32

The Valley County Courthouse in Cascade resembled a giant block hammer, but until now it hadn't occurred to me its shape might symbolize the way it dispensed justice. Not that I was a huge believer in legal justice—driven as it seemed to be by preconceptions, resources, and the parsing of language—but whatever hope I'd held in the past for outcomes involving other people faded to a murmur compared to the white noise in my head as we approached the courtroom. We had dropped off Minta in McCall for summer school. Derek had reassured us that an officer would make sure all was well while we were down the road. Ornice met us in the hall outside the courtroom and the mere sight of her produced an instant placebo effect. Probably neither of us paid much attention to the substance of the calming statements she delivered in her mellifluous voice, as her musician-like fingers swooped through the air and touched the lightest of arpeggios on our sleeves, but I appreciated her warmth.

It wasn't a trial yet, and we knew that only the attorneys would speak unless the judge had a specific question for someone, probably Fabienne. Documents had been submitted to the court by the state and by Ornice, although Fab apparently had filed nothing on her own behalf. Still, it was impossible not to think about Ornice's warning that Judge Totorica had a history of supporting parental claims to child custody even when evidence was strong of neglect, so long as it didn't tip into flagrant abuse.

We saw Fab when we entered the courtroom, sitting alone on a middle bench. She had her head down and didn't look at us. On the other side of the aisle, Darlene Carmody gave a little wave and a smile. Her husband Hank, in his go-to-meeting suit, nodded solemnly. Graham Wheeler entered just after we did and took a seat near the back. The FBI man tipped his Greek fisherman's cap at us and then took it off in a manner that managed to combine amiability with menace. It looked like both a greeting and a challenge. The paneled room held a few other onlookers, who perhaps awaited their own moment in the statutory gloom. We sat in the front row across the aisle from an attorney who represented the state. The court reporter sat at her desk below the bench and at a far end of the bench the clerk announced the judge.

After we stood and then sat again, I slipped into autopilot mode, which didn't keep me from following the proceedings but set them at a distance, allowing whatever was left of me to function in the background at least partly freed from the stress of powerlessness. I thought about the upcoming antiques exhibition where Ellis Trask would give a presentation and considered how best to extract from him whatever he was hiding. Meanwhile, I regarded Judge Totorica as he told Fab that a lawyer could take her through the steps necessary to settle this matter without a drawn-out and expensive process.

If she couldn't afford representation, the court could appoint an attorney.

He said his usual inclination would be to award custody of a child or children to one parent and to set the amount of time each parent would have with the offspring, unless circumstances made it unsafe or otherwise imprudent to do so. In this case, the mother's competency to care full-time for the child was under question, and the legal father was deceased. The state maintained that because no guardian had been appointed, foster care was required. Consequently, today he would examine the child's current situation and establish a temporary order of custody to ensure her safety.

"Your honor, with respect, your position amounts to an indirect dismissal of the question of my client's claims to custody," Ornice said.

The judge wasn't having it.

"As you're aware, counselor, any such claims your client might have are addressed in the statutes. Moreover, the main objective of the system is to maintain or return the custody of children to their natural parents whenever possible. The question of abandonment by the mother is germane in the legal sense of a failure to maintain a normal parental relationship with the child, including reasonable support and regular personal contact. These are the issues. I will entertain no further comment on them and counsel is instructed to constrain her arguments to these ground rules."

Tireia sat completely still, her face a study in enigma, which made me wonder if I had the same expression. But Ornice was practically hopping, which boded well for a push against the prejudices of the robed figure, at least as far as he would allow.

Byron Allen, the state's attorney and a thread-perfect

exhibitor of the decorous mask, pointed out that no legal guardianship had been set up and Fabienne had not formally designated a first responder in the case of any emergency that might affect her own capacity to care for the girl. He said as the biological father I'd relinquished my parental rights in Pennsylvania through a court order and he sketched what had happened after that, including Stuart's death followed by the arrival of the mother and child in Idaho. His take was that Fabienne and Tireia conspired to delude school authorities about who was raising Minta, even to the point of Tireia getting on the list to pick her up and to be copied on school emails.

Tireia acknowledged only by the tiniest twitch at the corner of one eyelid that she'd noticed. The part of me that wasn't listening to the lawyer went back to the old question of who had disrupted our lives by going to the authorities and why? Was it tied to the business of the statues?

Allen pointed out that Mrs. Sansverrou and Mr. Mencari both were at the scene of the recent death of Jim Davenport.

"Objection," Ornice said. "Mr. Davenport's death has nothing to do with the case today. No criminal charges have been laid."

The judge asked Allen why it was relevant and he said while it was true neither of us had been criminally charged yet, we were the only two at the scene and we were being investigated by the FBI, as indicated in an affidavit from Agent Wheeler. The issue went directly to the question of the mother's fitness to resume custody. Totorica said he would let him proceed for now but warned him to be cautious— whatever the hell that meant.

Allen reported a "violent altercation" I'd had with Davenport at Foresters, a drinking establishment in downtown McCall.

Ornice demanded to know what connection this had to anything. The magistrate asked Allen where he was going with this and he said he wouldn't take it further but it was germane to establishing the necessity of placing the child in foster care. Totorica said he'd leave it in the record.

Allen went on that after Davenport's death I kept up with my investigation and subsequently was assaulted and received a threat to both Minta and Tireia. Clearly, the child was in an unsafe situation, he said. This time, Tireia looked right at me and the question on her face was the same one in my head. We had told Ornice about the ominous slip of paper but she wouldn't have been obliged to relay that information to Byron Allen, would she? Would it be considered relevant to our case?

"Darlene," I whispered to her. "I told her."

My bet was her sense of duty had outweighed her loyalty to us. Maybe this was why she had seemed almost guilt-stricken the other day when she had offered to take Minta. But no, Darlene wouldn't have any regrets about doing her job the right way.

Ornice stood up.

"Your honor, my colleague is attempting to blame my client for a threat directed at her own safety."

Once again, Totorica told the prosecutor to proceed with care.

Allen thanked him. He said Tireia and I had a romantic relationship outside the formal and common-law bonds of matrimony. This prompted Ornice to declare, not in so many words, that now she was really pissed off. The judge told Allen to move on. The lawyer said school officials had reported that Minta was headstrong and used foul language, including taking the name of the Lord in vain, which he argued was evidence of poor parenting.

When Ornice got her turn to talk, she went on about Tireia's impeccable reputation—including her professional standing in both Silicon Valley and in academic circles—and emphasized she had provided a warmly nurturing home to Minta for several years. The judge told her to stick to the points he had identified at the outset as pertinent, which were the safety of the child's current circumstances and whether she should be in her mother's care.

"Yes, your honor, I'm trying to do that, although it's difficult to follow such narrow guidelines when the prosecutor has framed much of his remarks as an attack on my client's respectability, even to the point of questioning her personal relationships and her parenting abilities, which does not strike me as conforming to your honor's directive."

Totorica waved this away without comment.

"Mr. Allen's contention that Minta's use of language indicates behavioral problems is incorrect and misleading," Ornice said. "This matter concerns not only which words a family considers to be taboo but also is an indicator of the child's precocity in the process of testing her personal freedoms, as is her so-called headstrong nature."

Actually, Tireia and I would have taken back permission for the kid to cuss, except we didn't want her to think we were phonies. Nor did we want to risk rebellion that could prolong the phase. And then there was our mutual conviction that sometimes the rules should well and truly be damned. All this delicacy about words was for grammarians, we had told ourselves. In the end, the child would be stronger and wiser for the experience. Meanwhile, we kept trying to impress on her that profanity was most effective when used sparingly. But it's tough to convince a child that her new toy should be played with only occasionally. What Tireia had neglected in her strategy was the aesthetic offense of a kid enamored with profanity. That did bother us although not nearly as much as it seemed to shock the judge.

Ornice pointed out that CFS personnel had visited Tireia's place and attested to its exceptional fitness, while school officials had expressed satisfaction with Minta's scholastic achievement. The county sheriff's department had placed a watch on the child at school and now at summer school, to help ensure her personal safety. Tireia's marital status was clearly not relevant to the legal considerations in this case, she argued.

While she delivered this speech, the judge did a bench-bound St. Vitus dance. He then managed to say without too much irritation he'd take all this into consideration but would base his decision on the principal issues, which did not include whether counsel's client was fit to be a guardian. He confirmed Ornice's suspicion by announcing he'd appoint a guardian *ad litem* to act on Minta's behalf. This person would conduct an independent investigation and submit a report. A second appearance would be scheduled as soon as possible. In the meantime, as the parties had failed to agree on a temporary living situation for the child, he ordered she remain in her current home until questions surrounding the natural mother and the best interests of the minor could be resolved. Adjourned.

Ornice seemed relieved the judge had left Minta with Tireia but disappointed about his decision to bring a law guardian into it. And his attitude angered her.

"The problem with the legal system is too many judges can't leave their personal opinions at the courtroom door," she fumed.

"It went all right," I said. "You did well."

"Thanks. It's just that Judge Totorica has telescoped the thing to the question of Fabienne's competency, which will take some strategizing to get around. We'll do it, don't worry. It's just a little frustrating."

She touched the sleeve of Tireia, who looked impressively calm.

"You're doing fine," Tireia told her. "But I agree, it's strange the judge almost seems to think you should be representing Fabienne."

Before the lawyer could reply, Darlene and Hank stepped up to shake hands and offer words of encouragement and then hurried home to their children.

Fabienne materialized.

"I hope I won't have to speak next time," she said, and glanced nervously at Ornice.

No answer came and she remarked to the blank space within our little circle, "I could need a lawyer before long."

"Much of this might be cleared up if you'd agree to support Tireia as guardian," Ornice said.

Fab refocused on her from wherever she had gone and said, "Sorry, I meant the case of the statues."

She smiled sadly at me, said goodbye to Tireia, and wandered away. We all looked at her go, just as Stuart and I had watched her walk away that day I first met her on campus. But our gaze was different this time.

"I wouldn't be surprised if Judge Totorica's real problem is he objects to you two being unmarried," our attorney remarked.

It wasn't meant as an irritation but it galled nonetheless.

33

The California Militaria Exhibition in San Francisco where Ellis Trask would give his talk was at the Hilton off Union Square. It would be packed, so I stayed at the St. Francis for its lobby and the gracious rooms in the main building, even though they weren't big unless you went for the view, which I did not. Unwilling to push the Husky that far, I'd taken a commercial flight, and then a cabbie left-and-righted the traffic on 101 until we arrived at the hotel with a couple hours to spare. The online schedule Tireia had shown me said Trask's presentation was titled, "Admiral Nelson's Relics," which caught our interest but seemed a curious choice of topic, considering the military stuff in this event would be overwhelmingly American.

It was a glorious day outside, the square full of loungers and the sidewalks populated with striders who radiated the conviction you can sense in the citizens of great cities that they're part of a grand enterprise. At the Hilton, I skirted the NRA table by the entrance to check out the crowded exhibition hall. Long rows were crammed with all manner of paraphernalia from U.S. hostilities here and abroad through the decades, but mainly Vietnam and the other unwinnable wars that came later in Muslim countries. It was a dizzying array of pistols and rifles, binoculars and bayonets, flak jackets and telescopic sights, peppered throughout with hot warnings on patches and bumper stickers about good guys with guns, treading on me, and standing to fight. The attractions of weaponry and its associated trappings to those who felt besieged had never been hard to understand but long ago had become uninteresting and soon the prospect of an aged apple brandy drew me to a place darker than this one, literally if not metaphorically. The brandy was good and I was a few minutes late for Trask's spiel.

The deep narrow meeting room was set up like a theater, with chairs on both sides of an aisle and a screen in a corner offset from a podium where Trask spoke into a mic and clicked the slides. He wore a tailored seersucker blazer in thin stripes whose hue matched that of the bags under his eyes. My getup was jeans and a polo shirt, the Phillies cap still parked in my bag at the hotel. Tireia never understood why I wore it. You hate Philadelphia, she reminded me. Brilliant as she was, I had to explain that Philthy wasn't the Phillies' fault. Ah, like Russia and Solzhenitsyn, she said, which I took on faith as a logical response.

I chose an aisle chair in a middle row but there were few enough bodies that I could have sat practically anywhere. Trask's pictures showed the admiral's medals and all kinds of other stuff, including an ornately decorated rifle and canteen, swords, porcelain displaying his coronet, a tubular celarette full of crystal glasses and decanters, a silver tureen and goblet, a silver collar inscribed for his dog Nileus, a combination knife-fork, his rings and gloves, his coat, tunic, and breeches damaged from battle, even his funeral carriage. All through it, Trask talked about the volume of Nelson memorabilia and how it had been dispersed around the world, inherited, sold, stolen, misattributed, forged, but always desired, ever since his death at the Battle of Trafalgar in 1805.

He talked a lot about Nelson's gold watch and seal, which were among items swiped in 1900 from a display at Greenwich Hospital. He said a seaman later claimed to have gotten those two things from a drunken sailor, and the man offered their return for a reward but instead got seven years for an offense against the nation. The watch and seal were discovered in a railway station cloakroom, in a package that held a portmanteau containing a concertina, inside of which the treasures were concealed. Trask's sparse audience rustled to attention when he went on to one of the other prizes missing from that theft, the hilt of a sword presented to Nelson by the captains of the fleet after his heroics in the Battle of the Nile, its golden grip in the shape of a crocodile. He said the chief inspector on the case later wrote he figured a collector had the hilt and other booty, most likely in America.

It was an impressive presentation and several folks gathered around him for a while afterwards although I also overheard a guy tell his buddy on the way out he wasn't surprised Trask knew so much about the 1900 theft, when you considered that he himself was an infamous receiver of stolen goods.

After the fans dispersed, Trask approached and held out his hand underneath that solid-gold grin, Mephistopheles bamboozling Faust. He was happy to see me, had been wanting to catch up on our business, was glad I could stop in on the lecture. It was high quality, I said, although the topic surprised me for this convention, even coming from the owner of Anglophile Antiques. He replied that he couldn't resist indulging his special interest in British naval collectibles, particularly Nelson relics. He said he knew a place nearby where we could get oysters with our cocktails and led me outside.

We walked up Mason Street, took a right on Geary and crossed the street into Hotel G. Near the front desk he went up the stairs, opened a door into a hallway, and led me to the bar. It was quiet at this hour and we sat under a curiously modern black-and-white portrait of the bar's namesake, an ancestor of the owners named Benjamin Cooper, whom Trask seemed pleased to inform me never existed. My pick from the cocktail menu was a French Bobcat: bourbon, cognac, strega, alpine liqueur and vermouth. Trask got something similarly dangerous and we ordered oysters.

I again brought up the mourning ring and the Nelson box Stuart had given me.

"In Philadelphia, you said you couldn't recall who you'd bought them from. So we looked into it. The seller was a relative of Rowena Pascoe-Leyland."

A shadow flitted across his face and disappeared, like a time-lapse video. "You're right, I remember now," he said. "They both were from Rowena Pascoe-Leyland's brother-in-law, her younger sister's husband. That's right, the family was upset about him selling their heirlooms."

The oysters arrived and with his little fork he severed the lashings of one, as intent as an archeologist over a shell ring. The morsel disappeared into the yellow grinder and then he casually asked how progress was going with "the project" we discussed last time.

I told him I'd visited Faulkner, who had Geyer's two paintings in his office. This made him snicker.

"He finally got those, did he? Lou Faulkner's into film noir collectibles, you know, especially paintings featured in those old movies. Of course, most of them are just big photographs varnished to make them look like paintings but they're rare. And the stories behind them, you know, that's what counts. But Geyer's two, those are actual paintings, real prizes."

"He has others?"

"Oh, yeah. A lot of the pictures were supposed to have been lost or destroyed but he has a talent for digging them up. He has Alice Reed from the *Woman in the Window*, he has the portrait of Laura Hunt from Otto Preminger's picture, he has Matilda Frazier in *The Unsuspected*."

"You know a lot about his collection."

"People in certain circles are aware of it. And I checked around before visiting."

"The Balzac Club?"

"Yeah. Did Faulkner take you in there?"

"He didn't. What's it like?"

"Great, in a gothic way." His grin lit up like a jack-o-lantern. "A gentleman's club for black marketeers. It's the actual business in that building, you know. But none of his best art is on display. They say he keeps most of the stuff in free ports around the world to avoid taxes and as collateral for loans. No doubt it's a laundering exercise, too."

I sampled my cocktail, which was disturbingly tasty. Young Benjamin Cooper in his tux gazed seriously at some place beyond us.

"When I visited his office, he pulled curtains over Geyer's paintings."

Trask laughed and said maybe hiding everything had become a fetish.

"So, did you try to sell him the Irwin Raptor?"

He stopped poking the corpse of another oyster and I could see he still was reluctant to let go of the pretense that all this was hypothetical, that he never had the statue. But I was tired of the game. I said I understood he hadn't wanted to tell me in Philadelphia that he got the mourning ring and the Nelson box from Rowena's family because it would put him too close to Rowena and the whole mess with the two birds. But there was no longer any point in his evasions. I told him I'd spoken to Davenport's widow, who said Trask had hired the P.I. to get both statues for him after they were stolen.

"If you want your golden bird pried out of someone else's hands, I'm your best chance."

He gave in. "Yeah, I hired Davenport, and now he's dead. I've never been a part of anything that involved murder."

"Good for you. Thievery has its limits."

"I'm no thief."

"Me either."

We clinked glasses and then he said, "The Irwin fell into my lap. I didn't go looking for it, but the chance was too good to pass up. Rumor got out in certain circles that I had it, and Lou Faulkner invited me to come see him. He gave me the VIP tour of the Balzac Club. Maybe he thought he'd wow me enough to accept the price he offered for the statute. But it was an insult to be low-balled by that thug, so I decided to hang onto it."

"I wonder why he'd even want it."

"Why wouldn't he?"

"Several reasons," I said with a shrug. "It wasn't made in the time that interests him and it's not from the movie industry. It's famously stolen property, so it would be hard to resell. And it isn't a painting."

"If paintings were the only things he collected from the period, he wouldn't have much."

"Other statues?"

"Well, not statues specifically that I can think of but he

had a projection room in the club where Forties films played continuously, and it was decorated with all sorts of things: first-edition posters that had never been folded, guns, jewelry, clothing."

"No statues, though?"

He stared. If he didn't know Faulkner had the Ottoman Osprey, he wasn't going to find out from me.

"Don't be thick," he said. "The Irwin was a special deal."

"All right, then, tell me something else. How did the trade with Rowena for her prop come about?"

"That started during the same trip," he said. "I met her and her husband at the Balzac. He was an American, one of Faulkner's buddies, which of course by definition means on the shady side. Rowena's a blue blood, so the marriage raised eyebrows, but he did have dough, a lot of it. Like Faulkner, he was a fan of film noir and gothic melodrama of the Forties and Fifties. We had dinner together. Cassim Geyer was there, too. We talked about the Irwin and the falcon. It struck me Faulkner was more interested in the prop than my statue. He just about watered when they described it. Quite a while after that, Rowena contacted me. By then, a heart attack had gotten her husband. She was the one who proposed the trade—her falcon for my raptor."

"Why would you want to trade gold for lead?"

He finished his cocktail and dabbed his skinny lips with a napkin.

"For one," he said, "because Rowena agreed to cut me a check that helped to make up the difference in value. Two, because I knew Faulkner wanted the falcon bad and would pay big."

He toyed with an oyster but then let it go.

"The strange thing is, he's a fake enthusiast and doesn't

even realize it. The falcon, the paintings, the other collectibles, the films, none of it actually interests him. That's why he doesn't show his items to anybody, just keeps them locked up in climate-controlled storage vaults."

He waved a hand, long and slender like that of an artist. An artistic ghoul. What if he had followed in the direction signaled by the expressiveness of those hands? What kind of man would he be?

"It's criminal," he said, "hiding it all away, perverting the intent of the artists. But he's a criminal at heart, by which I mean he's about himself. Ownership is all that interests him. Possession. My own failing, if you want to call it that, always has been I'm interested in the art."

It wasn't likely Trask had kept the Irwin Raptor on a shelf in his antiques gallery with an NFS sticker on it but this was easy to let go.

"Rowena would have noticed Faulkner was keen on the falcon. Why didn't she sell it to him?"

"I think she didn't care about the money, she had plenty. She wanted a trade, a rare and beautiful thing in return for what she was giving up. My guess is she got a kick out of the thought of showing off the Irwin Raptor in secret to her snooty friends. 'Look what I have, and it's ill-gotten, isn't it thrilling?' Some of her old man's larceny rubbed off on her, that's what I figure."

The afternoon was waning, and the bar began to fill up. A couple sat at a table near us. Trask dropped his voice.

"My turn for a question. What news do you have for me about the Irwin?"

"Making progress. We're closing in," I lied. "I'll get my hands on it pretty soon."

"Good."

"Sondra Davenport told me her husband had seen texts between you and Fabienne on her phone."

Trask hesitated and then said, "I called the first time but then she started texting. Obviously, I shouldn't have allowed it."

"Why did you pick her to carry the raptor?"

"I heard a while back she'd moved to Idaho. That's what made me think of her. And you can't trust just anybody with a thing like this, some hired hand. She was a woman, you know? It seemed unlikely she'd cross me. Not that I'm really too scary or anything."

His hooded gaze came out hard at me.

"Geyer was the one I shouldn't have trusted. My guess is he found a purchaser for the Irwin, which is a feat in itself." He leaned forward. "You get the bird and there won't be anything hypothetical about that fifty grand. I don't like taking a loss on my property. I hate it. But it's a pay-to-play game."

"I might find the falcon along with it."

"Listen, no matter what Davenport's widow told you, I'm a straight guy," he said. "Anyway, you'd be looking at a reward from Rowena for the prop, wouldn't you?"

"Could be. I'll keep you posted."

34

Tireia was in town for groceries when I called. The weather was beautiful, so we decided to meet at a small park that descended to the lake. Down the hill from my cabin and across the street, I found an empty bench on the lawn below an ensemble of bronze bears. She showed up moments later, vivacious in chocolate culottes over a beige leotard top, her straight hair in a ponytail. She took off her sandals and we sat quietly for a moment. We gazed at a cluster of docked sailboats whose bare masts of varying heights extended up beyond the blue water into the contour of the mountains, like a cardiograph of the landscape.

The law guardian had visited while I was away and Tireia gave me the rundown. Jeanette Welgate was a volunteer who had gone through a training program. She was from Donnelly, in her early fifties, two grown children. She had no legal or medical background but was supposed to ferret out what was best for Minta by talking to us. She and Tireia chatted over cups of chai. Jeanette noted that Minta was a charming little girl who said she was happy here. "She's quite well spoken, not a hint of the naughty talk. It's as if she were coached but maybe she was just on her good behavior." The child's room was lovely, Jeanette remarked, and everything was very much in order, although in her work it could be amazing sometimes how a shiny surface could conceal grubby facts. "Not usually, mind you," she added.

"I might as well say I've had a lovely time, although I'm really supposed to keep my professional distance. Don't tell me you can get those cream puffs in Valley County. Actually, you might enjoy my church's monthly Sunday socials. Everyone brings their home-baked goods. But you don't go to church, do you? I almost forgot."

Jeanette worried about people. She wanted everything to work out nicely, but sometimes things happened that made her shake her head. Tireia figured that for certain folks fascinated by the details of their neighbors' lives, Jeanette's job was perfect. The woman meant well in the worst way.

Tireia's rendition would have been more amusing without the waver of anger in her voice. Succumbing to it, she said Jeanette Welgate had already made up her mind and nothing she saw or heard would change her conviction that the state knew best, although of course she knew nothing, she was a bureaucratic automaton. No, I argued, it was clear the woman was impressed. Everything would work out fine, we just had to get through this bullshit and we'd keep Minta in the end.

I described the meeting with Trask, including his reluctant confession that, yes, the Irwin Raptor had been in his possession. We agreed he probably was uncertain I'd actually return the statue to him, even for fifty grand. He had been willing to talk because he really did hate the thought of Geyer getting away with ripping him off. When I mentioned he'd said Lou Faulkner kept his art in free ports around the world, she nodded.

"I read somewhere that UNESCO's been trying to crack

down but it isn't easy. Stolen art can sit in those vaults for decades, undisturbed and unseen."

"I wonder why Faulkner didn't stash those two pictures he got from Geyer."

"Maybe he wanted to look at them for a while … gloating."

"Maybe."

"Have you noticed the paintings in those films are almost always portraits of women?" she said.

"You're saying he wants to keep the women in his office for a while?"

"He likes film noir, so it makes sense. The portraits in those movies are almost characters in themselves. They're intense, mesmerizing."

"Ah, he likes dangerous women."

She arched an eyebrow.

"Or he likes to control dangerous women. You put a woman in a picture and what do you do to her? You immobilize her. You make her into a possession. You put her behind a curtain, so you're the only one who can see her."

A motorboat came into view. A water-skier careened behind it, carving a white scar that was rapidly reabsorbed by the blue.

"OK, cool," I said casually. "Men try to control women through the paintings, but then they get mesmerized. And is this something we can use?"

"*Cherchez la femme.*"

She smiled. It occurred to me that despite her flare of irritation when she recounted Jeanette Welgate's visit, she was more relaxed today than in the recent past. No doubt because Totorica had let her keep the kid. For the time being, anyway.

A teenaged couple walked past us hand-in-hand and sat

close together near the water's edge. They ate ice cream cones while their dog rolled on his back in the grass. We smiled at each other and I kissed her. As always, I got a mild shock of surprise at how full those thin lips felt when they met mine.

She put her hands on my chest and said, "An interesting thing that came out of your tete-a-tete with Trask was he didn't know Faulkner had the Ottoman Osprey. Although maybe he's just a good actor."

"It didn't look like he was acting. Given Trask's obsession with Admiral Nelson, the osprey would be way up on his personal dream list."

"It's something to keep an eye on, as if we had a spare eye. Speaking of which, I looked into that 'RPL' note you found in Geyer's trash."

"And?"

"There was no code to break in the numbers. Once it occurred to me that 75 could be Highway 75, I got onto a Forest Service map. The road and trail numbers head into the Sawtooth Wilderness. The last number, after the dirt road ended, is a loop trail. Nothing out there but a canyon full of Douglas fir, aspen, and a ridge with views of the Smoky Mountains, except for one cabin in the woods about a mile-and-a-half to the west on the loop. Probably an old homestead, looks dinky. I checked out the county records and guess who owns it?"

"Rowena Pascoe-Leyland."

"RPL."

"Makes you wonder, doesn't it?"

"It makes me wonder if there's any fuel in that airplane of yours."

"Why would Geyer hole up in the cabin of the woman he

stole the statue from? Unless maybe he knew nobody ever went there."

"It would be delicious, hiding in the victim's house," she remarked. "But I wonder if she really is the victim."

"What do you mean?"

"I mean Geyer might still be working for her."

"Are you saying after she arranged the secret trade, she had Geyer swipe the birds?"

She didn't reply.

"But if she wanted to keep both statues, why not just buy the Irwin Raptor directly from Trask?" I said. "It wouldn't be free, but she has plenty of dough. And it would be a lot safer than stealing from him."

The teenaged couple's dog, a collie, trotted past us on the way to the lakefront.

"Besides," I continued, "if Geyer stole the birds for Rowena, there would be no need to hire me. She wouldn't have had to make a payoff to get the prop back."

Tireia remained silent.

"And even if you have an answer to that, why would he take off with the falcon and the money? Unless he decided to double-cross her."

"Let's just say for a second Geyer was working for Rowena all along," she said. "And let's say he didn't double-cross her. If those two statements are true, then there's only one other explanation of what happened. The whole thing was a ruse of some sort. And it was put together by Rowena."

"Are you really taking it in that direction, or are you just asking?"

"Right now, just asking. It seems to me Rowena would need a purpose for such an elaborate scheme. Something that went beyond cheating Trask out of the Irwin Raptor. But what could it be?"

"Anyway, I think my mechanic should give the Husky a once-over. I'll fly south tomorrow."

"That gives us time."

"For what, me to paint your portrait?"

She stuck her feet in the sandals while I looked at her legs.

"Why bother?" she said. "You're already mesmerized."

35

ighway 75 north of Ketchum is a highway only by rural state standards. The turnoff was one of those paved lanes occasioned by houses behind woods on lots enclosed by low picket fences, all of which made the drive a holiday. You wondered how anyone could live here and get anything done beyond gawking at the mountains. And then the houses and the pavement ended and the mountains got closer.

As the vehicle approached the trailhead, I thought about Tireia's theory that Rowena Pascoe-Leyland was behind all this, that she was working some intricate scam for an unknown purpose. It seemed incredible, but it never was wise to dismiss Tireia's theories until she did.

I parked in the empty dirt cul-de-sac and started hiking west, moving upward for about twenty minutes through several switchbacks into a large stand of fir. Off the trail, on a spacious ledge that interrupted the incline, the cabin appeared in a small clearing, its log frame squat and purposeful like a man with folded arms. I stepped into the trees and trudged through the undergrowth in a wide arc below the cabin, circling upward to approach it from behind.

When I could see the cabin again, there were no immediate signs of occupancy. I approached slowly, and kept my eye on the small window in the back, looking for movement. At the last tree that protected me from a stretch of open land, I took a breath and then emerged in a crouch to hurry toward a back corner of the little log structure. No response. If Geyer was in there, he either had fallen asleep or didn't want to add to his list of misdeeds. I took another breath, not as deep as the first one, and peeked through the bottom corner of the window. It was a tiny bedroom, not much more than an oversized closet, with a cot that held the first sign of habitation, an unrolled sleeping bag. Against the wall, a shirt protruded from a carry-on.

I crept around the far side of the cabin, ducked under a window, and passed a Honda dirt bike that stood on its kickstand. To get below another window at the front of the building, I went down on all fours, and then stood sideways at the doorjamb. I reached across the door, turned the knob, and shoved inward. The door floated open with a creak like a hello from a nonchalant cat. Nothing happened. I stepped forward. From behind the door, I exposed half my body to the interior. Directly in front of me, Geyer's man Jonathan Evers sat on a couch and stared up, his mouth half-open. On the coffee table before him, cards were laid out in a game of solitaire. A cigarette burned in an ashtray next to a hot drink. In one hand, he held half a deck. In the other, a single card.

"Reese Mencari," he said. "What the hell?"

This being well up on my list of preferred greetings, I came inside and plopped down in a sprung armchair rocker suffused with mold and dust. I could see the kitchen and the open bathroom door in the little cabin. He was alone.

"Come right in," he said. "Don't bother to knock."

"What are you doing here, Jonathan?"

"I could ask the same. I'm having a quiet vacation here, is what."

"At Rowena Pascoe-Leyland's place?"

"Sure, why not?"

He put the single card in the discard pile and placed the remainder of the deck on the table. He was in jeans, barefoot and shirtless. His arms, neck, and face were equally broad and smooth, a pale continent of skin landmarked in muscle and bone. He was an unexpected catch but a useful one. Tireia and I knew if our theory that Wilber had taken the two statues from Cassim Geyer's place was to hold true, he would have needed help. Plus, the safe had been drilled. Tireia had begun looking into the professional background of Jonathan Evers and had learned right away he had a thing for safes.

"I would have thought Rowena was pretty rich for your blood."

His smile was lazy and self-confident. He picked up the cigarette and took a puff before answering.

"I met her through Mr. Geyer. She's a widow. She offered me."

He was too full of steroids for her marital status to be relevant, I wanted to suggest. But 'roid rage in the middle of the woods was to be avoided. There was no sign of weaponry in the room and I knew how to take care of myself if it came to it—yet even so, when you're unarmed, it's best not to rile a big guy.

"So, how can I help you, Mencari?"

"Not so much me as the police."

A shadow fell upon the pale country.

"Whatta they want?"

"To find out where your boss is, of course."

"No idea. What difference does it make?"

I folded my arms and played piano on my left bicep, a replica in miniature of his.

"He's not actually allowed to run away with Rowena's statue, you see. Nobody's happy, least of all me, coming all the way out here to find him and ending up with you instead."

"He stole the bird?" Jonathan's acting was as broad as his face. I just shook my head. He insisted, "I got nothin about that. He said he was taking a long trip, going around the world. He was closing up the house, and my services wouldn't be needed for a while. That's all I know. I turned off my cell phone as soon as I got here."

"Just escaping it all, huh? I can understand that. So you won't object if I ask the Blaine County Sheriff's Office to send somebody up here for a chat, will you?"

He looked at the cards lined up in order and said to them, "Nah."

"Good."

I took out my phone and was relieved to see the signal was strong; it wasn't hard to get into the sticks from Ketchum and we weren't that far away. I made the call, identified myself, and said Jonathan Evers was here with me, on vacation according to him and quite willing to talk about his employer, Cassim Geyer. I gave the directions and hung up. All the while, Jonathan sat rock-still in front of the cards, stoical if not for slightly elevated breathing and a crest of sweat under his close-cropped hairline.

"I could walk out of here right now," he said. "Get on my trail bike and ride away."

He hunched forward, as if about to stand or even leap up, but he stayed put. I luxuriated in my moldy chair, which was an unpleasant act but good for effect.

"Maybe I'll go around and visit Rowena. Not that you'd tell a story about her letting you stay here."

"Too bad you won't find her," he said childishly. "She went back to England."

He puffed the cigarette and stubbed it out.

"While we're waiting for the cops," I said, "I'll take a coffee."

He didn't budge, so I got up and took the few steps to the kitchen counter. A spoon lay beside an open jar of instant coffee. I turned on the kettle.

"I spoke to Rowena a while ago," I said over my shoulder. "She admitted she tried to trade her movie prop for the Irwin Raptor."

The kettle began to do its work. I strolled back into the living room.

Tireia and I had agreed that if I found Geyer in the cabin, I'd try a bluff. He probably would see through it, but we figured it was worth an attempt. The chances of bluffing Jonathan were much better.

"We know you and Wilber took both statues. But you weren't really stealing them. Not for yourselves. It was for Cassim."

"How do you know? Who told you that?"

"Fabienne."

I stood over Jonathan, who regarded the cards on the table.

"She had him wrapped around her finger," he said. "I warned him."

The inside of my head flashed red as a taillight, and then everything funneled down to some deep place, leaving nothing but a static hum. It was like an instant brainwash with no replacement of what was gone. I went back to the counter to turn off the kettle, and to hide my face. I found a cup, spooned powder into it, and poured in the water. I came back, stirring as I walked.

"How did she find out, anyway?" I asked.

"She didn't tell you? She was there."

"At Geyer's place on the night of the theft. Yeah, she said that."

"She came downstairs in the middle of the night. Snagged us red-handed at the safe. She just looked at us and went back to bed. Wilber said he'd take care of it, and he left with the birds."

I gulped coffee. Shit, was all I could think. Shit, Fabienne.

"What then?" I managed.

"Wilber went over to her place to deliver the falcon statue, like they agreed."

"Did Geyer know about this?"

"You mean about Fabienne? Nah, he thought it would just be you and Wilber."

I sank back down in the stinky chair.

"Who pulled me into it?"

"That was Wilber. The boss asked who would be good for the handoff and Wilber said you."

I put down the coffee cup near Jonathan's card game.

"What do you know about the shooting?"

"Zip. Never talked to either one of them again. They were the ones who double-crossed the boss. They kept the Irwin bird. They were in it together, definitely. Wilber wouldn't of did it without her. And my bet is they would've kept the money for the falcon, too, except something went wrong. Somebody plugged the P.I. But honest to God, I don't have a clue who."

The door hinges rattled from a thumping. I opened it to two cops. Jonathan looked at me, looked at them, and put his shirt on.

36

The access road to the Carmody ranch in Donnelly was a straight shot of maybe a half-mile. You could spot outbuildings from the highway but the house, positioned north-south, was flanked by trees. Darlene had invited us over for a chicken dinner. We sat at the kitchen bar watching her bustle around her pots and bowls. Outside, Minta was in heaven with the Carmody kids, as they caught salamanders in the creek-fed pond behind the house, rode a pony in the paddock while Hank looked on, and chased around after the excited dogs.

"Tell me how you got onto the whereabouts of Jonathan Evers," Darlene said.

I said it had been garbage pick-up day at Geyer's place. She didn't press me. We'd hoped the directions on a note I found would lead us to Geyer, I said, but Jonathan was a good consolation prize.

"Chuck Palmer at the Blaine County Sheriff's Office stuck to the white lie you told that Fabienne put the finger on Wilber and him for breaking into the safe," Darlene said. "Chuck said Jonathan squirmed like a pronghorn trying to crawl under a barbed wire fence, but he didn't deny it."

She transferred pieces of chicken from the deep-fry onto paper towels. I waited for her to bring up Fab.

"He told Chuck all about how they staged it," she said. "The safe was disguised as an end table. Jonathan drilled into its side to avoid the hardplate. He stuck a long borescope in there to get close enough to the change hole to figure out the combination. Quite a piece of work. It must have convinced Mrs. Pascoe-Leyland's people that the burglary was for real."

I didn't mention Tireia's theory that Rowena Pascoe-Leyland had masterminded the theft. Tieria and I had agreed it was a little early to say anything.

"Did Jonathan give up Geyer's whereabouts?" I asked.

"Swore up and down he didn't know."

"I'd like to have another word with him."

Darlene confirmed this should be achievable. She picked up tongs and transferred the chicken to a giant serving dish, which Tireia took to the table.

"Looks like we turned up the right cards," Tireia said over her shoulder. "Wilber, Jonathan, and Cassim."

"And Fabienne," Darlene said. "Unfortunately."

"Or so Jonathan claims," I put in. "She knew about it, but that doesn't mean she planned anything. Wilber could have dragged her into it."

For a moment, Darlene busied herself in silence with the potato masher.

Then she said, "You remember asking for a list of Fabienne's phone calls? Well, Agent Wheeler did you one better. He got the number from Harold Irwin of the woman who offered to return his statue for a payoff. It was Fabienne."

She put the potatoes back on the stove.

Fab, you're the world's worst crook, I thought. First you leave your texts to Ellis Trask on your phone for Davenport to find, and then you make an extortion call from your own number.

"We know for sure now that Wilber had the Irwin Raptor," Tireia said, "but we're no closer to who took it from him and left him dead."

I appreciated that she sounded sad about Fabienne.

"At least Fab's not suspected of that," I said. "Unless someone thinks she climbed out of the hospital bed and went to work, like they do in the movies."

"Those are usually heroes," Darlene responded drily.

She turned off the water under the corn on the cob.

"Anyway, Wheeler gave me one piece of encouraging information. He decided there isn't enough evidence to charge you, Reese, with Davenport's killing. Based on what Jonathan told us, he figures Wilber most likely was the one who took the falcon to Fabienne's cabin. He thinks Wilber came back later and when he found Davenport beating her up, he shot him."

"You're off the hook, Reese," said Tireia.

"Not so fast," Darlene cautioned. "Wheeler now thinks it's possible Reese shot Wilber and took the Irwin Raptor from him."

"Oh, for God's sake," I said.

"He figures Cassim Geyer set up the double steal of the birds and you were in on it, Reese. But after Wilber shot Davenport, he got spooked and took the Irwin Raptor into hiding. You returned the falcon to Geyer and then drove to Warren, plugged Wilbur, and brought the Irwin to Geyer."

"Ridiculous," I said, too loudly. "Wheeler had a better case against me as the shooter of Jim Davenport than of Wilber Arndt."

One of the Carmody kids burst through the side door, Minta

on her heels. Delirious, they motored past us down the hall, around the far turn past the stairwell, down the backstretch, and did another lap before they careened out the door they'd entered.

When they were gone, Tireia said, "She'd be fine here, I guess."

We were silent for moment.

"It won't come to that," Darlene said. "Even if it did, it'd be practically the same as keeping her at your house. I'll bet you could pretty much just drop her off here to sleep and then she'd go to school in the morning with my kids and you could pick her up after. Not that big of a change, really, among friends."

Tireia listened with a look of tolerance that wasn't far short of pity.

"Jeanette Welgate, the law guardian, came over to my place earlier today," I said. "Do you know her?"

"Yeah," Darlene said unenthusiastically. "She goes to my church. How was it?"

"She must go to church more often than you, because she's definitely holier than you are. Tireia knows what I mean, they talked awhile back."

Jeanette had an unusual take on us, I explained, which seemed to be a philosophical view about the temptations of the chosen. The way she saw it, we had just about everything anyone could want, especially Tireia, who was smart, talented, rich, and lived in a lovely house. Plus she had a charming little girl at home, even though she wasn't the mother or guardian. Jeannette asked me if it was all right to say that Tireia also had a man who was not so hard to look at. But there still was the father issue, not that Minta didn't have a father, at least biologically speaking. It was a question of commitment, and men—especially perhaps the self-made type, the independent ones, the adventurers and pilots—could sometimes be a bit slow on the uptake when it came to the responsibilities of fatherhood.

Jeanette deigned to explain that marriage was an important institution, which had been around a very long time. She found it rather amazing that such blessed people as Tireia and I—and Fabienne as well—ended up having the same problems as folks without the looks or talent or brains or, at least in Tireia's case, the money. Then Jeanette observed that she shouldn't really be surprised, though, because people are people. Anyway, she was here to collect thoughts, not give them, she told me. She was a gatherer of opinions and facts, like someone conducting a survey. Once she put together all the ideas and information, she'd write up her recommendation, but it would be confidential, not for me or Tireia to read. She'd be fair, she promised. It would have nothing to do with people's looks, that was for sure. And then she asked if I got along well with little Minta.

Darlene put down a chopping knife and stared up at the ceiling. When she brought her face level with us, her eyes practically rolled into place like berries on a slot machine reel, her head wobbling a little. She asked how the Jeanette encounter went for Tireia, who said hers was much the same: religion, cussing, unmarried, nice place, though.

"And Minta? Did she say anything about Jeanette?"

"Mostly noncommittal but unimpressed by the baby talk," Tireia said.

"Fabienne was pretty brutal about her interview," I reported. "She served Earl Grey, managed to prevent herself from pounding the sherry, and claimed Jeanette just about climaxed over the cream cookies. When we spoke, she still seemed astonished at how someone so harmless could be so dangerous."

Becky, the niece who was helping with the new baby, carried him in from the bedroom. We cooed. Tiny, cute, reminded me secretly of not wanting to see Minta as an infant. Becky took him to a couch beyond the dining room.

Tireia went outside to call everybody in while I set out the rest of the meal for Darlene.

The crowd entered, and she told the kids to go wash their hands. They were back before you could say gimme the soap, piling into their chairs and into the comfort food, but not before Hank got in a hurried blessing that Minta witnessed with curiosity. Becky stayed on the couch with the baby. She said she'd eat later. We dropped talk of the case during dinner, and never did get around to mentioning the hardest thing of all to figure about Minta's fate, which was what Fabienne would say to the judge if he questioned her in court.

37

"**J**udge Totorica will do what he can to wrap this up quickly," Ornice told us outside the courtroom. "Even so, he might well order a psychological assessment of Fabienne. Whatever he does, our position looks stronger in light of the law guardian's report."

The details were confidential, as Jeanette Welgate had said, but Ornice was allowed to tell us the recommendation: Tireia should get custody and a regular visitation schedule should be worked out for Fabienne. But when Jeanette filed her report, she didn't know that Jonathan had incriminated Fab. At any rate, Ornice figured the report might open the way for her to make our case to Totorica. She still was concerned that the judge's moralistic streak could lead him to ignore Tireia as a potential guardian, because she was unmarried and didn't belong to a Christian church, even though he wouldn't say so explicitly.

"He'll know about Jonathan's confession, which he might interpret as a reason to agree with the state's argument. In other words, Minta should get a clean break from everyone," she said, "possibly to be placed with Darlene's family. I spoke with the prosecutor. Unfortunately, he's still firm in his opinion that Minta should have new custodians. But keep your chins up. Like I said, the situation looks better now than it did."

When we took our seats, Jeanette was one of the few people present. She sported a large blouse patterned in leaves over pedal pushers, sequined sandals, and reading glasses that dangled from a string of plastic beads. Under graying hair cut like a helmet, her expression was one of forced gaiety. She raised a hand in greeting to us, showing a wrist adorned with a rubber bracelet that I knew had to do with missing children.

Graham Wheeler was absent, which I took as a hopeful sign that the prosecutor, Byron Allen, might not try to conflate the criminal case with the custody hearing. It would be a bit of a surprise if he didn't, though, with neither of us in the clear. Maybe he figured he could discredit us without venturing into any unproven suspicions that might raise the judge's ire.

Ridiculously, we three adults who had the most at stake would once again not be allowed to speak unless questioned by the judge. The legalists probably figured we'd ramble or yell at each other. Fab still didn't have a mouthpiece and as soon as court was in session, Judge Totorica asked if she was set on representing herself. When she said yes and he asked why, she replied vaguely that she didn't feel an attorney was necessary. He sighed and remarked, in a manner both weary and edgy, it was her right to be wrongheaded. He asked for confirmation of his understanding that she did not intend to request a trial, at which witnesses would give testimony. No, no, she didn't want that. All right, he said, let's get on with it.

Byron Allen got up and started talking about Edith Howard, Minta's teacher. I remembered her as a myopic woman in middle age, whose bent and stolid posture gave the impression of a rooted organism. He said she was worried about the child's rowdiness and propensity for foul language.

Great, I thought, and went back into autopilot, following the proceedings even as I considered how best to orchestrate my upcoming interrogation of Jonathan Evers.

Allen grated on about the teacher knowing nothing of Fabienne, whom she had never seen. She thought the mother was Tireia, the only one who had come to the parent-teacher conference, and she hadn't said anything about not being the mother. Tireia D'Silva was the sole name across from that of Minta Sansverrou on the contacts sheet, so Mrs. Howard assumed she was divorced.

"Why not Fab's name?" I wrote on a slip of paper and passed to Tireia.

"I told her I wasn't the mother," she wrote back.

Allen must have figured he'd deconstructed Minta's behavioral issues to his advantage, because he turned his focus on discrediting Fabienne as a mother. He said evidence from medical records and other sources showed she had a history of substance abuse, driving under the influence, depression, and promiscuity. All that was correct but to me it was like a police report that seems accurate until you do deeper research, until you pack enough substance onto the bare facts to see how misleading the skeletal truth can be. Fab had been fighting since an early age to get herself right and she'd made progress. Not that I was an expert on a woman who was herself expert at concealing her past but she had confided in Stuart. He'd let slip a thing or two, after making me promise not to reveal any secrets on pain of self-immolation. Like a bad Buddhist, I broke the vow. I told Tireia everything even before Stuart's death.

It used to amuse me that Fab claimed her parents lived in Belgium. Maybe she liked that story because Belgium was far away and unconnected to Philthy or maybe because who knew Flemish? Anyway, she replaced that yarn with a simple refusal to discuss her family at all. If anyone asked, she said, "I don't talk about them," which necessarily gave away something but not too much. When Stuart and I were breaking his health rules over a few toddies once, he said the main problem was Helen, her mother, an alcoholic nurse who went through a series of men while Fab was growing up. In the middle of the night, as Mom lay unconscious, one of them raped Fabienne. Stuart said she worried that she'd been complicit. He reminded her that she was just a kid.

She never knew why her mother drank so determinedly, why she suffered from immobilizing depressions. Helen's principle mode of conversation was sarcasm, usually uninventive, and her attachment to her daughter seemed to be composed entirely of need, which extended to Fab cleaning up her messes, material and emotional. Fab got away at age seventeen and never went back. At the time, they were living in a Gainesville apartment complex but they had changed cities and states often and now there was no telling where Helen was or even if she still was. Fab showed a photo of her to Stuart. He said although she was about forty when it was taken, she looked sixty: a grim, cratered countenance confronting the lens like a POW just out.

Fabienne's father was a med student from Romania who had met Helen at the Carolinas Medical Center in Charlotte when they were both working there but that was about all she knew or at least all she told Stuart. Once, she mentioned the idea of looking him up, but when Stuart offered to take her to Romania she claimed to not even know her father's surname.

"He would have returned there during Ceauşescu's regime,"

she noted dryly, "which means he considered it the lesser of two evils."

A weak spot in Allen's objective to wrest the kid away from all of us, to make her a ward of the state, was Totorica's allegiance to the natural mother. Allen had to make Fab look utterly unfit, which certainly was possible but wouldn't be guaranteed just by proving she had mental issues, Ornice figured. She had reminded us at her office that the judge had observed all shades of parental incompetence in his courtroom yet stuck to the natal family model or at least some part of it. Even what Jonathan had told me and the cops might not sway him. Plus if the prosecution brought it up, she'd argue it was inadmissible. She still bet the judge would order a psychological evaluation of her before taking the child away. That would be good for us, it would give us time. Right now, what we most needed was time.

But Byron Allen exploded my hopes by saying that until recently Fabienne had been on the FBI's list of suspects in the shooting of Jim Davenport and evidence compiled recently by the Blaine County Sheriff's Office implicated her in the theft of two valuable statues. Ornice objected and Judge Totorica made a show of agreeing with her. The lawyer then established that Fab's financial reliance on Stuart's dad was why she didn't have to work. He suggested this could engender fear that the payments would stop arriving or be reduced if a guardian were appointed for Minta or if she were adopted.

I imagined the prosecutor's mask hardening into steel mesh as the fountain pen he jabbed in the air elongated into a foil. Each thrust produced another spot of blood on the shroud of Fab's reputation. Allen probed at her agreement with Ellis

Trask to transport a stolen object. He acknowledged she denied knowing it was stolen but to weaken that argument he established her familiarity with the art industry through her late husband. When he went on to her "virtual abandonment" of Minta, the judge parried. He asked Fabienne directly if she felt she'd given up custodianship. She said no, it was a gradual progression of time spent with Tireia. It was never formally arranged.

"I was depressed after my husband's death," she told the judge. "It was such a bad time for me that I didn't really feel capable of caring for Minta all alone. Stuart's health was never good and he always said he wanted Reese to help look after Minta if he … if it became necessary. And when that happened, Reese brought Minta and me to Idaho. He was with Tireia by then and she and Minta liked each other. We didn't plan the way things turned out."

The judge asked if Fabienne gave any of George Sansverrou's payments to Tireia or to me.

"No."

Totorica got to the point of it all: did she feel competent and willing to take the kid now?

"I want to have her," Fab began. Her fingers wormed over each other. "But I don't, I'm not, it's hard to know if I'm quite ready for full-time. I mean, I'm not quite ready. Yet. Could I, maybe, if it's all right with Your Honor, have Minta part of the time and let Tireia keep watching over her the rest of the time?"

Tireia grabbed my hand and squeezed. The judge asked why Fabienne didn't say this earlier.

"It's difficult. It's a hard decision to make."

Did she want to formally name Tireia as Minta's guardian?

"Oh, I don't know if … I'm worried. Could that mean … is it

possible I could lose my parental rights?"

If she wasn't willing to agree to a guardianship and was equally unwilling to care for her child full-time, she might lose her parental rights anyway, he intoned.

Ornice dropped her head. She wasn't just looking at her notes. Tireia's grip loosened and her hand slipped back to her lap. Fabienne started crying.

Byron Allen talked about policy regarding guardianship—more precisely, the paperwork requirement, Tireia's weakness. Once more, he brought up the note that had threatened Tireia and Minta, and Ornice objected that the county cops were keeping an eye on Minta when she was away from home. Allen made little effort to attack Tireia, maybe because the judge said not to. But probably the main reason was she was unassailable. Instead, he lobbed a few broadsides my way, as if to tar Tireia by association. He began by characterizing my relationship with Darlene as a working partnership but Ornice clarified that the best way to describe it was cooperation.

"All right, cooperation," Allen said. "And Tireia D'Silva is also participating in the investigation. The woman raising Minta Sansverrou without legal guardianship is assisting in a murder case that concerns not only her own lover but also the child's mother. Obviously, she has a personal interest in an outcome that would exonerate both of them."

"Ms. D'Silva is not a suspect in that case," Ornice pointed out. "As for her personal interest, we all know personal interest can make people get a lot done fast."

"Finding truth is not about speed," Allen said. "It's about facts and evidence."

The judge told the lawyers to quit squabbling and get on with the facts and evidence.

As the prosecutor rattled on, part of my attention took

in his appearance—shaved, plucked, knotted, creased, starched, shined, redolent—an explosively perfect party balloon. You had to wonder how a guy like that treated his own family, how thinly stretched his emotional life must be, how easily it could collapse into airless tatters. Allen turned to my having given up parental rights to the child, of whom I was the biological father, and Minta never having lived with me and I never having lived with Tireia, to whom I was neither engaged nor married and therefore without even common law stature. Yeah, I thought, all of that's right. But none of it touched me beyond the abiding pique that this bag of gas, this besuited dirigible, was allowed to get up and wag his finger.

When it was Ornice's turn to make our case, she began by saying Tireia was careful to never describe herself as Minta's mother. She noted Minta's outstanding academic performance in graded classes. Allen countered with the teacher's concern over the kid's "poor deportment and inability to work well with others." If Mrs. Howard meant barking at other students who goofed around in class, yeah, that would be our girl. Ornice described how the classroom operated: Mrs. Howard sat them in straight rows, both feet on the ground, silent when not spoken to, raised hands and passes required for everything, dissenters put in corners or made to write repeated "I will nots" on the blackboard—a fourth-grade chain gang. I couldn't tell how Totorica interpreted all this. Maybe he thought it was perfect.

She submitted into evidence sheets of parents' and guardians' contacts from the years Minta was in second, third, and fourth grade. On the last two sheets, Fabienne's name was missing as the mom. A clerical error had been made, apparently by an assistant who was no longer employed at the school.

Byron Allen interjected it was odd that the mother's name wasn't on the list for two years and neither Fabienne nor Tireia contacted the school about it. That wasn't hard for me to believe, considering the ambivalence both women had, in different ways, when it came to Minta. In Fab's case, it manifested as oblivion. In Tireia's case, it probably resembled the worrying twinge of relief I felt on occasion over Stuart's absence as potential competition. This was a lousy thought and I expunged it as usual. Stuart was my friend, things had turned out the way they had, and that was it. Then another bad idea arose, like a floater in my field of vision: the child needed and deserved more from me. I expunged it, too. And I killed the other things that followed: the grim satisfaction that Fab's aimlessness gave me more of Minta, and my relief that Tireia had taken a responsibility I otherwise would have had to assume alone.

Ornice turned to the topic of me. She described how my connection with Minta had strengthened since I moved mother and daughter to McCall. Even though Ornice was trying to help, I had to conceal my annoyance at public discussion of my relationship with the kid. She attempted to illustrate our respect for the parentage of Fab and Stuart by saying Minta called Tireia and me by our first names. I suppressed the urge to add aloud that she also called me "little man."

Totorica interrupted her, asking me why I never had applied for guardianship. I looked up at him in his robes. It seemed wondrous that I somehow had become aligned with authority, had turned into a kind of lawman myself, albeit an ersatz one in a precarious position, which was reassuring.

"Your Honor, I wouldn't want to take the child away from Fabienne or Tireia," I said. "And I see no particular value in codifying my attachment to her."

Ornice winced. Totorica leaned back and folded his hands. Tireia's eyebrows and lips went horizontal. Allen looked like he wanted to sit on my lap.

Ornice went into salvage mode. She talked about my valuable cooperation with Sheriff Carmody, who vouched for my character and that of Tireia. Through a fog of dismay over my dumb statement, I thought about what a good buddy Darlene had been. Her straightforward loyalty represented what was best in country life after you filtered out the ignorance and bias, if that were possible. Ever since moving from the big cities to McCall, it had seemed to me that the schism between people who see humankind as fundamentally good and those who see it as bad was played out eloquently in country law enforcement. It allowed the survival of optimists like Darlene, whose idealism atrophied in places where people got murdered every day. Here, when you went for a walk in the woods, a doe would execute her balletic stumble into your presence, freeze, and power-glide back into the mosaic. Such scenes could convince even those without the sunny view that God's country was the one place where faithlessness made sense. And the best rural folk like Darlene Carmody, whether religious or not, somehow managed to become the deer, infused with the grace of the woods.

None of that saved me from what I'd just said to the judge. And the ridiculous thing was I didn't believe my own reasons why I hadn't applied for guardianship. It wasn't about unwillingness to take her away from anyone, and it wasn't about scorn of the law. The untruthfulness wasn't what bothered me so much as the truth it concealed. The judge's question forced me to face what I already knew. I had let Tireia do the hard work.

38

Blaine County housed Jonathan in its Public Safety Facility, a moniker that suggested expertise or technology designed to protect people from harm rather than what it was, a jail. Totorica had set a continuance of the hearing for a couple of days later, which meant I could have flown to Hailey. I could have strolled a few minutes down Airport Drive for a glass-fronted visit with Jonathan, but it was unlikely to accomplish more than the video connection that could be made from home, and time was a factor. Both Fab and I were still under suspicion, and the goal remained to clean up the case before Totorica decided who got the kid.

From cop shows, you'd think the old hand breaks down the con simply by virtue of experience and smarts. But Tireia figured that like everything else, success with questioning someone is about preparation. She said in this case, the big picture required more than a road map or the satellite perspective or even the street view. We needed the virtual tour, which she had taken of Jonathan Evers' discernible life and passed on to me. He'd been cased with a thoroughness that would impress the best of burglars, although this probably was lost on Jonathan, who despite an apprenticeship in safe-cracking was a smash-and-grab thinker.

We knew he and a partner had sliced through a back window in a Los Angeles mansion when Jonathan was just eighteen, and he used a skill he'd acquired from an errant uncle to break into the safe. The burglary happened at midday. On the way out, the pair encountered a couple of cleaners who had arrived to shampoo the carpets while the owners were away. Jonathan dropped his stash and occupied himself with beating up the larger of the two guys, during which the smaller one brained him with a hand-sized Buddha from the flower garden. Jonathan's partner, no doubt a pacifist, got away with his loot. A court-appointed defense attorney organized a plea bargain with the prosecutor to reduce Jonathan's felony grand theft and aggravated assault charges in exchange for ratting out his buddy. He did, they snagged the partner, and Jonathan served a year.

This was a useful indicator of the big guy's preference regarding the necktie of loyalty versus the open collar of me first, which I grabbed onto.

"You lied to the sheriff about not knowing what Geyer planned to do with the birds. Unless you're comfy in that jumpsuit, you'd better think again."

"I don't know nothin."

"You know where Geyer is."

No answer, but even Jonathan had probably figured out by now he couldn't stall his way out of this mess, judging by the crashing lines on his big clean face.

"You can't help me," he said in a monotone that lifted into uncertainty at the end.

"I'm outside, Jonathan, and I'm not under the illusion you're the brains behind this. I don't believe you killed Wilber, even though the cops might not agree, seeing how you two swiped the statues."

"I didn't kill Wilber. I didn't kill nobody."

"If your boss can pin the blame on you, he's going to do it. You know that."

He just sat there, white on orange, a bitten Creamsicle.

"Those birds are worth a lot of jail time for your second strike, not to mention two corpses."

"I already told you everything."

Jonathan rubbed his buzzcut, which looked good on the big man. I was confident he'd give me what I wanted although not without a little lexical dance first, as if he required that the info be drummed out of him with pit-a-pats.

"Let's start with something easy," I said. "Tell me what you know about Geyer's plan to steal the two birds."

"I already told you."

"Tell me again. What was Wilber supposed to do with the statues?"

"Like I said, he was supposed to give the movie prop to you and get the dough for it."

"And what was he supposed to do with the dough?"

"Give it back to the boss."

"To Geyer. What about the Irwin Raptor?"

"Give that back to him, too. Then he'd have everything."

"So you weren't surprised when Cassim kept the money and the statue."

"Nah, that was the whole idea."

"But it went haywire when Davenport got shot."

"Right."

"And Wilber shot him?"

"Like I told you, I don't know. It don't seem likely to me.

I mean, Wilber a shooter? But the P.I. definitely was in the wrong place, wrong time."

"All right, let's look at Wilber. He had the other statue, too. The Irwin Raptor."

"Yeah, he had both."

"And he was supposed to give it to Geyer."

"That's what I said."

"But before he could do that, somebody got to him."

"So I heard."

"Who do you think that was?"

"Honest, I got no idea. Coulda been anybody."

Everything Jonathan said came straight out of him, unadorned. It didn't mean he was incapable of a convincing lie. But none of this sounded planned to me.

"What did Geyer expect to do with the statues?"

"Don't know."

"Take a guess."

"All we knew was he was stinging Rowena."

"So he had another buyer for them."

"That's what Wilber figured. Somebody who'd pay more."

"Who was it?"

"Don't know."

His blue eyes cloudless: an overgrown adult loitering at the age of reason.

"C'mon, Jonathan. You worked for Geyer, you kept your ears open. What's your best guess?"

"I can tell you why he needed money," he said. "He gambled all the time—casino, horses, dogs, fights, football. He'd bet on two ants headed for the sugar bowl, and he was bad at it. Real bad."

"Bad enough to be worried about his personal safety?"

"I was his bodyguard, wasn't I?"

"Lou Faulkner's not a man to anger," I said. "Maybe that's why you don't want to tell me he was the one holding Geyer's note."

He frowned into himself, like the victim of a crossover in a pickup game.

"I'm not afraid of him. Wilber thought the boss might give Lou Faulkner the falcon as repayment but that didn't make sense to me. A lead bird instead of cash and vigorish?"

"I know what you mean."

Jonathan looked out of the screen, mouth slightly agape. He was the perfect subject for an online interrogation, because he seemed to have no awareness of the electronic infrastructure. He couldn't have been more immersed if we were face-to-face.

"Jonathan, where's Geyer?"

"Told you, don't know."

"Not to split hairs but you didn't tell me that. You didn't answer the first time. I think you do know where he is and you're not saying out of loyalty to your boss, who gave you a good job when times were very rough for you, weren't they? And all because you were trying to help your sister, as any decent brother would do."

At the mention of the sister, he zoomed in like it was the key scene in his favorite series. Tireia had tracked down the big man's only sibling and had spoken to her. She was two years younger than Jonathan. At sixteen, she'd wanted to be an actor but was advised by an undoubtedly impeccable source that she needed breast enlargement surgery. Tireia said it was easy enough to read between the lines of her story: she had pestered her brother mercilessly to get the money. He did the burglary to escape the browbeating and maybe also out of a sense of duty. After jail, it was hard for him to find work. He kicked around for years and when at last he landed the job with Geyer, he was grateful.

I recounted all this in a soothing way to Jonathan. His protection of Geyer was understandable but even so, he couldn't deny that his boss had used him. He got him to swipe the birds, which was a crime any way you looked at it. Cassim intended to make off with both statues and the money. And who would be left to take the rap for the heist? All this—you could trace it back—was just because Jonathan had wanted to help his sister.

"Whatever happened to her, anyway?" I asked. "Did she get the operation?"

"Some guy came up with the dough for it."

"And did she work in films?"

"Yeah, but . . . not exactly what she hoped for. It was a short career."

"Uh-huh."

We were buddies now or close enough in his mind to give up Geyer, on the assurance that I'd help him with the cops as much as I could. He stalled a little more and then said he'd found a refurbished trailer for him behind the lodge at Smiley Creek near the ghost town of Sawtooth City. I'd never heard of the place. He said it was over Galena Summit from Sun Valley.

After a guard led him away from the communications pod, the sheriff, Chuck Palmer, came on and said his people were already on their way to Smiley Creek. We said "good work" to each other but we were online, so we didn't hug or anything.

39

The day was sunny, pine-fragrant, and Fabienne sat on the porch taking it in with the gratitude people in cold country have for the seasonal gift of warmth. The bruising on her face was no more than a flaxen shadow and she looked alert and healthy in her sleeveless sundress, barefoot, toenails freshly painted. I never understood why women painted their toenails but for her it was a good sign. It was afternoon and she offered booze, which was OK because not to do so would have been far enough out of character to make me suspicious. When I asked for ice water instead she gave herself a glass of it, too. We sat at the little kitchen table by the front window and she pulled her chair out sideways, the better, I suspected, to give a view of her exquisite legs.

"I'll bet you want to talk about Minta," she said.

"Always happy to," I replied, "but at this point there isn't much more to say, at least in terms of the court case. I wish things could have continued the way they were, but now we just have to wait for the judge's decision."

"Don't tell me it's a social visit, then."

She tilted her head down and looked up from under her eyebrows.

"No. Tireia and I need to clarify something you said."

She gave a little shrug; keep going.

"The thief called and told you to pick up the statue at the end of your property."

"And?"

"Did you recognize the voice on the line?"

"No."

"You couldn't recognize Wilber's voice?"

"Who says it was Wilber?"

"Jonathan Evers. You know him, Geyer's guy. He confessed to the Blaine County cops that he helped Wilber steal both birds for Geyer."

Fab sipped her water and regarded the glass with contempt.

"Even if he's telling the truth, Wilber could have disguised his voice."

My laugh was deliberately unpleasant.

"Fab, you're insulting me. No mysterious man left the falcon in the bushes at the end of your driveway. Look, I'm less interested in that than I am in Wilber's death. I want to know who shot him. He must have decided to keep the Irwin Raptor. He tried to double-cross Geyer."

She got up, went into the kitchen, ran a finger over the counter, came back. It was practically a fashion show and about as useful. I held the applause.

"Whatever Wilber might have been planning had nothing to do with me," she said.

"Of course it did. You called Harold Irwin and offered to return his bird to him for cash."

She sat down again, crossed her legs with a flourish, and adjusted the dress. My guess was you'd call her toenails fuchsia.

"Why in the world would you think that?" she said.

"Because Harold Irwin told Tireia it was a woman."

"A woman. Somebody telephoned Harold Irwin and you decided it was me. Was I supposed to have given him my name?"

She portrayed the sort of disappointment you might expect of an acting student, brows colliding, lips stitched.

"Harold Irwin gave your phone number to the feds," I said.

"Why are you making up situations that put me in a bad light?" she said shakily. "Why aren't you focusing on the obvious truth, which is that Geyer ran away with the statues? I'll tell you why he did it—because Jim got killed. Geyer didn't anticipate a dead man on my floor, which meant a murder investigation. And he was looking like an accomplice at the least, so he decided to disappear along with the birds."

"You could be right that Geyer ran because of Davenport's death. But only with the prop. He wanted both birds, but he didn't have them. Wilber had the Irwin. And you two figured why should you give it to Cassim? Why let him take the profits, when all you had to do was return it to Harold Irwin for big money?"

"Do you really believe what you're saying?"

Until recently, what I believed tended to be whichever scenario was being fleshed out at the moment among the many Tireia and I had gone through. Belief was a whim. But the fog was clearing now.

She ran her fingers through her hair, pulling it back even though it didn't need to be pulled back. It was perfectly tousled. She always did the country woman thing very well.

"Geyer hadn't counted on you and Wilber having the guts, or was it the stupidity, to keep the Irwin," I pressed.

She didn't respond so I laid it out, beginning with the night she stayed at Geyer's place. It would have been hard for a high-strung person like her to get to sleep in a strange house and she would have seen all the first-rate booze Geyer kept in his study. She also would have experienced how stingy he was with it. She went downstairs in the small hours, probably for a nightcap or two to calm her nerves, and came across the two guys in the midst of the heist. I told her that Jonathan had described the scene to me. Later, Wilber came to her cabin. She asked what he intended to do with the birds and he confessed it was a setup. Geyer planned to make an exchange of the prop for cash he'd squeeze out of Rowena, and he probably was going to fence the Irwin Raptor. At this, Fabienne saw an opportunity. She told Wilber they could keep the payoff money for themselves and she'd arrange return of the golden statue to Harold Irwin for more cash. Wilber regarded her scheme as evidence they'd get back together as a couple. She didn't dissuade him.

The signs of contempt on someone's face are close to those of repressed fear. In both, the straight line of mouth dips incrementally, but when fear is being contained, a slight widening of the eyes is the giveaway. Wearing just such a subtly fake look, Fabienne dismissed my deduction as foolishness.

"One thing that interested me," I continued, ignoring her protest, "was who dragged me into this? Jonathan said it was Wilber who told Geyer I should deliver the prop to him. That's when I knew how it had played out. After you stumbled downstairs at Cassim's place in the middle of the heist and persuaded Wilber to go partners, you had him set me up with Geyer as the delivery boy. You knew it would be safer that way, because I'd be sure to get the job done quietly if you were involved."

The strength of her stare began to wane as her face and

body succumbed to the gravitational effects of defeat.

"Everything worked fine until Davenport showed up," I continued. "What happened then, Fab?"

"All right, I'll play along with your guesswork," she said wearily. "Let's say Wilber gave me the statue. Then he must have come back to my place after Davenport arrived or maybe he was shadowing me. And then he shot him. Does that sound exciting enough?"

"And we can assume that for Wilber to not search for the prop and take it away after he shot Davenport suggested a measure of loyalty to you," I prompted. "Or maybe he just didn't know what to do except run."

"But he put the pistol in my hand. Why would he do that? I guess you could say because he wasn't very bright or trustworthy or brave. He was just another thug with a gun."

"Or he might have framed you because he was hoping to keep the cops from looking for anyone else. He may have figured you wouldn't get in trouble because it was self-defense."

Recovered from her funk, she was up and at it again: the hair, the swishing dress. You could practically hear the flashbulbs popping.

"Oh, please. Wilber anticipating what the police would conclude? That's your most outlandish idea yet."

She was probably right but it didn't matter. The objective was to break her composure.

"In any case, I would have liked to protect you from prosecution, Fab. But you've made it impossible."

She took a few steps in front of the table, turned, came back. She looked at me silently, considering.

"One thing I definitely don't believe is you intended to stick with Wilber," I said.

She sat and folded her hands, a benign gesture I found discomfiting under the circumstances.

"There would have been no reason for you to even suspect Wilber if he hadn't been dumb enough to let himself be spotted the day you came over," she said.

We let this hover and fade.

"You're right, Wilber was a dummy," she said at last. "And I had no time for him beyond his temporary usefulness. But I didn't get out of the hospital, drive to Warren with a busted-up face, and shoot him."

"Of course not. Why was he in Warren, anyway?"

She ran a finger under her eye and then flicked her hand away.

"Harold Irwin was sending someone there by charter flight to make the exchange of the money for the statue. I have no idea who killed him. For all I know, it could have been Irwin's men."

I remembered that Bill Atman, the neighbor, had mentioned an aircraft landing in Warren the day after he saw the Hyundai SUV at the cabin where Wilber was staying. If it carried people sent by Harold Irwin, they arrived too late.

"All right," I said. "But Wilber shot Davenport?"

"I don't know that either. Maybe he came back, like you said. I was unconscious by then."

She leaned toward me on the edge of her chair.

"Reese, you and Stuart and I go back a long way." She reached out and put her hands on one of mine. "You're the only two men who ever mattered to me. I made a bad decision to get involved in this whole mess. I don't know why I did it. The excitement, probably. I've made other poor choices, it's true, but you've always been there for me and you can be there now."

I took my hand away and went for the water. She moved back a little.

The truth was I hadn't always been there for her, especially before Stuart's death. I tried to avoid her. We got along but it was never easy. I was a third wheel and Fab made it worse when she'd flirt and pretend it was private, even though we both knew Stuart was aware. He'd joke that when he was gone, the two of us should marry. There was always her beauty to contend with, her sensuality. She never let me get beyond that to the person she really was.

"Believe me, I appreciate how much you've done over the years to help and protect me, even from myself," she said. "You've fought for me, and Stuart would have loved you all the more for it. You can help again but this time you don't have to do anything. Just let it be. The police will regard me as someone who was used by the thieves, nothing else."

"Darlene knows you called Harold Irwin and so does the FBI agent, Graham Wheeler."

This stopped her for a tick.

"But I didn't have Harold Irwin's statue. You're Darlene's friend, you could convince her that Wilber forced me. If she's on our side, the feds won't be able to make anything stick, not with Wilber dead. Who did the killings? That's the issue. I'm just a pawn here."

I was intrigued but not in a good way. How far was she willing to take this?

"Tireia knows everything I know."

She laughed, too eagerly.

"She won't say anything. She doesn't want Minta's mother to be behind bars. And you don't want that, either."

We both knew this was accurate. But she also must have known I wouldn't cover up a serious crime for her. Even so, she couldn't stop now. She put her arms behind the chair and pulled her shoulders back. A ray of light from the window crossed the table and cut into the fern-green of her sundress. No longer a fledgling, bruised now, she still was a magnificent reminder of how fleeting it all is.

"This is our time, Reese. We always had Stuart to consider and then Tireia but we can't let it go on like this forever. I see how you look at me. You still want me. We've waited years and now it's perfect. We'll keep Minta, you'll have Tireia, and I'll be there for you, whenever you wish."

Pity is a bad emotion to offer a person. It degrades someone once admired, maybe even loved. From a distance inside myself, pity struggled to arise.

"If it hadn't been for Stuart, we would have been together anyway," she said. "It'll be our secret. And that will make it even more exciting."

"And if your plan had worked out, what were you going to do? You'd have had to ditch Wilber. That would mean running away." My voice went flat, pitiless now. "And what about Minta? You'll excuse me if I find it hard to imagine you'd take her along."

For once, she didn't have a response.

"We need to secure Minta's future," I said. "After that, I'll do whatever I can for you. But don't expect the world."

40

Early on the day of court reconvening in Cascade, I called Ornice and told her Tireia and I had decided to tell the judge we wanted joint guardianship. There was a silence, and then she said it was a nice thought and she understood where it was coming from. But it wasn't going to happen. I tried to bully her but she rolled over me. A revision now of our strategy would be foolish and she wouldn't accept it. If we insisted, she would be forced to step away from representing us. She sounded incredulous when she asked if Tireia really had agreed to this notion. I said of course she had. And then I admitted she'd also told me it wasn't a smart idea. Her tone became melodic again. She said I'd been right that this ultimately wasn't about the law, even though the law had a place in it.

"Let's win custody," she said. "That's the only thing we're here for."

It occurred to me this was why Tireia had agreed to my proposal. She knew what our attorney would say.

In the courtroom, Ornice was first up. She tried out her strategy of using Jeanette Welgate's report as a springboard to talk about Tireia's strong and positive relationship with

Minta. The judge wasn't having it. He wouldn't let this become a debate about Tireia's fitness for custody. Ornice said she understood. She said she only meant to point out that the relationship between the two was high quality and the child also expressed affection for me.

It was a nimble dance around the glaring judge. She even got in a short elaboration on the mention she'd made at the first court appearance of Tireia's educational and professional achievements. If Totorica had been the least bit interested, if he had asked me, I would have loved to relate some of the stories Tireia's mother told about her. I would have described how she took algebra in fourth grade and the system quickly moved her into the higher maths. Your honor, that was on Cape Cod. Her father, Martin D'Silva, was a senior researcher in the Marine Biological Laboratory. He specialized in the relationship between telomere shortening and cellular senescence in the aging process, at the time an odds-on ride in the Ponce de León Stakes. Tireia's mother, Leticia, was principal cellist in the Cape Cod Symphony Orchestra and gave private lessons. I mean, judge, you have to realize this was an elite family but without the ostentation. Her folks still lived in the same two-story clapboard house with a cedar roof, a second-floor deck on the front, and a corbelled chimney, nicely spaced among other salt-weathered residences on a tiny paved lane accented in rock fences and trimmed hedges.

You need my image of her, your honor, as the only child of parents who were decent folk, if a bit detached in their academic way. They accepted on faith that the school officials knew what they were doing in pushing Tireia along but when she agitated at age thirteen to take online courses at home instead of in brick-and-mortar schools, they turned their attention to her complaints and gave permission. Judge, when I first heard this story from her folks, who were visiting in McCall, it impressed me she had the maturity and presence of mind to know she was growing up too fast, losing friends, being directed by others for reasons not necessarily in her best interest.

She studied at home and renewed old friendships through a neighbor girl, which was good but the other kids she knew wanted nothing to do with her. She was a freak, a brain. Two years later, she aced the SAT and was deluged with college offers. She picked MIT, your honor, because it was at least in the same state although a couple of hours away. She lived on campus but came home every weekend as soon as she was old enough to drive and at age seventeen got a degree in physics and returned to Cape Cod "to finish childhood." Can you appreciate that by now she felt a hundred years older than her peers? She spent much of the next two years alone, working on projects that applied power laws in nature to resource management, which she told her father about but nobody else. He had left the marine lab to found a biotech start-up in Falmouth on the Cape to develop a gene therapy technique he had pioneered, which showed potential to help combat certain age-related ailments by helping healthy cells to continue replicating beyond their normal span. But as that work went on, he realized mutated cells also arose, which could cause cancer. He turned the little company's efforts toward stopping cell replication rather than encouraging it, toward treating cancer rather than forestalling the ravages of age. Tireia and her father discussed their different studies often, which she told me, judge, was probably the most fun she ever had with him.

When she decided to get her PhD, she chose Stanford over regional options, not so much to get away from her folks as to try out her self-sufficiency now that college would be less emotionally and socially challenging. This time she took it easy, your honor, at least for her, emerging with a Masters in systems biology and a doctorate in theoretical physics at twenty-four. She then went to McCall to stay at the cabin her parents had purchased that year, after her father's replication-inhibiting molecule had been tested on animals with promising results for a type of cancer and was ready to enter the long and very expensive human trials. He sold the patent to a pharmaceutical giant that would try to prove it up for the marketplace and he bought the McCall hideaway with part of the proceeds.

As Ornice and Byron Allen droned on, I was well into autopilot, even though Totorica would never hear any of this. Nor would he be the least interested in what Tireia was like when we first met on a Hollywood film set. The shame of it was if he had seen her through my eyes, the pointlessness of this courtroom charade would be obvious to him.

I smiled at the thought of the movie, which was about a pandemic sent to Earth by aliens with erase-and-replace intent. Tireia was a consultant whose brief was to ensure that as the disease spread, the spiraling of events was believable. She advised on realistic emergency response, attempts to isolate infected populations, and even how fear could affect ethical and strategic decisions among professionals and everyday folks.

And what was I doing at the time, your honor? You want to know about me, do you? I was thirty-one, working at a think tank in the D.C. area, specializing in gun safety policy. Pragmatic about the job, not trying to eliminate guns from American society but intent on realizable ends like registration, training, improved restrictions on sales. And how did I feel about little

Minta? You want to know about that? Well, I felt relieved yet guilty, unable to shake the notion, however unreasonable, that I had abandoned both the man I had come to regard as a little brother and the infant I technically had fathered. OK? Happy now?

And how did I get from D.C. to Hollywood, you ask? It was after a producer approached the think tank for help with a documentary film he was developing about restraints on gun legislation. I provided research on the issues: bump stocks, silencers, concealed carry, sales to fugitives with guns. You know why this was a tough assignment, judge? Because for years, the funding for that sort of research had been virtually nonexistent, thanks to politicians in the pockets of lobbyists. But the producer was pleased with the chronicle I compiled of ideas squelched, movements countered, initiatives strangled in infancy.

He mentioned me to a director in search of an armorer for an independent feature. It was kind of funny, don't you think, Judge Totorica, that the director would hire a guy who had no guns and opposed their use on the street in real life? But he said the job would be to make sure people were safe during a scene or two in which blanks would be fired. He just needed somebody with gun safety credentials. To be honest, your smugness, I expected my supervisor at the think tank would put an end to it but he decided it would be related training and was willing to grant me time off as unpaid leave.

Tireia and I met there on my second day. We had a chuckle over how her studies in complex adaptive systems were roughly as applicable to the work as my qualifications were to being an armorer. It very soon became clear I was no intellectual match for her. But the thing was, neither of us minded. She was friendly yet wary, which at first I tried to overcome. But then I realized it was her way, a distance she either had developed in response to how people treated her, or had learned from her preoccupied parents, or maybe it was just a trait she'd always had. It didn't matter which to me, because she glowed like an underground wildfire. That's how I came to think of her, your arrogance: a snowy forest warmed beneath the mantle by a smoldering fire that could blaze again with a turn in weather.

What happened then? She moved to McCall. The pandemic film didn't attract a distributor but it helped her to snag an assignment from a tech firm that wanted to develop an improved system for recommending movies, books, and other products to customers. She took the job for a miniscule upfront fee in return for the potential of a back end percentage, as if it were a movie. She developed a probabilistic model that more accurately captured a customer's range of taste across genres or categories. The tech company sold the model and algorithm, she got a big payout, and promptly bought the cabin from her parents.

I followed her to Idaho, your pompousness. Who wouldn't, given the chance? But I lived alone, I gave her space, because she needed it. The McCall smokejumper base kept three DHC-6 Twin Otters, similar to aircraft I had piloted for charter work. The training was easy, a demonstration of steep turns, stalls, bounces, and a safety check ride, although management was cautious at first about sending me into the thick of it. They kept me clear of the low-level firefighting work. I did a lot of patrolling and hauling of supplies and smokejumpers to other bases. I liked the men and women who jumped, not only for their courage and commitment but because the varying reasons they were in it generally had to do with the independent life. For them, it sure as hell wasn't the money.

You live here in the mountains, you can picture what it's like to drop smokejumpers onto fires or to be those smokejumpers. The challenge, the exhilaration.

Ornice was still talking. She didn't mention any of this and wouldn't have been allowed to even if she knew about it. Maybe it didn't matter. Totorica had a few options concerning who would get Minta and he clearly had wanted to give her to Fab but that now looked like an extreme choice, especially after what Jonathan had said about her. Tireia figured he'd avoid extremes and go for an intermediate option. In a cocky moment before the hearing, she'd been harsh on the magistrate.

"He doesn't have the brains or guts to make a decision independent of the other choices. In the end, rather than picking what's right in his opinion, he'll head for the safe middle."

If she was correct, we might be OK. But the question was did he see Tireia as another extreme? That was the infuriating thing: how determined he seemed to be to keep his ignorance of her intact.

Ornice snowballed through the fluff about a secure and loving environment for Minta and then Byron Allen's death mask floated up again, replete with insinuations of collusion, lies, moral decay. He summed up that Tireia, not a blood relation, had no legal standing whatsoever, while Fab was an emotional and psychological wreck, completely incapable of being a decent mother. And I had agreed to disqualify myself as a parent from the start. He managed to concede that Minta's current home environment was stable but then he again brought up the criminal case and the anonymous threat to Minta as a safety issue and said given that Tireia already had flouted the law by not applying for guardianship, she was a bad choice. What's more, look at the behavior and language of Minta, who obviously needed firmer guidance. The paternal grandparents, who were divorced, had shown no interest in assuming guardianship and nobody knew where the maternal grandparents were. No other family members, namely Stuart's sisters, had voiced willingness to act as custodians. Allen strongly requested that the court assign the minor to qualified guardianship with an aim to adoption.

Ornice did her best to scoff at her opponent's arguments, even though scoffing didn't suit a person whose speaking voice sounded like song. Minta was doing great at school. She was well-liked, and her occasional penchant for stepping outside the behavioral box was evidence of leadership potential. She and Tireia clearly loved each other. The living conditions were first-rate and the police were helping to ensure she was safe while we provided valuable assistance on the case. Tireia was eager to become Minta's guardian but had been thwarted by Fabienne's reluctance to cooperate, as the court had seen. Neither Tireia nor I wanted to interfere with or in any way harm the relationship between mother and child. There was never any question about Stuart having been the legal father but after his death, I had filled in ably.

Ornice was smooth in her delivery of these points and if she fumbled a little when she got to Fabienne, we couldn't blame her. She said no written agreement existed between Fab and George Sansverrou. He was helping her because he chose to do so and he never had threatened to stop payments to her under any conditions. She was the widow of his only son and the mother of his granddaughter. Fabienne's questionable behavior had abated since she moved out of town to the cabin and she had less incentive to drink once she was away from the bars. Time had allayed the psychological wound of losing her husband. The friendship of Reese and Tireia had been invaluable, as had been their support in helping to care for Minta. It was a positive thing that the girl's mother didn't want to let go. But right now, even though everyone was eager to keep Fabienne in the picture, Tireia—a person of high standing in the community, who provided a loving home, and whose partner was the child's biological father—obviously was the right choice.

Totorica said he'd take under advisement the law guardian's recommendation. However, there were other aspects to be considered as well, not least of which concerned Mrs. Sansverrou's legal issues and mental and emotional condition. Accordingly, he would give careful attention to all submitted materials and confer again with counsel outside court before reconvening to issue his decision. He expected to accomplish all this without undue delay.

Adjourned.

The judge's pronouncement that his decision would come soon seemed to free Tireia to focus on the crimes. The emotional lockdown that had plagued her on and off disappeared. She returned to herself, the cool yet combustible analyst, the passionate over-achiever who made me think hard to keep up. That night when Minta was tucked in bed, we sat in the living room and I told her I had a big piece of news about the case. She pressed up to me on the couch, ran her hand through my hair, and no doubt didn't miss a syllable of what I said, although my narrative line wandered once or twice. She was in her fractal kimono and a chemise, her hair newly washed.

The information I had was that Darlene had phoned to say the Blaine County officers found Geyer at his Smiley Creek hideout, where he was packed and ready to catch a charter flight at the airstrip. He didn't have the statues. All he had was a receipt for a flight from L.A. to Montevideo. The cops had insufficient cause to hold him, but he was warned not to leave town.

When I said Geyer had agreed to meet me at his home, Tireia reacted to my impending trip in the old way, as if it were a mating call. She proposed we continue our conversation in the planetarium, her nickname for the bedroom because of its stuccoed ceiling, where she claimed to do her best thinking while stargazing. In an effort to ramp up the moment with the verbal cosmetics she liked, I agreed we should repair forthwith. Our flurry of preparation in the new locale included mutual help with fastenings that was more fun than necessary to provide, accompanied by sound effects from us both that were perhaps not entirely involuntary but atmospheric for sure. When it came to making the music, we weren't jaded enough at the moment to require variations on the theme and our rendition left us, performers and audience alike, impressed. Then we lay staring upward, adrift in the plaster universe.

She made a pistol with her forefinger and thumb, and fired upward. I'd never seen her do this. It unnerved me enough to ask how her shooting lessons were going, a topic I didn't really want to discuss for fear it would get nasty.

"I've only taken one," she said lightly. "It was kind of fun. The power, you know, the control."

This was a response I thought it best to ignore.

"I'll have to buy something pretty soon," she said. "Maybe you can advise me."

"I'd rather not participate."

"Oh, you slouch."

She turned away from me on her side.

"Your purity annoys me," she said. "It smells of the proselytized."

This sent a flame up.

"I have been proselytized," I said. "By death."

It was quiet for a moment, and then she turned back to me.

"You have a story." She sent her deep green look into me.

"Something you haven't told me."

She was right, I hadn't told her about my friend Belinda Harris. I hadn't talked to anybody about it. Tireia knew about my early fascination with airplanes, the part-time job I got in high school as a drudge at a small charter company, the student pilot certificate, and the expensive and time-consuming lessons for my private license after graduation. I'd told her about finally amassing enough flight experience to get the commercial license, and how I was taken on as a staff pilot at the charter outfit, which allowed me to abandon roommates for my own apartment. But that was as far as I'd gone.

Now, the brightest person I'd ever known, one of the two most important people in my life, wanted to buy a gun. It was fucking anathema; she had no idea. And I realized she should hear Belinda's story. Even if it changed nothing, at least it should help her to understand my position. So I told her about the charter outfit's dispatcher, a woman several years older than me. I explained that we liked each other and started having lunch together, which excited the interest of just about everyone in the little company for more than one reason, I suspected. The obvious reason was that Belinda was married. But this didn't bother me, because I saw our relationship as platonic, even though I realized she might have other ideas. Belinda's husband was trouble, and she needed someone to talk to. Maybe it would have been preferable for her to find a female friend to confide in but the outfit was almost all men and besides, why shouldn't I lend a sympathetic ear? It annoyed me to think small-minded people would try to prevent me from having lunch with this likeable person who obviously needed support. Even the one or two who said they were on my side irritated me. I could do without their benediction.

Another thing our coworkers apparently didn't like, I told Tireia, was that Belinda's mixed heritage made her an unsuitable companion for me in their eyes. Her skin was burnished russet, her long hair sometimes curly, sometimes straight. She was tall, her face a small oval that dropped away steeply at the sides, magnifying the impact of heavy eyebrows that arched away from black eyes. Her parentage wouldn't have been an issue if people had just let us be friends and hadn't already assumed we were an item or about to become one. This attitude, expressed only in looks or statements so oblique the speakers might not have been aware of what they felt, was what annoyed me most of all. Belinda warned me that people were talking but I said they were ridiculous to concern themselves over who shared a meal together. Her smile blended approval with melancholy.

One afternoon, when I returned from a Chicago-area flight, she told me to check the local newspaper's Help Wanted section. A charter service was in need of a pilot. The company was unnamed in the ad and the sole contact provided was a nondescript email address. Our outfit was the only one in town. If we were on the lookout for a flier, everybody should have known. The boss was trying to fill my job on the sly for sure.

The company had been founded and was still headed by a pilot who didn't get in the air much anymore. He was easy to find in the afternoon, because he always occupied the same barstool. My arrival at the neighboring stool irked the old guy, I could tell. He gulped the Scotch he had just been served and roughly told the bartender to give him another and put some booze in it this time.

"I saw a want ad in the paper today," I said. "It had my job description."

The boss looked straight ahead. He was a scrawny man, clean-shaven, white hair bristle-stiff. He named a company out of Chicago that often flew to the airport at Champaign and said I should ask them what was up. I said I already had telephoned their personnel department, who knew nothing about the ad.

The boss got his gigantic fresh drink and practically bit through the glass.

"All right, you're fired," he said, and turned a fierce look on me. "Tell Arnold to cut a check for what you're owed. Clean out your locker and don't come back."

When I asked for a reason, the boss said it was my attitude. I didn't smile enough for the customers, who paid for gracious service and expected to get it. We both knew this was bullshit. He didn't like me associating with Belinda, the only person of color he ever had hired, his evidence of inclusiveness. I was incensed, but not about losing the job. I picked up my check and said so long to Belinda and the others, all of whom stopped and stared in alarm, no doubt relieved it wasn't them.

Two days later, before I had time to worry about income, the boss called. He was in a bind. A convention had come to town and its members had booked several days' worth of joy rides. The old man had come down with the flu and couldn't fly. He needed another pilot and couldn't find anybody to fill in on such short notice. In the thirty years since he started this company, he'd never shirked on a major charter. He had to ask me to come back for a week or so.

I laughed insolently and then said, sure, I'd fill in, on one condition. He had to say I'd been laid off through no fault of my own, so I could collect unemployment insurance later. I could tell by the old man's tone he didn't like the deal, but he agreed.

In the middle of that extra week, Belinda and her husband went to a night spot to listen to a band. After the show, the couple stood in a small crowd outside the place when an argument broke out. Shots were fired, panic ensued. When it was over, Belinda lay dead on the pavement.

The report on the local news said the dispute appeared to be drug-related. The husband was the probable target, the wife most likely an innocent bystander. Shock left me staring at the television set, where colorful shadows moved and mouths worked but nothing made sense. My neural circuits had been tripped, the power was off, and I sat immobile. As I slowly came back to myself, the shock bled into anger.

Strangely, the killing turned my thoughts to my own upbringing, the complacency of it, the apparent blindness of older people to the chaos churning underneath the thin mantle of suburban manners. But the nihilism of the young people was worse. After getting my own apartment, I had avoided my high school gang of would-be tough guys, kids with poor educations and no prospects who already scorned the Horatio Alger cheerleading they'd heard all their lives. Belinda had married a kid like them, and her husband had become trapped in the same slow flow of frustration and violence that pulled in so many of them. When the little life rafts of their dreams went adrift and began to sink in this sea of nullity, their occupants reached out for the one implement that might carry them to safety, the only tool that offered escape. They reached for the gun. And it pulled them under. But not before they took others with them.

It infuriated me, I told Tireia, but I was isolated on my own raft, where it seemed the only conduit to the sanity of justice for Belinda was the insane choice of a firearm. I tried to get more information from the police but they would say only that the case was still open. Everyone knew these inquiries almost always went nowhere, especially when people of color were both the victims and perpetrators. Reluctantly, I turned to my old buddies, and quickly learned from them that the shooter was a small-time dealer to whom Belinda's husband owed a long-overdue debt. Belinda, an innocent and good person, had been shot dead in the street over a drug deal she knew nothing about. What justice would come of this? None. Who would avenge her? No one. I went looking. But I told myself not to be a fool about it. I got a pistol from one of my pals and stuck it in my belt.

I found the guy in mid-afternoon, waiting to get into a pickup game at an outdoor basketball court in his hard-soled shoes. The others in the game backed off in fascinated alarm when I pulled the gun from under my shirt. The dealer, a skinny kid of about twenty, tried to brazen it out but my angry intent terrified him and he fell apart. He hadn't meant to do it, he was just trying to scare the dude, he didn't want to kill nobody. The kid had big brown eyes in a compact, pockmarked face. A swatch of hair tied at the roots listed like a burnt chimney atop his head. Tremors rippled up and down his emaciated frame.

Gripped by a sudden sense of power and fury, I aimed the barrel at the forehead of the kid, who shut his eyes, which was the best thing he could have done. He'd given up, it was over, he was dead, and I was the agent. All I had to do was pull the trigger and drag us both into the vortex. If the others were shouting or pleading or threatening, I didn't hear them. To me, the court was silent. All that existed in the moment was the gun barrel centered on the skinny kid. I was alone facing myself, the boy's jittery head merely a target under the ridiculous upthrust of hair. My focus narrowed and zoomed. A red film across my vision wavered in the heat. Everything I had become up to that moment awaited its fate and I knew it. I inhaled sharply and realized it had been a long time since I'd last breathed. Slowly, I raised my aim above the boy, lowered the weapon, and reached around to put it under the back of my belt. Then I knocked the kid down, which made a couple of the other young men grumble, but nobody challenged me. I looked at the boy sitting on the cement holding his jaw, wet with relief, and knew that although I'd made the right decision, it was still wrong.

For a long while afterwards, I was furious, I told Tireia. But the lesson that remained was I would not, could not, abide participating in the futility and stupidity of it.

To her credit, Tireia had nothing to say. I wouldn't have expected anything less. She just hugged me, kissed my cheek. People say it does you good to talk about stuff, but not this. Even so, it was important for her to understand I wasn't taking some armchair philosophical stance. Argument wouldn't bring me around to her point of view. But the waste of it was I didn't expect for a second she'd stop taking her lessons.

It was a relief when we both pretended to shake it off and get back to business.

She wanted to hear about my talk with Fabienne. I sighed, and talked about Fab's admission that she'd plotted with Wilber to keep Rowena's ransom money for the falcon and to sell the Irwin Raptor back to Harold Irwin.

"She wants me to protect her," I said.

It seemed pointless to go into the dark deal Fab had offered.

We gazed at the swirls awhile.

"She claims she did it for the excitement more than the cash."

"The trickiest motive," Tireia said. "Greedy people are predictable, because you can follow the money. But thrills have no rules, no parameters. Thrill-seekers don't make sense."

This made me smile sadly up into the smears and blobs.

"In a way, the statues only matter as a driving force," she continued, "but at least they have substance. They can be pursued and we can analyze their pursuers."

"Even that trail can get faint."

"Yeah, but I dug up something very interesting today."

She'd been thinking about Fab's information that Rowena's brother-in-law had sold the Nelson mourning ring and the silver-inlaid box to Trask. She had found the brother-in-law's name, Alistair Yardley. Like the Pascoes, the Yardleys were landed gentry. She told me the U.K. aristocracy still intermarried, still went to the best schools, owned much of the country's rural property, and passed on the wealth. But not all of them were good at compounding it. The Yardleys were among those on the diminishing end of the spectrum, just as the Pascoes had been before Rowena married into money. Through a genealogy search, Tireia discovered that the Yardleys had something else in common with the Pascoes: via ancestral marriages, both families were related to Admiral Nelson.

This revelation sent her on a quest to find out exactly what share of the hero's booty was owned by the two families. She learned that by the time Alistair married his distant cousin Eleanor, known to all as Nell, her older sister Rowena already had given up the Pascoes' Nelson effects. The family's country manor still held the collection but to avoid crippling inheritance taxes, Rowena had ceded ownership to the government. The artifacts were merely on display at the manor.

In the archives of the *West Sussex Gazette*, Tireia found a breathless story that contained what she was seeking: several Nelson pieces had come down directly to Alistair Yardley, including the pièce de résistance: the Ottoman Osprey. It immediately took pride of place in his in-laws' collection, but the bird undoubtedly would have been doomed for sale to the government if not for the fortuitous arrival on the scene of Victor Leyland. Researching the American financier, Tireia established that when he snapped up Rowena in marriage he also rescued the family from genteel decay, in what she said could only be called one fell swoop. Among other advantages, Vic's money made it possible to pay an enormous inheritance tax on the bejeweled osprey to keep it privately owned.

Years later, after Victor Leyland's death by heart attack, Rowena was left with stacks of money, while the Yardleys' situation had continued to deteriorate. Alistair must have decided to sell the osprey to Lou Faulkner, perhaps to help his natal family. Tireia said the property of married couples is held jointly in the U.K., and prenups aren't officially recognized. Even so, she didn't find evidence of a court challenge by Rowena's sister to the statue's sale.

"So," I said, "if nobody in Rowena's family legally contested the sale …"

"Maybe Rowena took matters into her own hands."

We turned our heads on the pillows to look at each other.

"It would hold with your theory that Rowena is our master strategist," I said. "You figured she needed a motive to set up the thefts of the birds and this could be it. She wanted to get the Ottoman Osprey back."

"Yes."

"But we need to examine a few details here. I mean, there are dots to connect between stealing the two statues and getting the osprey."

"I have those dots connected."

"Why am I not surprised?"

Over the next half-hour, she took me through her breakdown of how Rowena had schemed to retrieve the Ottoman Osprey. I thought these ideas were kind of a stretch but Tireia insisted the pieces fit. To confirm it, she said I should fly to London, lay the plot before Rowena, and watch how she reacted.

I said I'd have to go to the arranged meeting with Geyer first.

"Good. You can probe how he fits into all this."

"As a shooter?"

"I could imagine him hiring someone for the job, or jobs, but doing it himself seems too far out of character, don't you agree? There must have been another actor."

We talked about it a long time, way into the night. Using the theory Tireia had just described to me about Rowena and the osprey, we raised all the players into the sky of the ceiling and swirled them around, forming and reforming a map that showed how they could connect to where they were going, or where we thought they hoped to go. In fits and starts, something emerged. Something perhaps visible only from this viewpoint. The more we looked at it, the more sense it made.

And then we slept.

Cassim Geyer had told me his lawyer would be present at our meeting but when I arrived he said he'd changed his mind. He preferred to filter information to the attorney as necessary, rather than giving him or anyone else the details of his life carte blanche. It was fine by me, this byproduct of the invasive information age, but it was pretty dumb of Cassim. Details of his life? When even programmers aren't sure why their AI makes certain decisions, how do you convince yourself you have any meaningful control over what others know or can discover about you? And then you let me in and shut out your paid protector. Cassim's decision practically steamed from the funk of hubris.

The copies of the film noir paintings were no longer on the wall of his spacious study with the fireplace and the big view where we had our last talk. Had they been taken down because of me or, more precisely, because he'd told me they were fakes? A young maid came in, not the same as the last one, whom he presumably laid off when he closed up the place, but this one was also good-looking and also classically maid-clad. To Cassim's credit, he didn't order tea and cakes. Instead I got a single-malt Scotch, waived all nibbles, and turned my attention from her to him, blessedly sans smoking jacket, although still flaunting his barefoot shoes.

"So." I settled into my opposing armchair. "Where's the falcon?"

He chuckled, which is to say he didn't laugh, didn't titter or guffaw, he made it avuncular, patronizing.

"Ask Jonathan Evers."

"He told me you have it."

"I see. But what motive could I possibly have for stealing the statue after paying you to bring it from the thief to me?"

He clenched his little face into a fist of censure. I sipped the Bruichladdich, which on the way down felt as radiant as a cloudless sun.

"It was coincidence, then, that you closed up your house and went into hiding with a ticket to South America just when the falcon disappeared for the second time?"

"It certainly was not coincidence," he said, "and I was not in hiding. The treachery of my man Jonathan and that snake Wilber Arndt put me in a dangerous position, despite my innocence. To be honest, I wasn't eager to encounter Mrs. Pascoe-Leyland's disappointment when she learned I'd allowed her property to be stolen a second time. The prospect of a trip was compelling although perhaps not the best choice I could have made."

"Jonathan, the criminal mastermind, and the wily Wilber Arndt outwitted you. I agree, it does look bad."

He tried to stare me down. But even standing up it wouldn't have worked.

"The police have kept those two under wraps," I said. "How did you know they were the burglars?"

"Jonathan confessed to me. Before his arrest, of course. He'd been manipulated by Wilber and was remorseful, you see."

"Remorse? You'll pardon me if I think that's a cheap reason for such expensive information."

"Information, Mr. Mencari, is a currency whose value depends on the transaction. I can only assume he considered it worth spending on me."

Sometimes it was all I could do to stop myself from tossing Geyer through the window but other times, like this one, he made me grin.

"Witticisms aside, what looks worse than bad for you is that you weren't just running away from your client's wrath or even a frame-up, as you claim. There was also Lou Faulkner to consider. How were you going to pay your note to him?"

He propped his elbows on the chair's arms and laced his fingers.

"You are well-informed, aren't you? I won't deny it, Mr. Faulkner does have a reputation for testiness if provoked."

"Testiness?" I grinned again.

"Wouldn't it have been a lovely solution for me if I had the falcon? Sadly, I didn't. But even if I did, the thought of Mr. Faulkner, or any lender for that matter, accepting stolen property in lieu of cash is ludicrous."

"He took your paintings."

"A perfectly legal arrangement."

"More important, it shows he'd take goods instead of money, if it was the right goods. But I agree the stolen falcon might not be enough for him. It wouldn't be worth four million to him. It's worth only what a person could get for it, or what people agree it's worth . . . like information, wouldn't you say?"

"I would not. The value of stolen information is often high. The value of an item in the hands of a thief generally plummets."

"Which is why Faulkner would want more than the statue to unloose the bind you're in."

I finished off the Scotch and put the glass down suggestively, holding and twisting it a little before letting go, but he didn't react. It never had been totally clear to me if he was a cheapskate or a prig. Probably both. I got up and poured it myself.

"No, you'd have to offer even more than the prop you stole from Rowena, considering the debts you've run up."

It was time to set the notion afloat. Putting the drink on the mantelpiece, I struck a pose, wishing at the moment for a Montecristo, a waistcoat, a watch chain. Despite the rich-blood monikers, Levi Strauss and Polo didn't cut it.

"Faulkner wouldn't take the falcon alone but he'd take two statues."

"You mean the Irwin Raptor, I presume. Your argument is that two birds in the hand are better than one, even if both are stolen?"

"I wouldn't want to be argumentative. It's just that the lure of both statues would be hard to resist for a criminal like Faulkner. Everyone has their passions. For him, the perfect combination would be the prop and the Irwin in the bargain. They'd be worth a lot more than what you owed him, at least to him."

Geyer crossed his legs and bobbed five contoured toes.

"It's hard to know if you actually believe such nonsense," he said.

"Faulkner's not just a shady character. He's a fan of high-end film noir collectibles and he's your bookie and moneylender. It's easy to believe he'd go for the statues. Maybe you could sell them elsewhere but that's the problem, isn't it? Who would buy them?"

"Why don't you go to Lou Faulkner and see if he has them? That should take care of your preposterous theory."

"It wouldn't answer anything," I said. "He'll have those statues in such deep safekeeping, they might as well be at the bottom of a lake."

I took the drink back to the armchair, settled forward, and put the glare on him.

"You're in major trouble, Cassim. You know that, don't you?"

His laugh was easy.

"Am I? Based on your wild ideas?"

"Based on both birds are missing, you're the last one known to have them, your henchman admits to stealing them for you, and you had huge debts to pay. And two men are dead."

He tried a sniff of disdain but it got caught and twisted into an accidental sob, which he followed with a mean little chuckle.

"Let's see you prove something."

"You know the old saw: it'll go better if you cooperate."

"Do you enjoy my Scotch, Mr. Mencari?"

"You should have one, too, Cassim. It's a rare pleasure. And rare things have a way of disappearing."

43

I tried to ignore the air of satisfaction among the high-paying passengers in their roomy seats as I made my way toward the back of the Boeing. Tireia had offered to spring for business class but I said no dice. At least I was by a window, away from the aisle traffic during the haul across the pond. And next to me sat a small middle-aged woman who most likely wouldn't stick her foot into my legroom.

I buckled in and took stock yet again of what we knew and only thought we knew about the three birds and the two corpses. What we knew was that in the midst of the trade of the Maltese Falcon for the Irwin Raptor, both statues were stolen from Cassim Geyer's safe. We knew Jonathan Evers and Wilber Arndt were the thieves, working for Cassim. We knew Cassim had hired me on behalf of Rowena Pascoe-Leyland to retrieve the falcon. But when I returned it to him, he disappeared along with the bird. We knew Wilber had kept the Irwin Raptor, and someone had shot him for it. When Cassim was found, he had neither the falcon nor the raptor. We also knew Lou Faulkner had Admiral Nelson's prize, which was the inspiration for all this, the bejeweled Ottoman Osprey.

That brought me to what we only thought we knew. Faulkner might have agreed to trade the osprey for the other two statues. Rowena may have engineered the double theft so she could execute that trade and return the coveted osprey to her family fold. And the biggest thing we now thought we knew, which we had puzzled out as we lay staring at Tireia's stuccoed ceiling, was who killed Jim Davenport and Wilber Arndt. But we needed proof.

Rowena's townhouse in Chelsea was eight stories with seven bedrooms, an indoor pool, rooftop terrace, and views over Chelsea Physic Garden along the Thames. A maid took me into a sunroom off the ground floor, where you could gaze through tinted glass at a fountain on a patio of Italian marble before a wrought-iron pergola amid birches and a laburnum. Through the sunroom's transparent ceiling, the foliage of plane trees that filled the sky put you outside without leaving climate control. Part of me wanted to wear jeans to the place but Tireia had said that would be foolish and ineffective, so it was slacks and a sports coat, the better to extract information.

Rowena entered in a chiffon pantsuit, her confident glide blending athleticism and sexuality in a way that again struck me as an artifact in a woman around sixty, but then an admonishment from Tireia floated in from across the water: how was she supposed to walk? Stately, like a dowager, and wasn't that an act, too? Rowena's fulsome lips were set in a shape that suggested whatever I was thinking deserved tolerance, which made me concentrate. We sat in leather chairs at a glass table placed on a circular mirror in the floor, which reflected the plane trees above. Someone came in and served lemonade with little cakes that made me want to pocket one to show Cassim Geyer what a real treat looks like.

I thanked her for agreeing to see me. She was gracious and asked about my flight. I made the noises and admired her place and she said, yes, well, if I recalled she told me in Hailey she was a city person, although many of her oldest friends and acquaintances unfortunately had been forced by changing circumstances over the years to move south of the river. Some had retreated to their country homes, and she still enjoyed spending time on occasion at her family's manor in West Sussex, but it admittedly was unsettling that so many of the beautiful old houses had been opened to tours and that their occupants, her peers, had managed to retain only sections of their ancestral homes for private living. She was fortunate to have married Vic, a successful businessman, an American at that, rather Jamesian of her, although he was a lovely man despite his rough edges which, in a way, even enhanced his attractiveness. And his astonishing acumen in the world of commerce eliminated potential concerns for her about safeguarding the tangible qualities of her family's heritage.

She said all this in the same rattling conversational style she'd demonstrated in Hailey, which gave the impression of imparting information—probably because it streamed out in a breathless high pitch—but didn't provide anything new. Except she'd given an easily disproven impression about her country manor.

I sidled up to that lie.

"Your family's heirlooms would be in West Sussex, I guess?" This was not a guess but no need to underscore Tireia's research.

"Yes, why do you ask?"

"I'm interested in the Admiral Nelson materials. You have

a large collection, the biggest in private ownership, isn't it?"

"So the news reports suggest."

She looked away, as if to display her profile or dismiss an underling.

"Technically, I suppose it's not yours anymore, though. I mean, since you sold the collection to the government to avoid inheritance tax."

She turned a determinedly pleasant look on me, an acknowledgment that even a bug rooting in the dirt has value.

"Yes, that was just before my marriage changed everything. Until then, our family was headed down the same dreary path as the others. We couldn't possibly afford to keep such a large place operational without commercializing it in some way, and a first step was to avoid prohibitive taxes on the Nelson effects. Under the government program, we could retain the collection at the manor, with the assurance it would be protected in perpetuity as a national treasure."

More evasion. I nibbled at one of the goodies, and then popped the whole thing without warning and chewed like it was alive.

"But wasn't the other part of the government program," I said around the mashing, "to open your place to the public, like your friends did? That's a condition of the scheme, right? You get to hold the goods but have to show them to the people."

Her smirk ratcheted down at the edges in stop motion.

"Unfortunately, true, Mr. Mencari. Which is why I rarely visit the manor anymore."

"Yeah, I can see the bind you're in. You could close the place to the public but then you'd have to put the collection in the National Maritime Museum. And you don't want it to leave the manor."

"It's been in the Pascoe family a very long time, you see. There's a certain responsibility."

"A duty, sure, you owe it to the ancestors. Lucky you didn't have to sell the government every piece in the collection. I mean the Yardley stuff."

This brought us to the brother-in-law, Alistair Yardley, and left Rowena in no doubt about where we were going. The porcelain-like finish of her face didn't change but neither did she make me relate the story of Alistair selling the osprey to Lou Faulkner. She just said the best thing about her sister's husband was his Nelson collection. She bridled at my suggestion that the trouble might have been avoided if the Yardleys had gotten some financial help. It would have been beyond crass to offer charity, out of the question, nor would they have accepted. Anyway, she sniffed, who knew how much Alistair had kept for himself of the proceeds from what he had sold?

I asked why she had decided not to pursue the matter of the Ottoman Osprey through the courts. Would her sister not cooperate in a suit against Alistair? She didn't blink at the specific mention of the statue. She said the advice she received was that legal action would be extremely time-consuming, and there was the expense. Plus the outcome of what already would have been a complicated case was made even more uncertain because the osprey was in the possession of a foreign buyer.

"And who was that?"

"Alistair wouldn't give me that information. He just said it was someone overseas."

I settled back in my chair and didn't say a damn thing.

"Of course, the government was eager to retain the statue

in the U.K.," she tried, "but a private transaction made it difficult for them to intervene, even for a priceless relic."

She wasn't going to offer up Faulkner. She wouldn't go anywhere without a prod. OK, I could do that.

"So you decided to take the matter into your own hands."

"The matter was closed. What was there to take?"

owena acknowledged that her sister Nell and her husband lived in private quarters within the Pascoes' country manor, where their twisted arms performed the bourgeois task of corralling cash. With a barely repressed shudder, she admitted that during public visiting hours, Nell sometimes personally made the register ping its accompaniment to the modern mime of *noblesse oblige*. Rowena professed no concern about Alistair selling any more of the Yardley stash now that the osprey was gone, because the best of what little he had left was in her townhouse. It wasn't charity, she said, they had come to an agreement. In exchange for the stuff, she contributed whatever expenses weren't covered by the tourism operation to keep them comfy in the manor.

She took me into the drawing room to show off one of her Yardley goodies, a golden sword hilt shaped like a crocodile, which I recognized from Trask's images during his San Francisco talk.

"I thought that was stolen more than a century ago."

"Correct," she said, and bestowed a look of approval. "The

Yardleys had lent it as part of a display at Greenwich Hospital. There was a break-in."

"The rumor was somebody in America bought it. So how did it get back here all these years later?"

"Ah," she said, as she held it up to display Nelson's coat of arms on the croc's side and the closed-mouth needling of its teeth. "A sharp eye, determination, and wherewithal can be a powerful combination."

She proffered the hilt but I didn't take it, on the instinct that this might be a productive moment to piss her off. It actually just seemed to confuse her. She looked down dumbly at the thing for a few seconds before replacing it in the cabinet.

"I appreciate you know how to work the back channels, Mrs. Pascoe-Leyland."

"An unfortunate choice of phrase, Mr. Mencari."

She closed the cabinet door and led me back to the sunroom, tour over.

"Not compared to, say, black market," I replied, as I trailed in the wake of chiffon and the scent of wealth. "Or criminal connections. Or consorting with thieves and murderers."

She stopped outside the sunroom.

"It appears our conversation has run its course."

"Nah, there's a long way to go." I barged into the room. "Come on in, take a seat."

She hated that but sat down.

"First off, I went to see Lou Faulkner, who told me he had the osprey, so let's not prance around it. Second, when you approached Faulkner to get it back, you proposed giving him the falcon but he said no. He saw how much you wanted the osprey back and figured you could offer a lot more than that."

She crossed her arms and performed a single lazy

blink. Excess mascara. Fear of the great falling apart had compromised her taste.

"An extraordinary statement, Mr. Mencari. But all right, let's pretend your invented scene did occur. Do you honestly think I would pay an endless ransom for an inanimate object?"

"Money? No. Money's always a pleasing prospect but something else appealed more to Faulkner. He knew Ellis Trask had the Irwin Raptor. He tried to buy it himself but he underbid, which made Trask angry. Faulkner looked at you and thought, here's somebody with a huge need only I can fulfill. He figured he'd make you buy the Irwin and then give it to him, along with the falcon, in exchange for the Ottoman Osprey."

Her laugh was a tuneful blend of soprano and air.

"All your talk of criminality. Of course, as I told you in Idaho, I did intend to trade for the Irwin. I wanted it because of its beauty and, I suppose, for the, shall we say, stimulation of owning a contraband item. It was poor judgment. But I certainly didn't expect to buy the piece and then give it to Mr. Faulkner."

Rowena stood and glided to the French doors. She pressed a button and the glass doors receded into the glass walls, which turned the sunroom into part of the garden. The fountain burbled. Everything flowed around here, even the way she moved into the courtyard.

"Your logic is faulty on more than one count," her breathy child's voice floated back to me. "First, if I needed both statues to retrieve the Ottoman Osprey, why would I trade away the Maltese Falcon? Why wouldn't I just purchase the Irwin Raptor from Mr. Trask?"

I went outdoors and stood next to her. She looked straight

ahead. I put out a hand and let the fountain's cool water trickle through my fingers. It was a dappled day and temperate, London trying harder than usual. Finches chittered in the arches of the pergola and two lilac bushes were in fragrant bloom.

"No doubt you tried," I said, "but Trask already had rebuffed an offer from Faulkner and you got rejected as well. Trask probably thought you were lowballing him, too—and there was a limit to how much you were willing to get gouged. So you proposed the trade. Trask agreed, because he knew Faulkner was eager to get his hands on the falcon and was likely to pay well for it. He didn't realize Faulkner had your osprey, so he was clueless about that whole part of the scheme. A cash differential you promised to throw in made the trade especially attractive to him. What he didn't expect is that you never intended to go through with the exchange."

She stalked back into the room, her flow gone stuttery, as I hovered like a purse-snatcher.

"But Ellis Trask knows the wrong sort of people, and it would have been too dangerous for you to just take his statue. Your solution was to arrange for a mock theft of both birds before the trade was completed."

"Your imagination astonishes me, Mr. Mencari."

"Thanks and back at you. But we aren't done yet, are we?"

Rowena put her hand on the lemonade pitcher. Neither of us had drunk much of what we had. She circled slowly around the table, and ran a finger along the tops of the chairs. I leaned against the wall and crossed my arms. It seemed likely she was better at chess than she let on.

"My head's awhirl," she said. "It's an amazing story and in a way delightful, because it makes me sound quite diabolical. But if I'm following you correctly, this mock theft would leave me with both statues. So why would I need to hire you?"

"That's what we wondered, until we looked at it from Trask's perspective. When he found out his statue was gone, he immediately suspected you. Even if he couldn't get it back, he certainly could look for revenge. You had anticipated this. You needed to convince him the theft was real. That's where I came in: you set up an elaborate return of your statue. You figured when Trask found out about it, he'd shift his suspicion from you to Geyer. But then Jim Davenport interfered and got himself shot."

She stood still, waiting.

"The killing brought in the police. You realized the best way to keep yourself clear of everyone's suspicion was to make Geyer take off."

"A remarkable theory," she said. "But tell me this: how in the world could I persuade Cassim Geyer to take the blame?"

"Easy. You convinced Lou Faulkner to erase Cassim's debt as part of the deal for the statues. Faulkner appreciated it was better for him and you if the heat was on Geyer. From Cassim's perspective, to owe a guy like Faulkner and not be able to pay up was a major threat to his health. Cassim would have preferred that the cops suspected him of making off with the falcon. But it was a sham, of course. The two-for-one trade was still on."

I see," she said. "And in this fanciful scenario, who would you say was responsible for the death of Jim Davenport? And why was he killed?"

"You want to answer that?"

"I want you to leave my premises, Mr. Mencari. I've entertained enough conjecture for one afternoon, thank you."

"OK, you don't have to get huffy."

I launched off the wall and made for the door, where a man

in a suit miraculously loomed. He motioned me out, I nodded, and then paused to make sure the needle stuck.

"I'd advise you to consult your solicitors, Mrs. Pascoe-Leyland. Two men are dead, a lot of valuable stuff is missing, and you're up to your ruffles in it."

She said nothing, but the veneer was showing its fault lines.

I got out of the merry old country and back to the mountains as fast as wings would carry me. Two days later, the Dodge took the curves on the way to Cascade without help from the brakes but I had to keep a close eye on a river of vehicles running the opposite way. Tomorrow was the Fourth, and McCall's population was swelling fivefold in anticipation. Holiday crowds drove the locals nuts but the permanent vogue of complaining about them, partly a way of asserting fidelity to place, had the unacknowledged flip side that crowds brought fun. And, of course, business owners loved the Fourth almost as much as Minta did. Still, it was annoying to see the sedans and RVs, the trucks and SUVs laden with noisy toys for water and woods, as they alternately bumbled and raced around bends unprotected by guardrails to save them from the Payette River's punishment for their bad driving. It amused me to recognize I was annoyed because the place was mine, not theirs, mine.

When I entered Darlene's boxy office at the county sheriff's department, her optimism that the judge's decision would be favorable to Tireia had something strangely abashed in it, which made me think she might be worried for Fabienne. I didn't know if that was really how she felt, but the supposition helped me to fess up. Fab's position had worsened, I told her. She made a questioning expression and I filled her in on Fabienne's confession that she had concocted the scheme to ransom the Irwin Raptor to Harold Irwin. And then she had tried to get me to tell everyone she'd been coerced by Wilber. Darlene said she appreciated the information. Maybe we should let it sit for now. This was more than OK by me. My part was done. A weight dropped, as if I were in a balloon as it shed ballast.

I quickly moved on to a description of how Rowena had masterminded the double steal of the falcon and the raptor to keep the suspicion off her while she traded them to Lou Faulkner for the Ottoman Osprey. It took a while to describe and Darlene listened patiently. I could see the skepticism in her face, although none of it was theoretical to me anymore, not after the London visit. Rowena had tried to brush off the guilt but it was all over her.

"OK, you're saying Geyer was both the middle man and the fall guy. He carried out the swap of two birds for one. But to protect Rowena, it had to look like he stole the prop from her. He didn't have any statues with him when he was taken into custody. If the trade had already happened, that would mean Lou Faulkner has the falcon and the Irwin Raptor. And Rowena has her precious Ottoman Osprey again."

She edged a hand through her tousled hair.

"Your inventive theory doesn't tell us why Jim Davenport and Wilber Arndt are dead."

Given that she found it hard to accept Rowena's role in all this, now was not the time to unveil the theory of the shootings that Tireia and I had concocted while we lay looking at her ceiling the other night. Anyway, I saw little difference in telling her or keeping quiet for the moment.

My chair in front of her desk started to feel confining. There wouldn't be much to see on a stroll: filing cabinets, blinds, the latest presidents' portraits lined up high near the ceiling. The U.S. flag on a United We Stand poster. Her bar fridge, by now probably devoid of Gorgonzola.

"We'll get there," I said. "It helps that Minta's future isn't a distraction at the moment. But it's too bad the holiday promises to be a loss of time."

Darlene had that upset expression again.

"What's wrong?" I said. "Was it poor form for me to badmouth Independence Day?"

"No, I'm just thinking . . . to be honest, I feel guilty for the trouble I've caused you."

"You've caused me? What're you talking about?"

"All these hassles about Minta wouldn't have happened if I'd kept my mouth shut. I had to go and tell Graham Wheeler the story of you and Fabienne and her husband. I thought it would help to dispel his bizarre idea about you shooting Davenport and maybe it did in the long run. But he focused on the bit about Minta's parentage. He had Family Services check the records and everybody realized Tireia wasn't her legal guardian. I wasn't thinking, Reese."

So that's what she had meant when she said being Minta's foster parent was the least she could do for us. A guilty conscience over well-meant decisions. The plague of decency.

"I want to talk to Wheeler."

"That won't be comfortable. But I guess if he buys your theory about the deal between Mrs. Pascoe-Leyland and Lou Faulkner, he can help with interstate jurisdiction."

"Wouldn't that be nice? Where's he staying?"

She gave me his cell number.

"Last I heard, he was at the Hunt Lodge."

"All those stuffed heads. Perfect."

"Watch it, my Hank is a hunter."

"Nothing wrong with hunters. It's the stuffed heads."

The huge log beams and stacked-stone siding of the Hunt Lodge made it a defender of the the old-timey contingent amid the architectural hodgepodge on McCall's main drag. The motel had long ago become a Holiday Inn but had stubbornly avoided homogenization. I parked and walked past the big old wooden bear at the door to enter the lobby, where all manner of horned meatheads stared in fierce disapproval from the walls. A pleasant person explained that Mr. Wheeler had left yesterday. No sir, no forwarding information. I thanked her and called Wheeler but got voicemail. I phoned Darlene.

"I'm at the Hunt Lodge and Wheeler's checked out. I left a message for him but in the meantime, could someone call his office to see if they know his movements?"

"Yeah, and if you don't hear from him soon, we can try other lodgings in the area. Who knows, maybe he's off to see Faulkner."

I got back in the Dodge and drove around the lake up to Tireia's cabin. As soon as I got out of the truck, Minta was at me: we had no fireworks and we needed fireworks right now. Non-shitting-negotiable. Or words to that effect. Actually, it was please, please, which did not brook argument, especially in the cross-armed presence of the perhaps soon-to-be-ratified mother figure. Catching bad guys had to take a back seat and the kid got up front with me. Accompanied by a pyrotechnical display of nine-year-old babble, I wheeled back down the road and up to the fireworks tent in a parking lot in town. This foray was the last thing I needed right now. But of course there was always the argument it was the only thing I needed.

On the drive back to the cabin after we made our purchases, I thought about how Minta was at the peak age for fireworks as a major life event. She'd lit a few herself last year, getting the hang of long-handled matches. This year she had insisted on a promotion to principal firestarter—not that we were setting off bombs in the woods. She'd light the fuses of the little turtles and trucks and snakes placed on the dirt and gravel of Tireia's driveway, where they'd screech and scoot and whirl unto death. She'd wave sparklers and dance through colored smoke to our applause. And then we'd pile into the vehicle for the big show staged by the city over the lake.

Our tradition was to be out there in the motorboat Tireia's parents had bought, which we otherwise seldom used. We preferred the potential of sneaking up on beaver or otter in our canoe where the river narrowed and quieted above the lake. But tomorrow night we'd approach the flotilla from the north, cut the engine on its outskirts and practice fringe participation, a forte well-admired in these parts, which made it a challenge to reach the fringe of the fringe. Tireia was determined to go through the ritual again in this summer of law, which had all but scorched us and required the salve of routine.

46

On the afternoon of the Fourth, we went into town and let Minta go wild in the bounce houses set up at Legacy Park. We watched the volleyball tournament for a while and toured the vintage car show, wending through cheerful crowds in the sunshine. After a day we called celebratory and made a heroic effort to not feel guilty about wasting, we went home and had dinner. It was interrupted by a call for Tireia from Derek. His men had learned from the employee of a small Boise company that it had rented out a Hyundai with Washington plates on the day of Wilber's murder, which had been driven a long way, apparently into rough country. The company's owner, who was at home, was peeved about the condition in which the car had been returned. Derek had badgered him for the name of the renter but the owner said the contract was on computer and not in the cloud (only his head was there, Tireia said), so he had to go into the office, which he insisted on doing tomorrow, after Independence Day, for God's sake, or at least after the damn fireworks.

Around sundown, we performed our minimalist fireworks

show and later that night took the boat out of its shed beside Tireia's dock. As we motored down the lake toward town, all three of us were expectant and hopeful, Minta because of the holiday and we adults because of the call from Derek. We passed through the gap between the western shoreline and the peninsula of Ponderosa State Park that jutted into the lake's long center.

My phone rang. It was Derek again, with more news. He'd put out the word to watch for Graham Wheeler, and one of his men had just discovered he was staying in the only cabin, a leasehold, on Shellworth Island.

"This can't wait," I told Tireia.

She put a hand on Minta's shoulder. "Reese has to take the boat to see someone, honey. When we get to town, let's you and I go to the beach so you can play with your friends."

That was a hit. Minta liked the boat but kids on the beach at night with fireworks was fine. We entered the fray of watercraft in the bay and managed to reach the marina's dock. Minta set off running toward Legacy Park but Tireia, still skittish about danger, called her back to a manageable pace. The park, the shoreline, and the lake itself teemed with merrymakers.

I turned the boat away from the dock and made for Shellworth Island in the lake on the eastern side of the peninsula. To get there, I wended through a crowd of waterborne revelers cutting across each other's wakes in skiffs, sailboats, and pontoon fishing boats decked out like floats in flowers and flags. The mess thinned out as my craft approached Wagon Wheel Bay on the west, where families kept cabins that had been there since way before the shoreline's value was measured in square feet down to the inch. Their docks, which jutted like gapped teeth from the lip of the beach, were filled with people whose laughter and shouts traveled to me over the water and the sound of my motor. The boat gunned into The Narrows, between a quiet stretch of Warren Wagon Road along the shoreline and Porcupine Point in the state park, and then powered between Cougar Island and the northern tip of the peninsula. The A-frame cabin where Wheeler was staying sat on the southern end of Shellworth, not far from shore behind a few trees. The island was mostly rock, with a smattering of pines. From the air, it was shaped like a raptor with folded wings. There was only one dock. I motored down to it and tied up beside an eighteen-foot Stingray sport boat.

Wheeler stood on the verandah, hands on the railing, watching as I mounted the wooden stairway.

"Mencari," he said. He crossed his arms, perhaps in avoidance of a handshake. "Surprised to see you here. I should think you'd be with your woman and the child tonight."

"Yep, I'll be going back soon. But I heard tell you were here and I wanted to come talk business."

I didn't ask why he hadn't returned my call.

"You heard I was here, huh? Well, come on in."

He led the way into the living room, which was positioned behind the verandah to take advantage of a picture window facing south. The sides of the A-frame came down below the raised porch, making a hard-shelled tent of the place except for openings on either end of its two floors. He motioned to a black leather couch, which formed the long end of an "L" with two leather armchairs around a coffee table. One wall was occupied by a woodstove on a tiled dais. Wheeler took the armchair farther from me, next to a bookcase crammed with paperbacks, in front of which lay a valise. On the end table beside his chair sat a glass of red wine and a Beretta.

"Got your pistol out, I see."

He glanced over but didn't touch it.

"Just about to do a little maintenance."

No maintenance materials were visible but I let that go. He didn't offer me a drink. Without the usual fisherman's cap, his curly hair increased the blurry impression of his face as he regarded me.

"The Beretta's a good gun," I said, "but not standard FBI issue, is it? Maybe you're one of those agents who don't like Glocks."

He shrugged.

"They're ugly, is all."

"They won't win any beauty contests. I remember for a long time the agency didn't trust Glocks because of the safe action trigger. Too many unintended discharges, right?"

He looked at me for a moment in silence. Much less garrulous than the time he tried to grill me in Darlene's office. Almost surly now.

"The Beretta, on the other hand, was the Army's service pistol for a long time."

"You probably learned that in school, right?"

A hint of malice. Good.

"You were in the Army, so that's probably why you have a Beretta. The Army has replaced it with a SIG, as I recall. But that was pretty recently, well after you were discharged."

His grin was part snarl in the fuzzy midst of his beard. Excellent dentition.

"You've done your research, Mencari, although why you would want to look into my background is a question."

"We look into everything, don't we? You look into mine, I look into yours."

"There's reason to look into yours. You aren't out of hot water yet, mister."

This was easy to ignore.

"It's interesting you don't like the Glock, especially with that shooting of a suspect on your record. You were using a Glock then, weren't you? Had trouble with the point-and-shoot, maybe? Is that why you switched back to a Beretta?"

Wheeler reached over and picked up the gun by the handle, finger away from the trigger. He stood and went to a small table against a wall near the kitchen, opened the drawer, and took out a cloth while I watched intently. Coming back to the armchair, he sat down and began to rub the barrel. The sight made me think of the debate with Tireia about martial arts versus a pistol at close quarters.

"The suspect made a move for a weapon," Wheeler said. "It was dark. Turned out he had a criminal record."

"Turned out he was unarmed. And the criminal record was speeding tickets."

"I thought you wanted to talk about the case, Mencari."

"That's right." I tried to look eager as I came closer to sit in the armchair beside his. "But pistols are related to it. For one, it's interesting the firearm found in Fabienne's hand after Jim Davenport was killed was a SIG Sauer. The same model that the Army now uses as its service pistol."

"So?"

"Well, it's also interesting the SIG was expected to be the FBI's replacement for the Glock. But then at the last minute they went for a new Glock. So, if someone who was in the Army and the FBI—like you were, for example—happened to dislike Glocks, maybe because of a bad experience with them, then that person would be likely to have a SIG or a Beretta or both."

Wheeler sighed, put the pistol down on top of the cloth, and picked up his wineglass. He took a sip. It was impossible to tell if he had forgotten to offer me a glass or was just a dickhead.

"You think a serviceman plugged Davenport. That doesn't narrow the field much, does it? Anyway, the same SIG Sauer has been manufactured for public purchase since the mid-2010s."

"True," I said, and shifted my body toward him.

He held the wineglass close to his mouth, as if it were a shield.

"But Davenport being shot with a SIG is only the half of it," I said. "Forensics show a Beretta was used on Wilber Arndt."

He put down the glass and turned a glare on me.

"You think that kind of information adds up to evidence? You don't know much about police work, do you?"

"I know Wilber didn't kill Davenport. His gun was found in the cabin at Warren. And guess what? Wilber didn't own a SIG … it was a Glock."

"Bad guys tend to have more than one gun, Mencari."

"You want me to lay out how this went down? All right, I will."

47

"For a while, Tireia and I couldn't figure out how you got here so quickly after the Maltese Falcon was stolen. Nobody knew about it, not even the police. Who tipped you off? Then we found out you knew Ellis Trask. You had interviewed him in Philadelphia, during the investigation of the Irwin Raptor's original theft in Honolulu from Harold Irwin. You also talked to Trask's regular customers who might buy the statue, including Fabienne and Stuart Sansverrou.

"Trask sized you up at the time, didn't he? He realized your interest in the Irwin was more than just professional. The sheer value of it got you going. What did you say to him, Wheeler? How did you show you were the kind of lawman who could be turned? Is it some sort of instinctive recognition criminals have of each other? Do you let off a stink?"

His snarl indicated he didn't like that. Too bad.

"After the prop was lifted from Cassim Geyer's place, you visited Ellis Trask in Philadelphia. We knew it was to discuss the statue that had been stolen with it, the Irwin Raptor. But that didn't answer who had told you about the thefts. At last, we realized Trask had contacted you, not the other way around. He knew you'd shot an innocent person and were on thin ice at the agency. There were only two ways out for you. One was to crack a big case and the other was to steal yourself a parachute. His bet was you'd go for the second option. You'd come across a lot of valuable art in your job and what did you have for it? A bad reputation and a desk job. Trask understood the situation, so when he called and you met with him, he tipped you off in his oblique way that the Irwin might be in Idaho, where it might have been part of a trade for the falcon that turned into a double-cross. And the payout to anyone who could get the two birds for him would be big.

"This was pretty trusting on his part, but listen, it doesn't make him a great character reference for you. Don't put him on your resume. He knew it was very possible you'd bring the statues to your bosses to get back in their good graces. But to him, even that would be better than Cassim Geyer having them. So you struck a deal to get them for him."

Wheeler reached toward the end table and I tensed but he chose the glass over the gun. He held it in his lap with both hands and stared forward.

"Trask told you Fabienne had carried the Irwin for him, so you started with her. You jumped on a plane to Boise and drove to her cabin. But you heard the noise of a confrontation inside and drew your SIG. It was Davenport giving Fab the one-two and she was out. Maybe he made a move for his pistol or maybe you just thought he did. Based on your history, I assume you fired first and reconsidered later. That's a problem with weapons, especially in the hands of rash people, don't you think? Then you planted the gun on her. Wilber Arndt already had delivered the falcon but you had no way of knowing it was sitting in the linen closet. And Geyer got it, courtesy of me."

Wheeler stood up, which sloshed wine on his track pants. I rose slowly to put a hand on his shoulder, a finger really, and guided him back down. He sat and resumed the same button-eyed stare in front of him, man imitating a transitional object.

"That's when you started thinking. Somebody was dead, you had nothing to show for it, and nothing to lose. You figured Geyer and Trask were trying to cheat each other out of the birds. They probably knew where to sell them, which meant if you got your hands on the statues, all you'd have to do to make a real haul—not just some crummy fee—would be to find out who the buyers were."

He didn't even look at the end table when he returned the glass to it with his left hand, which nudged the pistol aside. Beyond the black window, the first of the fireworks boomed, blossomed, and collapsed over the lake.

"You went to Geyer and tried to worm into his confidence but he sent you packing. He disappeared, taking the movie prop with him. But then Wilber went rogue with the Irwin Raptor. Now Geyer wanted to hire you to get it for him. Good work: both the competing bad guys, Trask and Geyer, had become your clients."

At this, whatever cacophony was in Wheeler's head died down enough to let him say how ridiculous this was. For one, why would Geyer trust an FBI agent to bring the Irwin Raptor to him?

"You didn't have to make Geyer into a believer. You already had what amounted to a referral from none other than Ellis Trask. He first met Geyer at Lou Faulkner's Balzac Club. They spent the night talking about the Irwin Raptor. No doubt, your name came up. You had the rep."

He snorted and moved his furry head from side to side, letting it linger a tick too long on the gun's side, which put me on orange alert.

"Sheriff Carmody's deputy, Derek, told you where Wilber was hiding. You went to Warren and figured what the hell, you'd already killed a man, so you executed Wilber. The neighbor came to the door and made you nervous, but he didn't try to go in. And then you took the statue and got out of there in the direction you'd come from."

This drew a protest that I was crazy. He'd never been to Warren in his life. Wasn't it way out in the sticks somewhere? His defensive effort was weak but he probably was relieved to at least be back in full cry. I ignored his noise.

"You took the Irwin statue to Geyer. But you'd killed two people to get this far and your plan was to cut him out. He still figured Wilber had shot Davenport. And of course Geyer didn't know yet that Wilber himself was dead, so you decided to play the hero. This had all been pretense, you told him. Now both statues would go to the authorities and Geyer would go to jail. He probably didn't buy this change of tack, not totally. But it would have worried him enough to reveal he intended to trade the statues for Lou Faulkner's Ottoman Osprey, which was worth way more than the other two combined. And he had a purchaser for the osprey. He wouldn't say who it was, but the proceeds would be plenty for both of you."

"What a flimsy story," he interrupted. "Geyer must be the one who told you these lies, it's the only explanation. I mean, he says there's a buyer for this Ottoman Osprey but he won't tell who it is? You couldn't have dreamed that up on your own if you tried. Not that there's a shred of truth to it."

Did he understand that Cassim Geyer didn't have to tell me? That Tireia and I had deduced it, by process of elimination? That it was the only way things could have played out? Well, if he wanted to hear it all recited, wouldn't take anything on faith, it was all right by me.

"You agreed to trade the birds for the osprey. But you weren't about to trust Geyer to handle the deal. You wanted to know who the customer was and you threatened again to turn him in if he didn't spill. It was a good corner: if you went through with the threat you could claim you were playing him the whole time and who would be the wiser?"

Wheeler folded his arms and made a culprit's attempt at scorn.

"Don't tell me," he said. "Let me guess. We sold the osprey to the Crown Prince of Saudi Arabia for half his oilfields."

"That's the problem, isn't it? Or so Maggie Kornbluth says. Remember her, the art museum curator down in Boise? She told me you pointed out when you visited her that the hardest thing for an art thief is to find a buyer. And now you faced that very challenge.

"What you hadn't counted on was that Geyer's customer was none other than Rowena Pascoe-Leyland. And she wasn't a buyer at all. She had forced him to get the osprey for her. His payment was that she'd convinced Faulkner to cancel his debts.

"When Geyer finally confessed there was no cash to be had, you decided to turn that situation around. You figured Rowena would pay whatever it took to bring her osprey back into the family fold … or end up with nothing. You decided to make the deal yourself and cut Geyer out of it.

"You probably would have put a bullet in him except you might need him, and then he got arrested. That was OK, though, he wouldn't talk. He was in deep enough water, especially because he still believed his boy Wilber had shot Davenport."

Wheeler stretched his arms upward and craned around.

This kind of body language set me on edge. It wasn't the safest strategy to lay out our evidence when he was at arm's reach from his weapon but a part of me wouldn't have minded if he made a move. I'd snap that pistol away before he knew what happened. Stay focused, stay alive, my Krav Mag instructor used to say. Right now, every atom in me was vibrating.

"I'm amazed at how in hell you ever came up with such a harebrained notion," he said. "How could you possibly believe I'd be so corrupt?"

That made me squint.

"It wasn't just the Trask connection, if that's what you mean. We thought of you when someone clubbed me in the Boise airport parking structure and stuck a note in my pocket that threatened our little Minta. At first, I thought it was one of Geyer's thugs. But something about the note bothered us. It said, 'If you value your kid . . .' It said 'your kid,' not 'the kid.' That suggested whoever wrote it knew I was the biological father, which was not well known in town. And the note called Tireia a 'fake mom,' so they knew she wasn't Minta's real mother. This was before the custody case, when even Minta's school thought Tireia was her mom."

The button eyes jerked. The teddy bear was aflutter.

Go ahead, man, try something. I'll break your hand.

"And then Sheriff Carmody told me you were the one who tipped off Family Services that Tireia wasn't the real mother. You were trying to divert us from the investigation. It's strange, but of all the shitty things you did, even killing people, that's what pissed us off the most. You shouldn't have done it, Wheeler. It was a big mistake to drag our child into this."

He stilled but this time it wasn't the freeze of indecision. He was poised. His voice went low with menace.

"You don't have any evidence."

I pointed at the valise in front of the bookcase.

"Open it."

"What, you want to look at my boxers?"

"Funny. But if it's just your clothes in there, you won't mind."

He put both hands beside him on the armchair and shifted his body slightly toward me.

"You think I'm carrying the Ottoman Osprey around? According to your scenario, I sold it to Rowena. Maybe you think I have a suitcase full of cash."

"I think you're holed up here until her people come with the dough. Let's take a look."

Wheeler lunged for the Beretta, quicker than I thought he could go. But the cleaning cloth under it slid just enough to interfere with a perfect move. In the split-second it took to recover his timing, my hand was up to send the gun flying. He bent toward the floor in its direction and I draped myself over him.

The pistol was under the bookcase. He grabbed the valise and whipped it around, the edge connecting with my temple. I pitched sideways and the pain was sharp but I managed a palm strike to his throat that was strong enough to slow him. I dove for the gun, snatched it, and spun around on my back.

"Don't move."

He had one hand on his neck and the other held the valise. He sneered and went quickly toward the door. I aimed at the wall above him and pulled the trigger. Empty. OK, maybe he really was going to clean the thing. When I got to my feet, the room went out of focus, which stalled me for a moment. I put down the gun. My eyesight cleared but by the time I got to the dock, he had a head start.

48

Wheeler's boat was moving westward toward the tip of the state park peninsula, the same direction from which I'd come. I pulled away from the dock and snapped on the lights affixed to a bar on the tower. I steered with one hand across the chop while I speed-dialed Tireia to yell out our location and bearing over the engine's growl. Even though the inboard on the Moomba sounded like the MGM lion in an IMAX theater, it couldn't go nearly as fast as his Stingray. Not that I needed to catch him.

If he had a rental car, it most likely would be parked near the upscale condos in the opposite direction from where he was heading. He probably hadn't gone that way because he knew it would be easy to intercept him on the unpaved East Side Road, which went around the lake if you drove north and into town if you headed south. The only turnoff that went a far distance was Lick Creek Road, which soon became a wilderness track. He was a city boy trapped in a mountain village surrounded by millions of acres of forestland. The open water maybe looked like a better bet to him than the road.

He clearly wasn't bound for North Beach, where a mess of

watercraft formed a ragged line of lights in the distance. My guess was he'd shoot the gap between the peninsula and Cougar Island and try to make the western shore at Wagon Wheel Bay, where the number of vessels near the cabins would increase. It was a pointless strategy, unless he somehow got a vehicle. Even then, the road going south to town on that side of the lake had only one outlet, which would be blockaded by Darlene's guys. And if he went north toward Burgdorf and Warren, he was in wilderness again. If he tried to escape on foot, he'd have nowhere to go except up the mountainside into the woods. It was possible he'd stay on the water and head south after rounding the peninsula but that would be his worst choice. He hadn't been here on the Fourth and might not realize the logjam of vessels that awaited him at the lake's downtown end. The cops would hardly give him a free pass at the dock. Surely he knew there was no way out. The only explanation for why he was running at all was he couldn't give up now; the throttle was open.

To the south, fireworks loomed large and kaleidoscopic in the sky. I could hear or imagined I could hear cheers from the shore like a chorus to the engine's baritone. Wheeler was well ahead but he clearly wasn't much of a driver, chine walking all over the place, the hull rocking like a mad cradle. The water was empty of other boats this far from shore, except for two cruisers that had passed the peninsula's tip and already were beyond the Stingray on their way to North Beach. The pair of vessels traveled side-by-side and had created parallel wakes as they moved up the lake.

Wheeler's boat planed at high speed as he turned southwest to round the peninsula. It crossed the first of the wakes at an oblique angle. When it entered the trough, its stern cleared the water's surface. Still at speed, the Stingray bounced up, down, and the bow was once again very high as it reached the second wake. The craft faced west now, and leveled to the surface just as it crossed the wake, which sent it completely out of the water again. It stood in the air at an angle of about 65 degrees to the surface and was moving rapidly toward perpendicular when the rotor came down to touch the water. The boat twisted violently sideways. By the time it fully landed, it had done a 180 and was pointed east. It spun until it had completed a 360, the entire vessel almost invisible within a furious squall of spray. Wheeler was tossed side-to-side and flew headfirst into the lake as the boat finished its spin in a storm of churned-up water and stopped.

From the western shore, lights sprouted over the treetops and moved in the direction of the Stingray. A rotor's chopping sound came to me over the water. I dismissed an absurd notion that the National Guard was on the spot and realized it must be Rowena's people. They must have been in contact with him. The helicopter soon hovered over the crippled boat, ripping up whitecaps. The Moomba was still maybe fifty yards away. In the 'copter's searchlight, I saw Wheeler's form flail toward a low-hanging rope ladder. To the south, the sheriff's patrol boat cleared the peninsula and headed straight at him, its dark cabin windows on the high deck looking the business.

Wheeler made it to the ladder. The helicopter dipped so he could snatch the bottom rung. He grabbed it with one hand. Somehow, the sonofabitch had kept hold of the valise in his other hand. He scrabbled and struggled to hang onto the ladder as he made progress up it. It felt like I was puttering even though the Moomba was at full throttle.

Wheeler was about halfway up the ladder when a flare rose from the deck of the patrol boat. I recognized Tireia's form at the bow, her arms outheld like a rifler's as she watched the flare's passage. It arrowed over the water in an almost horizontal trajectory. My breath caught as the rocket's red glare flashed straight at the helicopter. The seconds slowed and I tensed in preparation for a direct hit. The flare lost a little altitude and aligned with the dangling figure of Wheeler. He saw it coming and spun on the rope in a frantic attempt at evasion. I wanted to close my eyes but couldn't. At the last moment, the flare dipped again and passed just below him. It missed him by no more than a foot or two and then buried itself in the lake. He grabbed at the rope and struggled to hang on. The valise flew out of his hand into the water twenty feet below. Just when it looked like he would right himself, the helicopter swung around toward the western shoreline. Wheeler was flung off the ladder and slapped into the lake. The chopper pilot turned eastward, shut off the searchlight, and retreated.

The patrol boat reached him first. I spotted the valise floating twenty yards north of the Stingray. I retrieved it, but the fall had broken it open. Empty. I turned on the blue water light and circled the area briefly, peering. The osprey would have sunk fast and very deep here.

By the time I reached the patrol boat, Wheeler lay on the deck while an officer pumped the lake out of his body. Tireia put up a hand in greeting as I pulled alongside. Her other hand still gripped the string of the aerial safety flare's tube.

"How is he?" I yelled.

"He'll live. No sign of the statue?"

I held up the empty valise.

"They'll take care of his boat. We'll see you at the marina."

I sidled up to the Stingray but there seemed no point in going aboard. I followed the path of the patrol boat through the jumble of sailboats and cruisers and jet skis to the marina.

Two McCall sheriff's vehicles, a Valley County patrol car, and an ambulance waited. At the dock, Wheeler was not exactly lucid as a couple of paramedics transferred him from the boat to the ambulance. Rubberneckers closed in behind the stretcher, which deprived my nemesis and me of the opportunity to strive for the cavalier and the pithy. Anyway, he wasn't up to it. We didn't even make eye contact.

Tireia approached with Darlene. She gave me a hug and asked if I was OK.

"Yeah," I said. "Nice shot. Was that luck or have you been practicing?"

"It wasn't exactly a sidearm," she replied.

"I'm surprised the officers let you do it."

"Yeah, well, I forgot to ask permission."

Darlene, who had remained on shore, tried to put on a grumpy face.

"What was with that helicopter?" she asked.

"It must have been Rowena Pascoe-Leyland's people," Tireia said. "Did you get them?"

"There's a private airstrip in the forest to the east, where they were headed," she said. "We'll get them. Why would Rowena have sent them?"

"Wheeler intended to sell the Ottoman Osprey back to her," I said. "It was in this little suitcase."

I showed her its empty insides.

"It's more than three hundred feet deep around there," she said. "Did you see him put it in the suitcase?"

"No."

"So you don't know for sure what was in it."

"We know," Tireia said. "We'll need a towfish. I'll bet we can get one on loan from the Navy's submarine testing station at Lake Pend Oreille."

"Sounds like a needle-in-the-haystack search," Darlene said.

"It could take a while," Tireia conceded. "I don't know if the Navy will help, but one way or another, we'll find the thing."

It seemed to me the private sector might have to come to the rescue but someone would search the lake bottom eventually. How could everybody resist the lure of such a treasure hunt? Still, Darlene might be right about the difficulty of locating a small statue half-buried in the loam.

"We got word on the rental car company's Hyundai SUV," Darlene told us. "The owner had a change of heart and went to his office on the holiday. He said his cars aren't supposed to be driven on unmaintained roads, so when one of the vehicles came back muddy and with a flat in the trunk, they checked the GPS tracking. It had been taken to Warren and was returned at night on the same day as Wilber Arndt's death. The renter was Graham Wheeler."

"You'll find Wheeler's Beretta at the cabin on Shellworth Island," I said. "It's unlikely to be the one used to shoot Wilber but I'll lay odds it was purchased around here very recently."

"He killed Davenport, too," Tireia said.

"I definitely want to know how you figure that," Darlene said.

Tireia offered an overview of the "aha" moment but it wasn't too helpful. She said we tried to locate a connection between the suspects' motivations and the difficulty of finding a buyer for pilfered art. We came to realize the thieves had created a market among themselves for their own stolen goods. Everyone was a buyer and a seller. The question was who had gone beyond underhanded dealings into murder? The big picture swirled like a pinwheel, she said. We had to defocus our gaze to make Wheeler emerge, as if he were the hidden 3D image in a stereogram.

Good luck to Darlene on that last part, I thought, which even I didn't quite get but she nodded and offered the crowded waterfront a serious once-over, maybe trying to see it in a new way.

"I'll need a bit more detail," she said, "but we can go through it later. Do we have anything that will stick on Mrs. Pascoe-Leyland? I mean other than trying to pull Wheeler out of the drink, if that helicopter does prove to be hers."

"Not without the Ottoman Osprey," Tireia replied. "She was very good about keeping her fingerprints off everything. Clearly, she didn't intend for anyone to die. She did try to get hold of the stolen Irwin, but I'd say her punishment for that has already been meted out."

"If we recover the osprey statue from the lake, it'll be the one piece of evidence to implicate her," I said. "She wants the very thing that would do her in."

We stepped off the dock onto the beach and the crowd oohed as the fireworks finale exploded over the water. Just as the last of the sparkles faded into blackness, Minta emerged from the edge of the crowd with one of her friends, whose parents were close behind. She waved at us and came running.

49

Not long after the holiday, John J. Totorica called us back to the Cascade courthouse to pronounce Minta's fate. Ornice said such a public show was not the usual procedure but this judge's fondness for pontification sometimes inspired him to present his findings and conclusions orally. Afterwards, a more succinct order would be drawn up. We all arrived before he made his self-aware entrance, like an athlete sitting down before the cameras after a big win—except nobody has to stand when the star player enters the room and Totorica had a tiny audience. Fabienne was there, Darlene, Derek, and even Jeanette Welgate. We'd left Minta with a school friend's family. Tireia reached out to squeeze my hand and then let go.

The judge began with the obvious, that the case was unusual. He repeated that the court's main objective was determining whether the child's custody could be reassumed by her natural mother, who had expressed ambivalence about her own fitness and willingness to do so. Her erratic behavior and wavering allegiance to the child cast doubt on her ability to properly carry out the duties of parenthood.

Near the far end of the row behind us, Fabienne hunched in a buttoned-up shift, her forehead scored as if this were something new. Totorica rustled his papers and leaned back. A big problem was the evidence of Mrs. Sansverrou's affairs, drinking, and depression, he said. Moreover, her potential complicity in transportation of stolen goods related to the deaths of Mr. James Davenport and Mr. Wilber Arndt was still under investigation. Nevertheless, a pending police case was not sufficient provocation to remove the child from her school and community under the immediate danger provision.

That last part was something, at least. It nagged at me that I'd had to tell Darlene about Fab's confession. It wasn't like I'd had any choice but it still felt like a betrayal of Stuart. Tireia and I wanted to keep Minta but not with her mother possibly going to jail.

Totorica noted again that the record showed Mr. Mencari had relinquished legal rights to parentage. It was laudable that he and Ms. D'Silva had played roles in the capture of the alleged murderer of Mr. Davenport and Mr. Arndt, which removed a threat to the child's well-being. Nevertheless, given the unconventional relationship between Ms. D'Silva and Mr. Mencari, there remained a lack of clarity concerning the best interests of the minor. This was mitigated by the appropriate living conditions provided for the child, by her expressed attachment to Ms. D'Silva and desire to retain her current living conditions, and by the length of the arrangement. Conversely, the judge's concerns were deepened by evidence of the child's unfettered behavior with regard to her language and her indifference to authority figures, exacerbated by her lack of religious training and the disadvantages created through the absence of a natal family.

Even from this windbag, it wasn't easy to shrug off that

last crack. But part of my attention was still on Fabienne. What bothered me most was her collusion with Wilber and especially the way she'd intended to dupe me into giving her Rowena's payoff money. Rowena was no angel and Ellis Trask was worse. Fab was nuts to be running with that pack of jackals. But trying to sucker me; that was what hurt.

Totorica finally got around to ordering a psychological evaluation of Fabienne, to determine her emotional and mental fitness to be Minta's full-time custodian. He said the evaluation period also would provide time for law enforcement to make further progress and bring charges concerning the theft or close the case. In the meantime, there was no extended family for the minor to stay with. He therefore ruled it was in her best interest to be placed under foster care until Mrs. Sansverrou's evaluation was completed.

Tireia and I gripped hands again between our chairs. Both Sheriff Carmody and Ms. D'Silva had applied to foster the child, Totorica went on. Then he finally got to the point. For continuity of care and in accordance with the guardian ad litem's recommendation, he ruled that Minta Sansverrou should remain with Tireia D'Silva. Subsequent to the approval of Ms. D'Silva's guardianship application, the child would continue to live with her while Fabienne Sansverrou underwent evaluation.

We breathed out.

Totorica said if Mrs. Sansverrou passed the evaluation and was not charged with a criminal offense, the child would go to her. This didn't surprise us. Meanwhile, he said, the mother was granted visitation rights. He stressed the door was still open for Mrs. Sansverrou to gain custody if everything went well for her. But if she was convicted of a crime or the psychologist decided she was an unfit parent, then the state would consider Ms. D'Silva's application for adoption if she so desired.

We stood up and hugged at the counsel table and Ornice joined the clinch. Fabienne approached us, smiling uncertainly. We broke apart and listened as she expressed relief it had worked out well and said she was happy for all of us. She didn't look all that happy but we assured her the evaluation would go well and in the meantime she could see Minta whenever she wanted. Nobody mentioned the criminal case. She hesitated, made an excuse, and left.

Ornice went to shake hands with Byron Allen—nice game, tough luck—and when she came back, we asked how long the evaluation of Fabienne would take.

"Three or four months, I'd say."

This was not bad news.

"Once you're approved as a foster parent, you'll be eligible to adopt."

"Depending on Fabienne's situation," Tireia said.

"Right. In any case, it wouldn't hurt your cause if you weren't single. Just saying."

Tireia accepted this with the grace of disinterest. Ornice probably figured it was wise counsel but she also probably realized there was no way the hardliners would force our hand. Evidence of the goodwill behind her suggestion, if we needed it, was she and her girlfriend were unmarried. Not that their vows would make a flood of friends here.

Darlene approached us. Hank wasn't with her but Derek hovered a few steps away. She came up and took Tireia into a warm embrace. Then she put a hand on my chest, made a loose fist and tapped me.

"I'm delighted for you guys," she said. "And Ornice, congratulations to you. Great job."

"Thanks."

Derek bounded forward and told us it warmed his heart to know we'd be keeping that little girl. Tireia gave him a hug. I executed a semi-awkward pat on his shoulder and said we'd better go get her right now.

"By the way," Darlene said, "I got a call from Ellie Crossfield at the bookstore. She has a serious family problem down in Idaho Falls. The situation sounds interesting and it needs investigating. She wants you to help but she phoned me first to see what I thought."

"No, no, we have our own jobs to do," I said quickly. "I'm already late for the start of fire season and the jumpers need another pilot."

"A few thousand acres are burning in Bonner County," Darlene reflected. "And of course, we've already had those two fires in the Payette from dry lightning. If these last years are any indication, it's gonna get bad."

"Bakersfield heard about my San Jose job and now they're after me," Tireia said. "For the water system, if you can imagine."

"So I'll tell her not to contact you," said Darlene. "I'll remind her it's not really what you do."

"Good," we said in unison.

"All right, then. I gotta get back to the station. Just wanted to be here for the victory lap."

"Thanks, Darlene. Incidentally, out of curiosity, what is it? What kind of problem does Ellie's family have?"

ABOUT THE AUTHOR

Steve Bunk has worked as a freelance magazine journalist for many years in the U.S. and overseas. He also has written travel books, young adult fiction, and co-authored a nonfiction best-seller in Australia. His nonfiction book, *Goliath Staggered*, about a people's environmental movement, was praised by Sierra Club executive director Michael Brune and environmentalist author Bill McKibben. Steve edits *Idaho Magazine*.

ACKNOWLEDGEMENTS

Thanks to Michael Donnelly for early advice and encouragement; to David Griffin Brown, Jordan Dane, Sam Wiebe, and to my editor, Bob Gaines.

EXPLORE THE HIDDEN SHELF